DECEPTIONS
OF POWER

G. E. FISHER

Fulton Books
Meadville, PA

Published by Fulton Books 2022

Registration Number: TXu 2-263-625
Effective Date: June 4, 2021
Registration Decision Date: June 25, 2021

ISBN 978-1-63985-911-5 (paperback)
ISBN 979-8-88731-513-3 (hardcover)
ISBN 978-1-63985-912-2 (digital)

Printed in the United States of America

Chapter 1

a dangerous road

Snow blanketed the world with a heavy silence. Large flakes fell straight from heaven in the small evergreen encircled clearing. On the south side of the glade, a small, seldom-used east-west track was the focus of attention. Riordan sat astride his tall pale-gray horse. Both were quiet, listening for sounds in what had become an oft-performed play. He was dressed all in black except his large-brimmed hat. In better days long ago, it was once a bright scarlet red.

Anticipation and focus were acute in the mounted pair as they heard the first creaks and groans of their expected visitor's cart. With practiced ease, he drew his worn but polished straight blade from its sheath, holding it up as a signal to his followers waiting at their assigned posts. The intruders' sounds grew to include the muffled stomp of hooves adding a counterpoint to the wagon's own. A wild grin blossomed on his face under the scarf he wore against the cold as his "guests" appeared into view from behind the trees. With a howl of feral delight, man and beast leaped out of the woods from the north and raced to the cart that had no hope of escaping the coming trap…

*****

A cold wind swirled the snow into little zephyrs around the cart as it slowly squeaked and rumbled its way east along the narrow, drift-covered road. It was harnessed to a single solid-brown mare. Towed rather indignantly behind it was a feisty stallion, darker brown than the mare and with three white socks on its feet. Three

1

Socks did not care to bring up the rear, but his rider was occupied with driving the cart.

The driver, hunched over against the cold, was wearing a long green robe with gold edging and a matching belt. All in all an unusual sight for these lands. Standing he would be about average height with a thin build. Gray-white hair, complete with long, thin beard and trimmed mustache would complete the picture of a stranger to these parts. His face and form suggested a noble build and upbringing; however, it was his eyes that immediately drew attention. They were a deep green and gave the distinct impression of seeing far more than others. This foreboding would be confirmed when any learned his profession. He was a mage from the legendary Sarrik school.

Wizardry as a profession was no longer considered respectable in these lands. In fact, most people held deep suspicions when it came to sorcerers and their motives. With that said, even other wizards spoke in awe or fear of the Sarriks' as their stories and powers were ancient and traveled back to the kingdom's founding.

The green-robed old man was not the only person in the cart. Huddled in the back, among the supplies and furnishings, was a young man, nineteen years young as measured against the bitter winter seasons. An adult, but inexperienced to the great wide world. He also wore a green robe, albeit without the gold trim. His almost black-brown hair was exposed to view whenever the wind could snatch his hood and throw it back from his face. Curious blue eyes drifted from his master's back to the surrounds as they passed through this deeply wooded area. The forest lay quiet and Kalamar's thoughts were drifting back to the events that brought him to this contemplative moment of his life.

He'd met his master while playing in the woods near his family farm about fifty miles west, he guessed, from their present spot. While wandering aimlessly among the trees, not really paying attention, he spotted a man bent over something near a tree.

"Hello," he'd said pleasantly. There had never been any trouble around his family's farm and he figured it must be someone from one of the neighboring homesteads. "Do you need any help?"

"Well, hello," his future master had replied. "I was just picking a few of these Chamoloi flowers. Have you seen these before?"

Kalamar peered around the man from where he was and looked. He had seen them around and said so. Now that the man had stood, he got his first good look at him. He was dressed simply, as most farmers would, with a simple white cotton shirt and brown pants. He seemed kindly enough. Although there had never been any trouble, his father had taught him to be polite but keep some caution when dealing with strangers that may pass through.

"Why would you be picking those flowers?" asked Kalamar.

The man leaned against the tree, flowers in hand and replied, "Well, they are good for treating ailments of the stomach, if properly prepared."

"Are you from these parts?" Kalamar asked.

"Not originally. I visit a cottage I have nearby from time to time. These woods are filled with flora hard to find in other places." He'd pointed vaguely south as he replied.

Kalamar was curious about this. There were no real roads around and he thought his family the farthest out in these woods. Also, how could someone earn a living while visiting places from "time to time" unless they were very well off? This man was dressed like any farmer but did not speak the same way the locals did. He sounded clearer somehow.

"Where are you from then?" he asked. He'd realized the man had not given him that in his answer and found he really wanted to know.

The stranger had put the flowers carefully away in a tan-colored bag hanging at his side. Studying Kalamar, he replied casually, "I was born in the Calledon Kingdom, over the Nantukk mountains."

Kalamar was stunned. That land was a place of legend. His father told tales from long ago that all people south of the mountains had once come from Calledon. Almost all contact was now lost and few people made the journey any longer. The original pass through the mountains had been destroyed somehow and the only way to make the trip now was by ship, a dangerous and expensive journey to take.

3

"You must come home with me!" he exclaimed. "We would love to hear stories from your land. Please?" he made this entreaty as only the young at heart could.

The stranger formed a rather-amused expression on his face and replied that he would, so they set off for Kalamar's home.

The stranger, whose name turned out to be Angus Crow, a very strange name indeed, became a frequent guest of their homestead. He and his stories were always welcome.

Crow was quite surprised to learn the entire family could read and write. Greer, Kalamar's father, had learned to read while working as a guard captain for a traveling merchant and together with his wife had taught all four of their children. Greer had brought his new bride far out west from the settled lands, where a farmstead could be claimed by anyone willing to wrestle it from the forest.

There were eight other families within ten miles or so that had similar stories and they formed a little community. They knew where each other were and in times of trouble, which usually meant a bad crop, would help out the others as needed. Also, as the children grew up, marriages occurred between the families and a new homestead would be built. Kalamar's oldest brother was approaching that age and his father had taken him on visits to the other families to meet possible brides. Life wasn't very exciting this way but nobody seemed to mind.

Crow's arrival, however, had changed everything for Kalamar. His stories created a longing in him to learn and do and see that he couldn't deny. Greer, of course, noticed this and on one of Crow's many visits, they'd taken a long walk. From that walk, the family learned that Crow was a master mage and he would be willing to take Kalamar as his student if he so chose.

Most people at this point would have asked Crow to leave and never return. Greer, however, was a more experienced man and in his youth, had worked for a short time guarding a wizard in his travels. As such, he understood that people were good or bad as they chose and that applied even to casters.[1] Because of this, he would allow his

---

[1] Caster was the generic term for wizards or priests, anyone who could "cast" a spell regardless of source.

son the choice. Kalamar leaped at the opportunity. While he'd never envisioned himself as a wizard, the thought of what he would learn and could do was a call he could not ignore.

Kalamar excelled at his studies. He completed his apprenticeship in five months when it usually took between one or two years. Master Crow frequently commented that he had a natural talent for the craft. Kalamar also learned that completing the apprenticeship wasn't the end of learning but instead was just the beginning. As a mage of the First Circle,[2] he now knew enough to really begin analyzing and studying the world around him and the powers and structures of that world. And that was what a wizard was, someone who could sense and manipulate the natural energies of the world for his own ends.

It was quite a surprise when his master informed him they were leaving the cottage he'd called home for years. The nearest lands to that cottage were under the control of the baron of Eddington,[3] Master of Stormlake, Lord Terrence Eddington. Lord Terrence had summoned Master Crow. Almost thirty-two years earlier, Master Crow had known and worked with Lord Terrence's father, Lord Edward. While Crow would not speak of the specific service, he left

---

[2] Circles were how mages measured their power and defined the spells they could safely cast. There were Seven Circles each split into Junior and Senior. After an apprenticeship you were First Circle and generally had the power to cast a few first-circle spells each day. How many was determined by your intelligence to hold the spell in your mind and your internal toughness to contain and control the power. A weak-spirited mage could only cast a half dozen or so but an iron-willed mage could cast far more. The title for First Circle was Initiate and you officially knew enough to begin your career in the art. At Second Circle you added the next level of spells and your title was Adept. After Adept was Journeyman, then Lessor Master, Full Master, Grand Master and finally Archmage. Most mages never progress higher than Journeyman. Since this affords spells that are quite powerful and the mage is experienced enough to pass on his knowledge, journeymen are sometimes called teaching master or instructors and they are recognized as such in their communities. It takes both dedication and extreme intelligence to rise higher than full master and only the most brilliant can reach the powers of an archmage.

[3] Eddington is the youngest and last of the lands founded by the Calledon Kingdom. It was created in the year 1328 from the founding of Calledon.

5

Lord Edward a thin band of silver that he'd crafted a recall spell into. With this, Lord Edward could insert a message and upon activation by way of spoken word, the circlet and message would return to Master Crow. The magic ring was left against dire need and Lord Edward had never used it. Obviously however, he passed it to his son.

Lord Terrence requested that Master Crow travel to Stormlake to discuss his appointment to the baronial court as Master of Magic in its preservation and enrichment. Master Crow's humorous translation was that he was being offered a job. The question was why. What need would cause the baron to hire a wizard on a permanent basis? Wizards were not generally well thought of by the populous and while some courts had wizards on their staff, it was considered an oddity or eccentricity.

His father was proud but concerned, his mother tearful and his siblings envious. It was quite an emotional whirlwind. It was...

Kalamar was pulled from his musing by a feeling of something not quite right. He quickly centered his mind and emptied his thoughts as he'd been taught. The exercise was now quite natural and automatic to him. The surroundings didn't feel normal. It was as if the forest was unnaturally hushed and waiting for something. He slowly shifted position and focused harder to locate the source of the foreboding. It was ahead of them, not behind, so he turned in that direction. He was just about to say something to his master when several men stepped out from the cover of the forest. Two men had bows and drew arrows to cheek for firing. Three others had swords and began charging the cart, loosing screams in the air. A rider was racing from the north across the glade and quickly outpaced the swordsmen.

Kalamar did not panic or even think. His training had emphasized over and over letting go of conscious oversight and to simply be. Emotions, particularly fear, clouded thought and when given enough energy, could paralyze, cripple or even destroy. The antithesis, however, the concept of thinking and doing in complete harmony, allowed a person to master his environment and himself. His repertoire of spells burned in his mind as clearly as would a scroll of parchment in hand.

Even as the lead attacker began his charge, Kalamar jumped down from the back of the wagon and steadied himself. Turning toward the horseman, he took a few steps away from the wagon as it shuttered to a stop. He began crafting a spell of attack. The words combined with his mind to draw the power of fire from the etheric plane. His hand rose to cradle the combined force of his will and the flame exploded to life in his palm. With his cupped hand now holding the ball of fire, he rotated his wrist, turning the palm, facing toward his attacker. A whispered release and multiple balls of flame shot straight and true into the charging rider.

Time appeared to slow in Kalamar's mind as his vision narrowed to only the two of them. The man seemed to be out of step with this new reality around them and the dance Kalamar was directing. The horseman proceeded from ferocity and rage to incomprehension of Kalamar's movements. This led to surprise at the flame, followed by pain, shock and fear. These steps all took place within the few seconds it took for the casting and direction of the spell, but each was one step behind Kalamar's actions.

While the damage was serious, it wasn't enough to kill him and with his horse pulled up in discord, he spurred him back into the race across the field. Kalamar had not stopped and already begun crafting the spell a second time while the man regained control and redirected his steed. The second spell slammed into the raider, causing him to crumple over his mount before falling off the far side. The horse seemed confused by this and pulled to a stop huffing and pawing the ground while shaking its head.

It took a moment for Kalamar to remember the rest of the attackers and shift his focus. As he looked up from the now small-seeming form of his attacker to where the others last were, he saw that Master Crow had not been idle. The other three sword welders were crumpled and smoking forms on the ground. The two archers had dropped their weapons and were on bent knee with hands held up in sign of surrender. Terror was the closest expression that Kalamar could distinguish on their faces.

Master Crow had already stepped down from the cart and was speaking soothing words to the mare. It amazed Kalamar that his master had retained control of the horse, cast multiple spells against the attackers and was even now calmly walking toward those remaining.

Kalamar reached back to grab the cart and noticed an arrow protruding from its side. He went to Three Socks and began talking and rubbing him to calm him down. As the shock of the moment passed through him, he kept thinking of what he'd done and his eyes were continuously drawn to the man he'd killed. A man he had killed. That thought above all else took hold of his mind.

He didn't realize he was trembling as he began to make his way over to the form on the ground. The rider didn't look terrifying at all now, just small and empty. The man had fallen over on his face. Only when he reached out to turn him over did he finally realize his hands were shaking. With a conscious effort, he mastered himself and turned the body over. The scent of burned flesh assailed his sense of smell and it was all he could do not to vomit.

He forced his eyes back to the corpse and his mind began taking note of little things. The clothes, except for the burned parts, were actually well made, if a little worn. The boots were also of quality make. The expression on his face was of terrible pain. There seemed no peace in his death. Everything about this man indicated he'd once known a better life but it was long ago.

This only raised the issue in his mind of why he'd be out here in the winter snow, trying to ambush a cart passing by. His eyes caught the glint of something about the man's throat. He leaned over closer and noticed what clearly looked like a woman's necklace. This raised more questions for Kalamar. Was it something he stole from some other passersby? Was it a gift from a woman who loved him and was waiting for his return? This last question was too much and he began to break down.

His master had trained him for combat using glamours that seemed quite real; however, once they were defeated, the illusions would disappear. This one wasn't doing that. He had taken a life and that reality hit hard. He knew life was a struggle. People died, with some deserved but many not. His father had certainly told of enough companions killed over his long years of mercenary work. Death was part and parcel of adventure and violence frequently stalked people's lives. None of this stopped the tears beginning to silently fall down his face and the shakes taking a fierce hold of his own now-crumpled form.

Master Crow had been watching to see how he'd handle the experience and was there for him. "It is a hard thing to kill a man and it is something that you never get used to, but sometimes it is not only necessary but the right thing to do." he quietly said. "I'll be close by if you need anything." With that, he walked Kalamar a few steps away from the corpse and left him to his thoughts.

Kalamar wasn't sure how long he stood there with the uncaring snow gently falling, oblivious to his concerns. He was unsure what had brought him back to the present but his mind quickly caught up. As he listened, he heard quiet voices and the thumping and grunting of men working the earth.

A burial. It all came back in a rush.

He understood clearly what was happening. Those men who had died in the attack were being buried. Not wishing to eavesdrop and feeling a bit foolish, he slowly walked over to his master, the cart and two men digging a pit in the ground.

Master Crow turned as he arrived and gave him a long look. "I want to introduce you to Edan and Tremain," he finally said.

At the sound of their names, both men looked up at Kalamar. They were gaunt and unshaven. It was clear they didn't eat well or regularly. Edan was tall in height with a long nose and chin. His hair was thin, but very blond. His clothing was tattered and repaired so many times it looked to fall off at any given moment. Tremain was dressed to match but that was the end of the similarities. He was shorter by a hand and wider by several. Stocky and barrel-like, with black hair gone to gray, his skin was drawn over bones in a severe manner.

His master quickly brought Kalamar up to speed on the circumstances of both men. They and one other were all that were left of Riordan's band of outlaws. They had a hideout not far from here from which they raided hamlets and farms to get by. They normally didn't raid so close to home, but it had been a harsh winter and as Crow and Kalamar were coming into the barony, no one would be looking for them. The local nobles didn't patrol outside their territory, so they were seen as easy targets.

Kalamar found himself looking once again upon the dead out-law but in addition to pity and sorrow, anger was now mingled in. Anger that their lives and any others that crossed his path were so cheap and could be so callously taken.

He found his voice was quiet but steady as he said, "You said there is another left?"

"Yes, young master," Edan spoke up quickly. "Gilles is watching the camp til our return."

"Master," Kalamar spoke, "we need to capture this last one so that no one else suffers what they tried with us today."

Tremain spoke up then, excited as he added, "There is a large reward to the person who brings in Riordan's head Master Crow. We cau'd be quite helpful to you, making sure you get to Lord Nellis and convincin' him o' tha truth."

"That's a right," Edan added right behind him. "We was only do'ng what we was told and not meaning no harm. We'd do any thing's you need doing and be grateful for it."

Master Crow, in his usual calm, said, "You boys will do what you're told regardless as we've already discussed." He pointed to the dead lying behind them. "As for what I'm going to do, I keep my own counsel. Any trouble from either of you will end in your immediate death." He spoke very quietly, "Are we clear on that?"

Nodding their swiftly bloodless faces, they quickly agreed and pledged anew that they would.

"Now, Kalamar, what did you have in mind?"

Kalamar ordered his thoughts and laid them out for his master just as he would any problem presented.

His master listened and agreed. "Very well, we try it your way. We shouldn't leave this last criminal out here and we won't make Nellis before evening now."

*****

Kalamar cursed himself a fool for the hundredth time. It had been an hour since they'd finished burying the raiders and proceeded with "his" plan. Every snapped branch from too much snow or bird call had him practically jumping out of his skin. He looked down at himself and shook his head ruefully. He was wearing a dead man's clothing and had glamoured himself to look like the fallen Riordan as he led the "victorious" bandits back to their lair to capture the remaining criminal. He was completely exposed and while his personal magical shield would help him, it was draining to hold both the glamour and shield. Edan and Tremain had explained what to look for in their camp and were driving the cart behind him but he had to lead them back as that was what Riordan had always done. His master was concealed in the rear of the cart.

It was with some relief when they came upon the landmark he was looking for. Two large oak trees whose branches were interwoven in front of and to the right of a large hillock that rose right out of the ground. The entrance to the lair was reached by following the hill toward the left. Gilles was to be watching from the oaks, but it was more than likely he'd come running out of the cave as he heard them coming around. The path leading here wasn't much but was just wide enough for the cart.

A clearing developed as they rode around the left and as promised, Gilles came around to meet them with a friendly wave. "Ho, Riordan," he called and looked to see his mates driving the cart behind him. "Looks like a successful trip!" he yelped in ghoulish delight as he continued walking to the right of Kalamar for the cart. "Our spy was correct again."

As Kalamar was adjusting to the shock of learning about a spy, several things happened at once.

Gilles looked up at him noticing the burned clothing for the first time, causing him to focus harder on what he was seeing.

Those driving the cart started shouting at Gilles to put down his crossbow and he wouldn't be hurt.

Gilles looked back to them and noticed that the others were not with the group and a cloaked figure was getting down from the cart.

Kalamar swung the sword that had been across his horse's pommel and pointed it at Giles, telling him to drop the bow. The problem, he quickly realized however, was the sword was much heavier than it looked and he had no skill with holding it. The end began

11

to waiver. Between that and his voice not sounding like Riordan's, the glamour failed and Gilles's eyes widened in surprise and fear. He jerked up the crossbow to shoot the impostor before him.

Kalamar couldn't hold the sword as well as cast, and in his panic dropped it, his magic shield and the now-failed glamour to cast a sleep spell on the brigand. His own fear of the rising bow lent power to the words and energies rushing to his aid as he raced through the chant.

Fear turned to alarm for Gilles as the chanting raised the hairs of his neck. He pulled the trigger, releasing an arrow just as the full weight of the spell hit his mind like a collapsing wall. He fell like a rock to the ground.

Riordan's horse stamped and twisted at the unsure rider on his back and Kalamar's efforts were consumed for the moment with getting his mount under control. Sawing on the reins back and forth until he calmed him down, it was only after, that he felt a terrible pain in his left arm. He looked down to see a tear in his sleeve and, on closer examination, noticed rather-profuse bleeding. Several fingers of skin seemed to have been ripped from the lower bottom half of his arm. Fighting down panic, he focused the remainder of his magic to stanch the bleeding and close the wound. As a mage and not a healing priest, this was the best he could do. It would be ugly, but he wouldn't die and that was his immediate priority.

As he finished the spell, exhausted from pushing his body and abilities so hard so quickly, he noticed his master at his side. Holding Shadow's bridle steady, he looked Kalamar over to judge the injuries for himself. Edan and Tremain were standing over Gilles, waiting for instructions from Master Crow.

His master's efficiency soon had everyone and everything in hand and he led them into the cave. Kalamar's exhaustion was overtaking him, mind and body and he couldn't really focus on much. His general impression was rotted goods and furnishings. His master quickly laid him down on some blankets and he was soon out cold, knowing that everything was in hand. His last thoughts were of a miserable end to the first sorry adventure of his new life.

Chapter 2

Rewards of a new life…

N ellis was the most westerly village on the main road through the Eddington barony. As a lordship created in the last twenty years, it had not been there when Kalamar's father, Greer, had come west to build a new life for himself and his wife. The town was a quiet place, in an out-of-the-way part of the world. The snow of yesterday had ended during the night and the sun was out in a cloudless sky, quickly melting yesterday's and the remaining winter snows. Freemen and Villeins alike were in the fields, breaking the ground, preparing for the new season's planting. Into this, Kalamar rode. As protégé to his master, acting as herald was among his many new duties.

Kalamar rode in from the western woods, where the path and river merged before it passed by the entrance of Nellis. There was no wall or even fence separating the fields from the town. The entrance, such as it was, consisted of a guard shack and two now curious-looking guardsmen.

"Who are you and what's your business, sir?" the shorter of the two asked.

"I am Kalamar the Mage, protégé to Lord Angus Crow the Archmage," he replied evenly. "We are invited to Stormlake by request of Lord Terrence Eddington. Here is our summons." He finished while withdrawing from a side pouch and then extending the written request for their inspection.

"Kalamar the what?" "Lord Crow?" they started talking over each other. It was clear his pronouncement and words had confused them, except for "Lord Eddington." That they knew and drew themselves up straighter. The first to speak stepped forward to inspect the document.

"A mage is what you might call a wizard or even a sorcerer. And my master, Lord Angus Crow, is an archmage, which is the most powerful kind." He began to explain. Further explanation would have to wait as the words "wizard" and "sorcerer" produced the immediate effect of both guards pulling back while spears were planted as if against a charging foe.

"Just hold right there!" said the shorter man. "Don't do anything, or we'll deal with you right off."

Kalamar continued in a calm and measured tone, realizing this was getting out of hand, "I have no interest in doing anything. Please contact your master and I'm sure we can get this settled to everyone's satisfaction." His quiet demeanor and reasonable suggestion seemed to get through and after a brief whispered discussion, the taller of the men jogged off into the village to Lord Nellis's estate. With the other guard just watching, Kalamar took the opportunity to look around.

The manor was obvious; one of the few stone buildings and the largest and best positioned of all. Most everything else was timber made or waddle and daub. The only other large building was a standard in every community. The temple of the god Telmar,[4] creator of communities and provider of civilization.

Young children were gathering for the excitement of a stranger on horseback. A few raced off to share the gossip. Within minutes, the adults began to arrive and inspect the scene for themselves. A rider from the west was very unusual, as no one was supposed to live out there. A mage with sorcerer's powers claiming to know the baron had them beside themselves with curiosity.

---

[4] Telmar is the god of communities. Considered first of the gods because wherever a few hundred gather a priest would arise and begin building both the temple and the community. Telmar's brothers, Veynar (farming) and Ohfrey (crafts) would soon follow as the community grew. The temple's design was always the same. A square building with roof arching to the center where a hole was left open for a fire's smoke. It was sometimes referred to as the First Fire of the community. Telmar was also referred to as the father of society.

As herald, Kalamar had ridden in advance. His master had not yet arrived but could be seen riding Three Socks with the cart following. Turning his attention back to the village, a better-dressed man with eight guards in tow now appeared coming up the street with the growing group of onlookers quickly making way. This man, wearing furs against the chill and fine albeit dirty walking boots, slowed as he approached the scene. He eventually stopped next to the guard whose spear was still planted against a charge.

The newcomer's eyes never left Kalamar as the guard whispered in his ear.

"I understand you claim to be a wizard and have a warrant to appear before our Lord Baron," he stated. His voice was deliberately even.

"I am a mage," Kalamar replied equally as calm, "and I have an invitation from Baron Eddington to my master, the archmage Crow, to join him at Stormlake as a member of his court." He extended the invitation once again for inspection.

The gentleman walked forward to take the parchment, leaving the protection of his men behind. After a brief moments review, his demeanor changed dramatically.

"Young protégé, I am Keene, chancellor to Lord Sart Nellis and on his behalf, I welcome you and your master to our home." He returned the invitation and extended a courteous bow. "I apologize for any confusion and offer our hospitality for such an honored guest."

"Please, think nothing of it," Kalamar graciously allowed. "It is certainly wise to be careful with the care of your people. My master will be delighted to accept your lord's gracious hospitality and, if possible, would like a word with him. There was a distressing matter upon the road your lord should be made aware of as quickly as possible." He finished in a slightly lower voice that would only project to the two of them.

"Of course," he replied just as quietly. "My lord will be anxious to meet your master and hear his counsel."

It wasn't long before the archmage arrived and further introductions were made. With that done, they all proceeded through the main street across the center market square to the manor. It was two stories of stone, a basic rectangle with a wing added to the western side. On the inside, the furnishings were solid but simple, without many carvings or adornments. *Practical not pretentious* was Kalamar's overall thought and he felt comfortable in the surroundings.

Visitors were always a treat in small communities and those with baronial passes were a must-see for the locals. Everyone who could, raced to the great hall to gawk at the visitors and hear what they had to say. As such, there were almost twenty souls with the connections to gain entrance to the court.

Master Crow entered first, with Kalamar slightly behind and to his right. The bandits-turned-servants followed behind, with one carrying a box and the other a leather bag. Kalamar glanced over the court as they entered but kept his main focus on Lord Nellis and his party.

"My Lord and Lady, members of the court, I wish to present Lord Angus Crow the archmage."

At this, Master Crow inclined his head politely, Kalamar bowed slightly from the waist and, while doing so, could see that Edan and Tremain bowed completely from the waist to the point of almost falling over.

Lord Nellis inclined his head in return. He was an older man, slightly gray and a small paunch giving evidence to the growing prosperity of his holdings. His wife, two sons and daughter rounded out the group; and all seemed pleasant in both temperament and countenance.

"Lord Sart," Master Crow began, "I am honored to make your acquaintance and gladly accept your gracious offer of hospitality. We've had quite an adventure getting here and there is an important matter we must discuss." He then began telling their story.

Kalamar had known his master was able to spin a great yarn but was amazed at what he was hearing. In his master's version, yesterday saw Kalamar leaping from the wagon to confront the bandit lord in single combat. After vanquishing his foe, he quickly created and executed the plan to capture the remaining member, thereby ending forever the plague upon western travelers.

It was something straight out of legend and he was the central character. While the details were all true, it was the drama and emotional additions that changed a young man reacting as best he could into a hero of old brought to life. He was embarrassed and nearly blushed when the assemblage began clapping and cheering at the end of the telling.

Lord Nellis waited until the approbation had subsided before speaking. "That is a fine tale," he began. "We are grateful indeed for the end of that foul band and its storied leader. Do you have upon you some token or sign that we may show the populace to ease their concern and fears?" Kalamar thought this a most clever way to demand proof in a way that would not cause offense.

Lord Crow nodded and turned to his newly acquired servants to step forward and present the evidence they carried. Both items were placed on the floor. The bundle was unwrapped to show the bandit lord's head and the box was filled with his personal belonging.

The assemblage gasped at the site. An older man, clearly a priest, stepped forward and stooped to examine the morbid offerings. He began mumbling an incantation to himself that Kalamar could feel even if he couldn't hear the words. They were minor powers being summoned, identification spells he suspected.

"It be him, my lord," the priest intoned in a formal voice as he stood up and turned. "Riordan the Scarlet Bandit is dead."

Lord Nellis raised his hands for quiet and pronounced, "Let the joyous news be spread throughout the land. The bandit is dead and the threat to the people is finished. Take his head to the wall and mount it on a pike as proof this brave deed is done."

As the head was removed, Lord Nellis continued, "Master Crow, you have brought us glad tidings and performed a great service to the realm. There is a knighthood promised to the warrior who vanquished this bandit and other gifts in thanks and appreciation. Step forward to be recognized."

"My lord," the archmage replied, "you are most generous in this, but it is not I who should be rewarded. While it is my right to accept, I must ask you to consider giving this to my faithful protégé who actually carried out the deeds in question. It is he who should be recognized and if you are amiable, I would ask you to bestow these well-deserved praises upon him."

There was a ripple of surprise through the crowd as they considered this. A lord would always accept the rewards and then share as he felt appropriate with his servants. Lord Nellis looked from Master Crow to Kalamar and asked, "What do you say to that, young man?"

"My lord, I was only doing my duty and it was through my master's training that I was able to act as I did," Kalamar replied.

"Well said young man, however, I applaud your master's generosity and agree with his judgment in this case. I will brook no refusal. Step forward to be recognized."

Kalamar did as asked and knelt when directed.

Lord Nellis drew a sword leaning against his chair and now presented it to Kalamar's right for him to hold the blade with both hands. "Be it known far and wide that we recognize the noble deeds done by this young man in service to his master and our person. He has demonstrated the highest ideals of valor and courage. It is with great pride that we confer upon Kalamar..." At this point, he trailed off and looked to Crow for a name. "Sylvicheld" was the reply. "Kalamar Sylvicheld," Lord Nellis continued, "a knighthood of the order of"—again, he stopped with concern.

Lord Crow stepped forward, recognizing the issue at hand. Kalamar was a mage, not a knight and no order would be willing to accept him as such. "My lord," began Lord Crow quietly, "perhaps it would be best if you made him a knight of the realm and then when he has proven himself ready, he can petition an order to gain admittance."

"A most agreeable solution," Lord Nellis responded, and began again. "We recognize and name Kalamar Sylvicheld a Knight of the Realm with all the privileges and responsibilities that entails."

"Do you, Kalamar, swear to uphold the knightly virtues?"

"I so swear," Kalamar replied.

"Do you, Kalamar, swear to protect the weak?"

"I so swear," he responded.

"Then let all know from this day forward. Rise and be recognized, young sir and go forth into the world as a light for justice and honor."

Kalamar did as asked and the room burst forth again in cheers and applause.

"Tonight," Lord Nellis shouted over the crowd, "we will feast in recognition and celebration. Let all preparations be made."

Kalamar was then overwhelmed with introductions and well-wishes from the crowd. During this, his master took Lord Nellis aside quietly and from his gestures, it was clear he was explaining the situation with the three remaining survivors. It seemed, however, that the archmage's promise to rehabilitate them was accepted as judgment and they were turned over to his stewardship.

*****

Today is a good day, Kalamar decided as he was exploring the shops in Nellis. His master had suggested he spend a good portion of his reward here so there wouldn't be any hard feelings that he was ungrateful or insensitive to the local community. He was happy to oblige. In addition to keeping all the possessions of the bandit lord as required by the code of Saa'Vey,[5] Lord Nellis had posted a reward of thirty pounds sterling and two horses with full tack which, in a community this small, was a fortune.[6]

He had his robes dyed a deep blue and cut shorter, with slits up the side and back after a design he'd seen in one of his master's

---

[5] Saa'Vey is the god of warriors and leader of the gods of good. He has provided codes of conduct and training for his followers that most gods recognize and respect.

[6] Pay and business arrangements are conducted in coinage or barter. In an average town, a poor person could survive on the equivalent of one pound sterling each year. Not a good living but survival. In the countryside, a pound sterling would see you living better, still poor but much better off than your city cousins. A farmer with forty acres could earn between three to eight pounds sterling each year after feeding his family. Horses were a luxury and could cost as much as two pounds sterling for a farm animal, not a warhorse, depending on peace or wartime. A knight was one of the most expensive professions to maintain and it could cost at least twenty pounds sterling to acquire a full suit of armor (plain with no engraving) and the weapons (average quality, no gems or customizations) needed for service.

books. Dark blue was his favorite color and matched his new heraldic device.[7] He'd found and purchased several bookshelves and a table he liked for his new home in Stormlake. What he hadn't found were books, but he and Tremain were heading now to a candle maker he was assured, claimed to have magick books from a dead relative. Since most people couldn't read, writing in itself was considered magical to the unlearned, so his hopes were not high.

The shop itself was in a poorer part of the community and the scent of beeswax was strong as they walked in.

A youngish woman was busy cutting wicks on a counter and said, "Welcome to my shop, young sir." She stood up and came around the counter. "How can I be of service?"

Kalamar replied, "Good mistress, I've heard that you may have books for sale and I'm hoping this might be true. I am a mage passing through to Stormlake and would be grateful for any help in this matter."

This was an unexpected turn for her, but she recovered and replied, "It is true. My grandfather was a great wizard, traveling far and wide. He always told the best stories." She said with a fond smile. "We have his chest of books and tools in the back. Beggin' your pardon, please excuse my ignorance, but what is a mage?"

"A mage is what you would call a wizard," he replied. "Would you mind if I take a look?"

Her expression brightened considerably at this and she quickly excused herself. After a few moments of calling to someone named Kellyn and some thumps and bumps, she reemerged with a young girl of about nine summers carrying a medium-sized chest between them. With a loud thump, they set it down and she, putting key to lock, opened the chest. She stepped back from the open chest with arms outstretched as if she'd just performed some type of parlor trick.

Kalamar walked forward to the chest, hopeful indeed, as he could see there were several books inside. Once he knelt down, he

---

[7] It seems his master had given some previous thought to a last name for Kalamar. Sylvicheld in the old speech means briar field. The device was blue covered with three golden long thorn'd briar strands, each ending in a red rose (Kalamar's mother's favorites).

noted written sheaves of parchment, a carved stick, and a man's ring in the corner. It was obvious as he held his hand over the open chest, extending his senses that a faint aura of magic was in the chest.

"There is magick here," he said. "Please step back and allow me some quiet to investigate."

"I knew it, Mom," Kellyn said excitedly. "I told you it was true."

"Hush, child, and let him look." She whispered back, "I always knew it too."

Kellyn looked askance at her mom but said nothing as Kalamar began quietly whispering words and gesturing over the items. After a few minutes of this, he'd removed all the items from the chest and laid them out neatly on the floor.

"All right," he finally said. "The large red leather-bound book is a grimoire and this wand is crafted to hold spells but currently has none. The ring and the sheaves of papers are not magical. These three books are also not magical. One is a history and the others deal with creatures and plants." He lifted up the parchments and began scanning the writing before continuing. "It looks like these are a diary, stories of a man calling himself Raghnall the Red Fox, a wizard who had all these adventures." He held up the parchment in his hand for emphasis.

"What does it say?" Kellyn asked with large, hopeful eyes.

Before her mom could object, Kalamar briefly described the first story in the diary about Raghnall being hired by a local lord to rescue his daughter from a bandit. After several failed attempts, Raghnall finally rescued her and fell madly in love with her on the journey back to her father. Raghnall asked the father for her hand in marriage but was refused because he was penniless and she had been promised to a rich lord in the neighboring land. The father kept his word and paid him the agreed price for her return and, feeling sorry for the young wizard, gave him the ruby ring with the foxes engraved on both sides holding up the stone.

Kellyn had been engrossed with the story and exclaimed, "What a wretched, heartless woman! To not marry the hero who saved her life. I hope she was miserable with her fat, ugly husband and had lots of ugly, ungrateful children." She stomped her foot at the end of this declaration for emphasis.

"Be careful what you say, little one," Kalamar gently chided. "She doesn't sound like she would have made your great-grandfather happy in the end. Maybe he finds his true love later in the story. After all," he added, "he must have found someone to love or you wouldn't be here."

"You're probably right," she added with the gravity of a child. "I wish I could do magick."

"Maybe you will. It's a hard craft but if you work hard and are dedicated, there's no reason that you can't," Kalamar replied.

"You'll teach me?" She gasped. "I can go with you to learn?"

Kalamar realized he'd just stepped onto unsteady ground with the child and cursed himself for not being more careful with his words.

"Can she really go with you and learn?" her mom added. "She won't have any kind of life here and she is a hard worker."

Kalamar's heart sank further upon hearing the mother's words. He'd hoped she would talk the child out of it, not encourage her. He collected himself and carefully considered the pit he'd just dug for himself.

"Madam," he began gravely, trying to regain control of the discussion, "magical study is a dangerous pursuit. It is not a decision of the moment. I am also not a master, so I cannot teach Kellyn myself or speak for my master in this matter. In addition, she is too young to begin studying at a school and I'm not aware of one around here.

"My remarks about learning are true and I meant them to encourage her if that opportunity came along when she is ready. It was not an immediate offer and I'm sorry for any confusion I've caused. If you're still willing to sell me these books and items, I'd like to discuss that with you but will understand if you want to keep them for sentimental value." He'd kept his voice calm and hoped he'd clearly sorted out the situation. Kellyn, however, was heartbroken at his words and was clearly fighting back tears.

"I understand," her mom replied, "and we're the ones who confused your words. The fault is ours, not yours. I would ask you to please consider taking her. I know you can't make promises to teach her but she will never find any teachers here and there is no type of life that I can give her that matches. I will certainly sell you the chest as it is of no use to me. I don't know what a fair price would be but will accept your honor in this."

Kalamar nodded at this and used the opening rune he'd discovered earlier with his identification spells to unlock the tome and look through it. He was using this as cover and knew it. He was about to make a rash decision that he hoped he wouldn't regret or his master be disappointed in.

After finishing his scan, he set all the contents back into the chest and stood up. Tremain was clearly studying him with a curious gaze, wondering which way he'd go. He looked to the mother, who was clearly anxious for her daughter. Finally, he turned to Kellyn, whose face was like a puppy he'd once seen. So pathetically hopeful it was impossible to not respond.

He cleared his throat and, turning back to the mom, said, "A fair price for the chest and its contents is thirteen pounds sterling." The mom gasped at hearing this as she'd never considered having that kind of wealth.

"As you can see," he continued, "that sum will considerably change the type of life you and your daughter can have. With that being said, however, I will make you this offer.

"I am not a master, as I stated earlier and cannot promise to train your daughter. I will take her as a servant to clean and care for my possessions. When she is older, and if I judge her to be qualified, I will train her myself if able or I will present her to my master for his consideration. I cannot, in any way, guarantee he will accept her. She will then have a choice to make. She can continue to serve in my household, she can find employment elsewhere or I will see that she is delivered back here to pursue another path. She will be fed, clothed and paid four shillings a year until a decision has to be made."

"Yes, yes, please," Kellyn shouted. Kalamar ignored the outburst and kept his gaze on the mother.

"Yes, she should go with you. Even with the coinage, there really is nothing for her here," her mom replied.

"Very well then," Kalamar responded. "My master and I will be leaving in the morning. Have her ready to go then. And you, young miss," he said, turning to Kellyn, "head over to Mahon's shop and tell him that you are entering my employ and need two suitable sets of clothes in my colors. I'll settle up the account with him later."

With a squeal of delight Kellyn ran out the shop.

"Now, mistress, let us settle my purchase, shall we?"

Kalamar left the shop with a half-empty coin purse. Tremain carried the chest over his shoulder. All things considered, Kalamar felt he'd come out well in the day's deals.

*****

Eolande watched Kalamar as he sat, legs folded beneath him, in the corner of his room. He was clearly meditating with the occasional spell cast between. The object of his focus was a small necklace that she knew well. It was now the famous locket of the Scarlet Bandit, whom this young man had slain to his newfound wealth and glory.

The celebration last evening had been a huge success. Both he and his master had been clever and witty, captivating everyone with their charm and grace. She was here in his bedchamber, having volunteered as a priestess of Telmar to guarantee the virtue of the young girl who shared his bed last night.[8]

There had been no violation of Nestor'Shath and the night had passed slowly. She found herself drawn against her will, however, to what he was doing. As a priestess, she was certainly aware of casting spells. His confidence and calm, his steady manner, however, were unsuited to someone so young. He did it almost casually, even as she felt the strong and powerful energies he was channeling.

---

[8] Nestor'Shath was an old custom. Through third parties to protect everyone's honor, a noble could share the warmth of the evening with the unmarried girls of court for an agreed fee. The fee increased with the desires of the noble. From sharing warmth to the capturing of virginity, it was all mutually agreed in advance to protect everyone involved. It allowed the (usually) poorer young servant women to quickly grow a dowry and the chaperons ensured that the noble didn't change his mind and demand more once they retired to the room.

He was now dangling the necklace in front of his eyes, watching the simple garnet catch and reflect the early morning sunlight. A contented smile was upon his lips in clear satisfaction of his work.

"What have you done?" she asked in spite of herself. She'd had no intention of speaking to him and was surprised to have done so.

"I've put a small blessing and protection upon this necklace," he replied. "It must have seen so much sorrow. I'm hoping it will bring its new bearer better fortune." He spoke quietly and his melancholy at the thought seemed quite sincere.

Eolande quickly drew in her breath at this. Several impossible thoughts raced through her mind at his words.

It was impossible he could so easily put permanent enchantments on the necklace.

It was impossible he could cast a blessing and not be of a priestly order.

And it was impossible that this murderer of Riordan could feel sorrow about killing him.

Her next words did not come from her head as she wanted but from her heart as she didn't.

"You sound remorseful over his death? Surely, a hero such as yourself wouldn't concern yourself over an outlaw bandit's death." She held her breath at her foolhardy outburst but he didn't appear to notice. He turned his head, appearing lost elsewhere as he softly responded.

"As the arrows were flying by and he charged sword drawn to run me down, I simply followed my training to save my life and that of my master. I will never know what choices he made that led him to those actions. I only know my own. I do know, however, there was someone that he loved or he would not have worn this." He held the necklace up higher in the light. "That probably means that he was loved by someone as well. What happened? Why were they not together? Are the stories true that her father separated them? Who can say?" He paused for a moment before continuing. "I do not like what I've done even though I know it was right. I have also shed my tears for this stranger, although my master left that part out of the story." He smiled gently at that. "I am leaving this necklace here with

Vevina"—he nodded to the woman sleeping still in the bed—"in the hope that, with her, it will see some happiness and joy and perhaps Riordan will find some peace wherever he's gone."

With that, he got up, went over to Vevina and kissed her on the forehead. He gently set the necklace beside the bed, nodded his thanks to Eolande and quietly left the room.

What he did not see was Eolande scrambling over to the table, reaching for the necklace—her necklace. Her hand was trembling as she reached for it, but paused as tears flowed down her cheeks. She had joined the order instead of marrying Dewitt, whom her father insisted she marry. Her father would not accept her true love because he was poor, so she'd been shipped out here to be far away from him. Riordan had followed her after he dueled and killed Dewitt, forever an outlaw on the run for his love.

After what felt an eternity she drew a deep breath and withdrew her trembling hand. Years of sorrow and pain were purged from her heart and she felt her god's love wash over her with it's peace. Kalamar was not her enemy and he was also right. Let the necklace find solace for them all with a new life and a new beginning.

Chapter 3

Stormlake

I t had taken almost two weeks to reach the town of Overlook,[9] just northwest of Stormlake. Every town and village they'd passed through meant a call on the local lord and usually a dinner and night's rest. This had given them the opportunity to make acquaintances with lords and officials they might need to work with in the future. Since they brought with them news and stories from other places, their visits were upbeat affairs. An additional benefit was to give the entire party opportunities to better understand their roles and adjust to the archmage's leadership and direction.

Kalamar hired two additional servants, Duer as a tutor for Kellyn and Sloan to see to his horses and gear. As was his station, he was riding about one-quarter mile ahead of the rest to announce his master's arrival and make preparations when necessary.

Their journey had followed the Stonewash River through most of the barony until Herford, where the main road diverted north around the lake's forest. As he rode up to Overlook, he noticed the unusual planning that allowed the forest to follow the road all the way to the edge of town. It was filled with evergreens that were so dense no view through them was possible.

---

9   Overlook—so named because it provided the best view of Stormlake Castle and Stormlake itself. The road leading into the town from the west had dense trees planted up to the edge of the town so the visitor was completely surprised with the view of the valley below to the lake. All of the town was to the north of the road, so those traveling through and the lucky few with homes directly on the road had the most advantageous views.

Normally, for security, the trees would be cut away and cleared from the town so attackers couldn't hide. While it's true there hadn't been any fighting in Eddington since its founding, the rules for security were always enforced. Almost always, he amended. While his master had mentioned the name and the nice view, Kalamar was speechless with what he beheld as he finally reached the edge of town and forest.

Stormlake Castle was straight out of a troubadour's tale. High white stone walls and turrets surrounded a beautiful castle with bright blue-and-red pennants flying high and proud in the breeze. The deeper-blue-slate roof seemed to gleam as it bathed the entire complex in a hazy glow. Upon seeing, it was not hard to imagine that a fair lady and powerful lord ruled there and all were subject to their benevolence. The power and majesty of the place were unmistakable. It was set upon a rocky crag thrust up from the bowels of the earth and stood guarding over the town below to its north.

All this, however, was as nothing compared to what awaited the viewer upon taking the next steps showing the entire panorama. Stormlake itself filled all the southern view. Its deep blue waters reflected the sun and sky with a clarity that was unheard of. At its heart was the sight that filled the witness with awe and even fear. A never-ending storm churned in the center of the lake. A massive water cyclone reached all the way to the sky, pulling in any clouds that flew too close. Lightning slashed and ripped through the atmosphere in a dance that never stopped with the slow, purposeful sunwise spinning of the storm. While the water was roiled and churned under the clouds covering the sky above, once outside of its panoply, it flattened smooth as glass.

This sight left the viewer moved on the deepest levels and Kalamar was no exception. The beauty, power and majesty of the lake struck him almost a physical blow, taking his breath away. Tears unashamed, rolled down his face at the sight and he could only stare.

It was a subdued group that finally made the last few miles to the town of Stormlake. While the view still overwhelmed, it was starting to become more manageable as the mind began to make sense of the myriad sights and feelings.

It occurred to Kalamar this was exactly why the first baron chose this spot to build his capital. The mind would naturally associate the power of the storm with those who lived here. *It was a very clever bit of manipulation*, he thought and he would need to keep that in mind. It was early afternoon when he rode up to the city's western gate to be challenged by the guards. His now well-rehearsed introduction was quite polished and he was pleased to see the swift, positive response. Obviously, they were on lookout for the archmage and quickly sent word to the castle to arrange an appropriate honor guard and escort for their arrival at court.

The town of Stormlake was double the size of anything else they'd seen. Its population of approximately eleven thousand permanent residents was the wealthiest and it showed. Every visage was about maintaining the expected image. The viewable streets were well kept. The clothing, noble and commoner alike, was of good make and condition. The streets were paved and without potholes. No detritus or debris was clogging the channels for drainage. The homes along the main thoroughfare were exceptionally well kept and of the finest craftsmanship available.

The main road didn't take you into the city but instead through the noble's district, making directly for the castle. The southern gate led straight to a short but steep climb up to the fortress itself. At each checkpoint, they were passed through alert and well-dressed guards. It seemed a bit excessive to Kalamar, but he suspected it was meant to impress upon any entering the status of those who lived in the palace above.

Once inside the fortress' outer walls, several beautifully maintained gardens were visible at the edges of the main courtyard. Their party was quickly escorted inside the palace proper to the main waiting hall to be introduced at court.

Only the archmage and Kalamar waited. Their servants had been taken elsewhere with their supplies, to await further instruction. He stood as they heard the rap of a staff on the other side of the entrance doors to the great hall.

"Hear ye, hear ye," someone's voice boomed with ritual emphasis. "My lord and lady baron, lords and ladies, esteemed members of the court. I present to you Lord Angus Crow, Archmage of Sarrik, and his protégé Sir Kalamar Sylvicheld, mage and knight of the realm."

At this point, the doors were hauled open, allowing a view of the court inside. It was a grand affair with large columns on both sides. There were about one hundred people on both sides of the aisle through the center. Upon a raised dais on the far side was clearly a throne and smaller matching chair for the baron's wife. The baron was perhaps in his late forties, his wife about a decade younger. They had six children of which four were present today. Stern and proud they looked with their gold stitched, fur-lined clothing.

Upon reaching the front of the court, the archmage gave a slight bow, with Kalamar bowing lower.

"I am honored to accept your invitation, my Lord Baron Eddington. Thank you for extending me the gracious opportunity to reacquaint myself with your beautiful hall," The archmage intoned.

At this, Lord Terrence rose and replied, "It is we who are honored, my lord, for your swift response to our cause. I remember well the high esteem my father had for you and your aide in his needs of the past. We would like very much to discuss privately the possibility of you joining the court on a permanent basis, to add your wisdom to the defense of this land."

"I would be delighted to hear your proposals and be of any help that I can offer," the archmage responded with a polite nod.

"Then let us retire to a more comfortable setting so we may discuss things in earnest."

Lord Terrence then waved to another man who stepped forward and announced, "This audience is ended. Thank you to all who have participated this day in the lord's justice."

As the formal dismissal faded, whispered conversations rose and swelled as the assemblage began exiting the grand hall. Kalamar and his master followed a much-smaller group through a small door on the left. This new hall led them to a smaller room, suitable for about twenty to sit comfortably on cushioned chairs. Several windows on the left looked out over a garden that was just beginning to bloom with the new spring.

Here they were introduced to the smaller group, whom they would learn were the privy council[10]: Lady Ula, baroness of Eddington; Lord Dugan of Highcliff, high chamberlain; Lord Malcolm Cherrheld of Bandon, high chancellor; Lord Owen of Greenfields, high justice; General Shay, high marshal; Ghan Teague high priest of Saa'Vey and high chaplain; Lord Willem Vestrum of Chandrom; and the baron's eldest son, Wallace.

While the introductions were made, drinks were served and then the serving staff withdrew.

"As we stated in the missive sent to you," the baron began, "we would like you to join this council. What we did not say is why. Ghan Teague?"

Ghan Teague was grey of hair but clearly strong in physic. As a high priest of the warrior god, he was required to be ever ready for war. He went straight to the point. "Our order has been troubled by dreams and visions over the last year. None of them very specific. No wordings or pronouncements as such. Usually just dark images that seem to swallow the light or blood-soaked images. Our best intuition suggests a war but not a traditional one. Many of the images seem sorcerous in nature. We also cannot pinpoint a specific threat. It is vague and ill-defined. I'm sure I don't have to mention to you that these are not the typical images that our order receives in times of war.

"As a separate issue, but one we think linked, we found a wizard's spy[11] here in the castle. We were unable to determine who sent it, but we don't like the idea of an enemy spying in our lands and what that might suggest."

"Have you seen any physical signs of an enemy? Anything on your borders?" the archmage asked.

General Shay spoke up, "No, we haven't. That is also a disturbing part of this. We have been additionally vigilant since the

---

[10] The Eddington Court was a more formal group and had several more members, thereby representing a much-larger selection of society.

[11] A Wizard's Spy or Occulari in mages terms, is a magical creation from many spells that function as a scrying device. A seeing and/or listening orb. The more powerful can even remember what they experience so that its creator only has to sporadically merge his senses to gain a full viewing of past events it witnesses.

dreams began and have found nothing to suggest or point to an enemy close by."

The archmage nodded and responded, "So that may be a clue in and of itself. The enemy may not be close and/or the time of danger may be farther out, which may be why the dreams are so difficult to define and explain." Many nodded in agreement with this statement or added a verbal assent to this logic. He continued, "The visions ambiguity may also suggest that the threat is not just this barony but all the lands, therefore, it is less specific to you here but a threat to everyone."

This was greeted with outright dismay at the possibility.

"What can we do against such a threat?" Lord Willem asked. It wasn't addressed to anyone specifically but all seemed to turn to the archmage.

"You do what it seems you are already doing. You increase your patrols, increase your soldiers and train them even harder. You run down any evidence you can and remain vigilant. Gather any allies you can find and maintain your faith in the gods," declared his master firmly to general assent from those present.

"And are you going to join us?" asked Lord Dugan.

"What are you asking of me?" was the archmage's reply.

It was Baron Terrance who responded. "We are asking you to join this court as High Wizard. You would be a member of this council and the greater full court. You would be responsible for and have jurisdiction over all things magical in my lands. I must confess to not knowing what funds you would need or any supplies or space available, but we will work with you to provide what you need."

"Fair enough," his master responded. "As for the rest, let me lay out what I've seen before in this type of situation. In addition to what you have stated, I will need a quiet place to work, preferably a tower in a less busy part of the castle. A single entrance is best. There will be times I have to make life-and-death decisions and I need the authority to do so. I, or my protégé will also need access to you specifically without going through others in times we deem an emergency.

"If there are any specific spells you request be cast, I will need you to provide all the necessary components for those. I will need the authorities and permissions to train students. While I will pay my own staff, I will expect that we can all eat from the castle larder with the rest of those residing here and that our animals will be cared for with the rest of your animals. I also require that mine and my protégé's patents of nobility be recognized. As for pay, I will need one hundred pounds sterling per month, plus any taxes I may be subject to."

The room exploded in noise once he'd finished his list. From the multiple conversations, it quickly narrowed down to his last demand of payment. The archmage remained calm throughout and Kalamar followed his example, saying nothing.

Baron Terrance brought the room back to order but it was young Lord Wallace who spoke up.

"How can you possibly ask for such an outrageous sum?" he demanded. His look was clearly affronted at the perceived insult.

The archmage responded calmly, "When I left the arch-chancellorship of Sarrik, I was invited by the King of Calledon to be the Royal Court Wizard. The offer included a private palace to work and study from, a paid staff of two hundred members plus ten master mages, thirty lesser mages plus any and all supplies. In addition, I was to be paid fifty thousand pounds sterling per year."

The silence in the room was complete.

"Now, I understand the economics of the barony are different," he continued softly, "which is why I have not asked for anything nearly as extravagant as all that. You are a quiet hardworking people and I respect that. I am willing to stake my very life to help you maintain that for your people, but I do ask that I be paid what, under the circumstances, is a very fair wage."

It was Ghan Teague who spoke first, "Every word he just spoke was true. While the mind boggles at those kinds of numbers, I don't see that anything he is asking for is unjust."

Baron Terrance cleared his throat in the silence that followed and asked, "May we see the patents?"

The archmage held out his hands and performed a simple summoning spell, causing both patents to appear, before handing them to the baron. It was not the spell that caused the room to hush anew.

Patents were wrapped with several bands representing the officials whose seals were involved in their creation. The first band is the patent holder's seal and colors. The second band is the seal and colors of the noble issuing the patent. A third band is possible once the patents are certified by the royal patent authority in the Calledon capital north of the Nantukk mountains. This set is always black with a gold thread.

Kalamar's patent had the first two bands. Lord Angus Crow's had four bands. The fourth band was purple with silver thread. Only a member of the royal house would be allowed the fourth band.

The baron's hands trembled slightly as he undid the ties and unrolled the patent for the archmage. He briefly looked over the patents and then exclaimed aloud, "This says you are almost two hundred years old."

"That is true, my lord. I will be 193 on my next birthday. Wizards can live a very long time."

Baron Terrance gently rolled back up the first patent, retied the bands, and handed it back very carefully.

No doubt as a courtesy, he then unrolled and read Kalamar's. This patent was different, as he was the first of the line, so it described the events of it's creation instead of the lineage he came from.

"So, you defeated the Scarlet Bandit and earned your patent," he remarked. "That is well done. You have done us all a great service in this and are welcome to this court.

"Lord Crow, we find that your terms are most generous and are honored to welcome you to this court. We will hold a feast in your honor this evening and let us all look forward to a long and prosperous future together."

*****

Kalamar entered the tailor's shop recommended to him. He wanted a new outfit for the dinner this evening.

"You lad, what master are you here for?" a thin, older man shouted across the shop from where he was busy sewing something.

"None" was Kalamar's startled reply. "Have a good day," he called as he exited the building. *That seemed rude*, he thought as he made his way to the next shop farther up the street.

Three shops later, he was getting annoyed. Everyone was treating him like he didn't have two pennies to his name and couldn't possibly be there on his own accord. He walked to the nearest intersection and turned right off the main street. He then kept heading east through town.

The farther east he went, the lower the level of wealth displayed. He stopped at an intersection with a stump on a small green patch. Looking all directions, he saw a tailor's sign to the right and headed south.

The sign was freshly painted and the windows were clean, but the building itself had seen better days. It was obvious the proprietor was making the best with limited funds.

"Welcome, young man" was the greeting he received from a thin man of average height. His clothing was spotless with intricate stitching of roses and vines. "I'm Master Taylor Cory Dresdon. How can I help you this fine day?"

Now he was getting somewhere. He didn't want anyone fawning over him. He'd already seen enough of that on his trip here for a lifetime, but he didn't believe a bit of courtesy and maybe even some honest friendliness was too much to ask.

"I'm Knightmage Kalamar Sylvicheld and I'm looking to have some clothes made for the baron's dinner this evening."

"I'm honored to meet you, sir," he responded with a slight bow, "and you have certainly come to the right place. Do you have something particular in mind? You said mage. Does that mean the rumors are true that a Sarrik has come to town?"

"To the first," he responded with a smile, "I like the cut of what I'm wearing. It allows me the freedom to move and ride but still has the look of a robe. To the second, you are correct. My master is a Sarrik archmage."

"Sarrik archmage! That is extraordinary. I'm stunned that there's one out here in the middle of nowhere," he said with a laugh. "Are you passing through to bigger and better places?"

Kalamar smiled at the imagery Cory's words conjured. "Actually, my master has just accepted the post of high wizard of the baron's court. I must ask, are you familiar with Sarrik? Also, Dresdon, there is a city in the Duchy of Genevieve[12] by that name, isn't there?"

"There is indeed, sir. There is indeed. That is where I was born and raised. I came out here as a young man to make my fortune in the frontier." He laughed to himself. "Finding my wife and then my children coming along has given me a quite different treasure than I originally expected. As for Sarrik, everyone in Genevieve knows of Sarrik. All the local wizards would go green with envy every time they'd be mentioned. If I may get back to business for a moment, sir, what are your colors?" he asked.

Kalamar created an illusion of his banner and was pleased to see that Cory didn't jump or startle the way everyone else did. He was clearly experienced in dealing with mages or at least had heard the lore.

"My father was born in Glendale, just north of Dresdon as I recall. He also came out here to make his place in the world. Brought his beautiful wife with him and settled down to property west of Eddington."

"Glendale! My, my, what a small world it is. I visited with some friends one evening, looking for a good time. We woke up in the sewage pit outside of town the next morning, heads ringing and bruised all over. None of us could remember the night before but we all swore it was the best night of our lives."

Kalamar had to laugh. "That sounds just like my father described it. A town of rascals and scalawags always looking for trouble." Kalamar was enjoying the conversation and company. It also reminded him a bit of home in this strange new place. He had to admit he rather liked this Cory.

"I am certainly able to make your outfits to this color with cotton but for a more formal evening, may I show you something?

---

[12] Genevieve is the only duchy south of the Nantukk mountain range. It is the oldest and largest of the noble holdings created by the southern immigration from Calledon. It was officially created in 946 of the founding and is far to the east of Eddington, along the Viliss Ocean's coast.

It's not suited to most people as it's a bit dark, but it's the finest cloth I have." He'd gone back behind a counter and pulled out a wrapped bundle. Unwrapping it, Kalamar saw a very dark-grey silk Coathardie with delicate, almost silver-ivory stiching. It was excellent quality and he was sure there must be a story of how it was left in the shop unpaid for. It was indeed dark and he could imagine most wouldn't care for it. It created a very specific look.

"I like it," he stated. "It's a bit different, I'll grant you but I think it will suit me. Can you have the modifications ready before dinner this evening?"

"Certainly, my lord. I'll bring it up myself."

"Will I get in trouble with the original purchaser?" he asked carefully.

"No, my lord. It was many years ago and to give it the shape you've requested will make enough changes no one will recognize it."

"Excellent. Now, if only I have this much luck with the rest of my purchasing," he complained with a clearly frustrated tone.

"If you don't mind my asking, my lord, what else are you seeking?"

"I don't mind at all," he replied and quickly gave him the items he needed.

After the privy council meeting, Kalamar and his master had been taken to one of the original towers built in the keep. It was currently being used for storage, but its out-of-the-way location was ideal and the archmage had accepted. It was five stories tall, not including the roof and Kalamar was being given the third floor for his own. Other than a few shelves and every book he could find, he hadn't purchased anything until he knew what his new home would be.

To his surprise and pleasure, Cory quickly gave him a list of sellers of all the items he needed and the prices they would probably accept. He also told him to not let them charge him for delivery because it was a point of pride to be seen carrying your wares up to the castle. They'd all be delighted for the opportunity to preen before their competitors. His local knowledge of everyone and everything was impressive.

"I greatly appreciate the advice, Cory. Thank you. What will I owe you for the coat and two working versions in cotton?"

"Eight pounds sterling," he responded without apparent thought.

Kalamar considered this against what he'd seen both here and on his journey. Silk was a great luxury and was almost nonexistent; he'd seen it almost nowhere on his journey here.

"That seems a fair price," he said slowly. "I tell you what. You deliver the coat tonight as agreed and I'll pay you ten pounds sterling." He continued, "And if you're interested, you can display my banner in your shop." It was an honor to display a noble's banner in your shop as a display of patronage and distinction among competitors. It also created a bond, as the noble would bring his business there and was publicly putting his name and honor on the shop.

Cory and Kalamar looked at each other and came to an agreement without words.

"I'm honored, my lord, truly, and would be delighted to display your banner in my shop. You will never have cause to doubt this decision or me."

"I know I won't, Cory. Now, I have some more purchases to make, so I best be about it."

Chapter 4

dinner and a show

Cory stood quietly on the balcony with the other town craftsmen as their handiwork was on display below. It was a well-known secret they all met up here to gloat over those who weren't allowed in. It had been almost three years since he was here last and that had been as a guest of someone else, so it didn't really count.

He looked down at the baronial dinner and all the guests as they wore the admission price for his fellow craftsmen to gain entrance to this balcony. Dresses and jackets, jewelry, hats and shoes. If an item you crafted was downstairs for its first appearance in society, you were allowed to witness its debut, discreetly, to the exclusion of your peers without such access. It was vain and petty, but it allowed those with the wit to observe much of the politics and intrigue in the capital.

As someone foreign born, Cory had been at a disadvantage with his competitors. In the beginning, his difference had been a novelty and gained him some work, but it had not lasted. As such, he'd been unable to secure permanent entrance to the higher strata of society. It was not because of his work or skill with a needle, which he could honestly say was of the finest quality.

He had to admit it was the superior attitude he'd brought with him from the duchy to this backwater, as he'd thought of it at the time. It had rubbed too many people the wrong way before he learned a bit of needed humility.

He shook his head ruefully. He'd learned the lesson too late to keep those rarefied doors open, but he had eventually managed to make a meager living and raise a family. Tonight, however, he had a second chance and would not fail again.

He turned about as his name was called by another sharing the balcony. Sullivan, the tailor and Keefe, the jeweler, held the patronage of Baron Eddington and as such were here every dinner, if they were not themselves guests. Cairbre, Broderick, Fionan and Donald were the other tailors present but it was Owen, an excellent jeweler, who said, "What an unusual design for that jacket you made Sir Kalamar. I see he purchased that dark silk you've had for some time, hum? He carries it well, I must say. He doesn't wear any jewelry, I see, but I have a sapphire I could put in a ring that would go beautifully. Don't you think?"

"I'm sure it would," he responded noncommittally. "Isn't that necklace your design Lady Avalbane is wearing? It's quite stunning with that dress."

"Well," Owen feigned forgetfulness, "I believe it is. She wears it very well."

"Of course, of course."

"I must say…" Owen broke off as something unusual was going on below.

"My lords and ladies, honored guests," Baron Terrance began with raised voice, "I am delighted to announce, due to the persistence of my youngest, Mahon, that Lord Angus, our new high wizard, has agreed to craft a small piece of magic for us." He nodded his head as the assemblage broke out in polite applause.

At this, the archmage walked from the place of honor around to the front of the main table.

"My lords and ladies, honored guests," Lord Angus began in a quiet voice that still managed to be heard clearly by all in the hall. "Young Mahon has asked for a display of magic and I am sorry to report that I don't do those very well." The guests were clearly disappointed at hearing this and began to whisper among themselves. "So," he continued as if there was no interruption, "I've decided to summon the greatest sorcerer in the known world." This now held everyone's rapt attention. "His name is Jack Bennibauk. I am sure he would be most delighted to put on a sensational show." The archmage paused for effect. "Now, I must warn you that he is a giant from Stormgate Mountain and while he might seem scary, please do not be alarmed as he would not hurt a fly." He once again paused and slowly turned to make sure everyone was agreeing to the terms.

When he'd completed his circle, he raised his arms and all the fires and torches dimmed to delighted oohs from the crowd. With that, he began a chant, slow at first, rising and falling in words that you couldn't quite make out. Louder and faster it grew until, with a great voice, he shouted, "JACK BENNIBAUK!"

At first, nothing seemed to happen; but within a heartbeat or two, a humming sound began to permeate the room, growing louder and louder until, with a tearing sound, a great light ripped open in the ceiling and a deep, angry voice demanded, "Who dares summon the Great Jack Bennibauk?"

Anger and no small fear began filling the room as everyone reacted at once.

"Calm everyone, be at peace," the archmage whispered, and all heard and obeyed. "All will be well."

Lifting his head up to the light, the archmage said, "Now, Jack, you are scaring all these fine folk. It is I, Archmage Crow, who has summoned you. Surely you have not forgotten my calling rune in your decrepitude," he chided.

"CROW," the voice returned. "I remember you well and not kindly if *your* memory has not failed completely." At this, a literal giant's head appeared in the light above the hall as if from a hole in the sky looking down. It was quickly replaced by what clearly were its feet then whole legs as it lowered itself down to the hall floor as if from a tree branch.

Shocked, stunned into immobility was the reaction in the hall and balcony as they gasped and gaped at the sight before them. A giant, twenty-five feet tall if an inch, towered above everyone in the hall, especially the puny-looking archmage who had dared to summon it. Wearing a bright-yellow robe with star and moon symbols that glowed in the darkened hall, with a matching pointed hat, the giant would have been comical if he didn't look like he could squish anything he wanted without a second thought.

"I'd like to introduce you to Baron Terrance Eddington, Jack. And especially his youngest son, Mahon, who requested your esteemed presence this fine evening." The archmage's tone was calm and matter-of-fact. As if this was a perfectly natural and normal introduction, the tensions and fear slowly subsided.

"Baron, you say?" Jack boomed. "Seems you're moving up in the world. 'Bout damn time, anyway," he said with a laugh. "I'm delighted to meet you, Baron of Eddington, and you too, young Mahon." He gave each a bow. "How can I help be of service this night?"

"CAN YOU SHOW US SOME MAGIC?" Mahon's childish voice shouted in delight. "Crow promised you would."

At this everyone laughed and as if a spell had been lifted, the nervousness seemed to flee the room.

Jack had joined in the laughter and said, "He did, did he? Well, well, well, I guess he will owe me a favor once we're through here. How delightful." He continued to more chuckles from the audience. "What shall we see? What shall we do? How about...got it. Would you like to see the four elemental planes, young man?"

"Err, what element planes?" Mahon responded, unsure of what they were.

"The elemental planes! You know, where all the material to build this world came from? Crow, have you not been teaching them anything?" He went on, "Never mind. Seeing is believing, and it's just the thing."

"Jack," said the archmage, "are you sure yo—"

"Pish, posh," Jack responded. "Of course, I'm sure. It will be a great learning experience for him. Now hush. Are you ready, young man?"

"YES," shouted the boy, not having the slightest inkling.

"Excellent. You've got an adventurous heart, most excellent. *Now*, the first plane to visit is AIR." Jack raised his hand; and with a snap of his fingers, the walls, the castle, everything but the floor and the furniture they were using disappeared.

Gasps of fear and not a few shouts and screams greeted the stunning vista before them. All around, for as far as the eye could see, was sky and clouds. A bright sun shone down, lighting the world they found themselves in. The sky was filled with every kind of flying creature imaginable, from birds and butterflies to winged angels and dragons. All manner of creatures they'd never dreamed possible were visible on every horizon. None came close, but all could be seen and heard, calling and singing to each other.

Jack let this go on for just a moment and, raising his hand again, snapped his fingers while shouting, "FIRE."

This time they did not jump as earlier but seemed to fly among the stars as the realm of fire grew larger in their vision. He did not take them into it, but they seemed to hover near as they saw never-ending fields of flame, raging volcanoes spewing lava, with fumes and smoke rolling every which way across the plains. Even here, though, they saw creatures of all kinds, in large groups or singly. Salamander to humanoid, flying and crawling.

"WATER," Jack shouted and they shot off again through the stars. From schools of fish in every color imaginable to a great beast that dwarfed the hall or even the entire castle, merfolk and all manner of eels, squid and whale swam by without a care for the visitors.

"EARTH," he shouted a last time, and they were off again through the stars. Now, however, they seemed to enter an impossibly large cave as they trespassed deep into the plane. Here were great slithering things glimpsed in the connecting tunnels with dwarfs, gnomes and a thousand other creatures busily digging, mining and building.

Between one heartbeat and the next, they returned home, the castle walls solid again around them as if they had never left. Jack also was gone with only the faintest sound on the air that seemed to say, "I hope you enjoyed your trip, young man."

"I DID," Mahon shouted. Everyone started talking at once. Many reached for their goblets and drained them dry, looking around for more.

Cory had never experienced anything like it in his life. What little he knew of magic told him it had to be an illusion, that it couldn't be real but he, like everyone else, was reeling from the experience. Everything had been so believable. *That was power*, he thought.

It was this certainty that allowed him to settle his mind down. He brought his attention back to what everyone was doing and what those in the room with him were saying. Who enjoyed the display and who didn't, lines were being drawn. It was inevitable. This he could understand, this was a game he longed to play and this was why he was here. *It was time to go to work*, he thought with a smile. His lord was counting on him.

*****

It was almost the second hour of night[13] and Kalamar was with his master as they were crafting the runes to protect the castle within a large magical shield. The dinner was over and Kalamar thought his master's display had been a great success. There were a few who seemed perturbed but most everyone else couldn't say enough about how much they enjoyed it. With the guest gone, his master wanted to get started immediately on encircling the castle. Once done, they could capture all the occulari spying on the occupants before their creators could hide or remove them.

The full spells of protection would take days, but for their purpose, they just needed to cut off the occulari from outside contact. This could be done by just creating the first set of basic shielding runes. They only needed a few hours *and* to be uninterrupted. It was this last part that was going to be the issue.

Orders had been issued to the guards, he and his master were not to be interfered with. Additional orders required no one could enter or leave the castle until the archmage gave orders otherwise.

The spell they needed to create was simple and straightforward, but tedious. A single mistake in crafting and all the prior work would be undone. A small personal shield involved fifteen runes connected

---

[13] Time is divided into four six-hour periods, named morning, afternoon, evening, and night. Morning and afternoon are separated by "official" midday on the longest day of the year. All other time revolves around that. Midnight separates evening and night. The first hour of night would be equivalent, in our counting between 12:00 a.m. and 1:00 a.m.

end to end. To shield the entire castle,[14] they needed to cast those fifteen runes in sequence over and over around the entire outer walls. It was the third hour of night and they were working across the main gate when Kalamar heard horse's hooves clattering up the paved road.

Kalamar looked to his master, who nodded but did not interrupt his rune-crafting. Withdrawing his senses from the shield, he quickly walked around his master and out the gate to the guards, who were pointing down the road and discussing the situation. The rider was pushing his horse hard and was only moments from the gate.

"You need to stop that rider," Kalamar instructed the lieutenant.

"I can't, sir, that's Lord Ferguson an—"

Kalamar ignored the rest as there was no time to argue. He stepped a few paces down the road and began chanting the runes to activate a sleeping spell. Instead of one individual like before, however, he needed to stop the rider and the horse. Hand outstretched in a halting gesture, the sleep spell hit both horse and rider like a wall. Lord Ferguson was asleep before tumbling off the horse, but the horse stumbled a few more steps before succumbing and dropping down on the road just a dozen or so feet from where Kalamar stood.

"Are you mad!" the lieutenant began but Kalamar was having none of it.

Grabbing the soldier by the arm, he steered him a few steps away from the men stunned by what they'd just seen. "Listen to me, you fool," Kalamar began in a hoarse whisper that clearly carried to the others. "Do you want to kill us all? Because that is exactly what could have happened if he'd ridden that horse through the shield before it's finished. You, me, all the men, everyone in the whole

---

[14] Normally, the shield would be built into the walls as they were constructed by placing specifically carved rune stones equidistant throughout the center most part of the wall. If a magic shield needed to be added after construction, conventional wisdom taught to cast each sequence of the runes and seal them into the wall. This took much longer but made it easier to work with. It also allowed the caster to complete a section without worrying about interruptions. Another benefit was, it allowed lower-circle mages to work on larger projects because they could stop to rest and regain their strength between sections. The possible drawback, however, was of allowing possible gaps in the shield.

castle could have been killed. Is that what you want?" Real fear was starting to show in his eyes as this lightweight youth still had hold of his arm.

"Your order," Kalamar continued remorselessly, "was to not let *anyone* through until we gave you permission. Anyone! Now"—he looked him in the eyes—"can I count on you to follow your orders or do I need someone else to carry them out?"

Finally, the seriousness of what was going on seemed to sink in and the very real fear of being disciplined for failing in his duties prompted him to say, "Yes, sir. You can count on me. Nothing will pass until you say so."

"Good," he replied. "Good. Now put a blanket over Lord Ferguson until we're done and take the tack off the horse so it doesn't hurt itself. I have to get back to my master." With that, he strode back to the entrance. The problem however, was his master had not been idle and continued on alone completing the current section.

Kalamar cleared his mind and extended his thought to the shield but did not enter. He waited patiently for his master's permission. Once granted, he slowly slid himself through the shield to get to the inside where his master was. All the soldiers watching gasped and jumped back as the shield flared and sparked around him as he went through.

His master obviously was aware of what had transpired and was adding "a bit of visual support" to Kalamar's words, he thought with a smile he kept off his face.

The remainder of the evening was thankfully uneventful and the spell was eventually complete. He and his master were now searching for any flaw or gap in the sequencing. It proceeded far more quickly and finding none, they now needed to give it power.

This was a simple thing that every mage learned in the early days of their apprenticeship. Kalamar began pouring his energy into the shield and if his power was like a rivulet of water from a stream, his master's was like the entire creek flowing to fill all the space within the shield both above and below the castle grounds. Both of theirs combined, however, were as nothing to the mighty river poured in by the guardian[15] called Tor. Tor had been the guardian at the arch-mage's cottage and agreed to relocate and continue his service here in Stormlake.

Even though Kalamar's contribution to the shield's energy was insignificant in relation to the others, it was necessary if he was to be able to claim authority and use the shield fully himself. As small as his contribution was, he was happy to see that it spread evenly throughout and he could sense there were no areas he didn't have access to. His master, also observing the shield and its rapidly grow-ing strength, finally nodded in satisfaction.

"Finish up here," the archmage said while looking in the direc-tion of the guards, "before you turn in. You've done well." He turned and walked inside.

Kalamar walked back to the lieutenant and his men. "We are finished for this evening, Lieutenant. Please see the men returned to their normal duties. I will go and wake Lord Ferguson," he said and began walking over to the sleeping form.

"Don't do that!" the lieutenant whispered in fear. "He's a nasty temper. 'Specially when he's up drinking. Let's just carry him to his bed and let him wake on his own. I'm sure that would be the wiser thing to do."

Kalamar noticed all the nearby soldiers were vigorously shaking their heads in agreement. "All right," he said. "We'll do it your way. If any trouble comes of it, just send it to me. I'll just go wake the horse. That is, unless you want to carry him in because he has a nasty temper too?" He added with a smile and noticed the soldiers were grinning as well.

---

[15] A guardian is a being from the higher realms that if they agree, usually for a fixed time (ten years and a day, one hundred years and a day, etc.), will protect a specific place using the spells they are given by the summoners. Their abilities make them especially suited for this task as they never sleep or rest. They generate large amounts of energy and replenish a shield that is being drained by attacks. The summoning mage also "teaches" the guardian all the spells he is allowing it to use. The traditional spells "taught" are missiles and lightning spells to repel attackers, open objects and create magical barriers for close range defense. As a final benefit, these shields can hold tremendous amounts of energy that the controlling mage can tap into in an emergency.

"No, good sir. The horse and I are old friends. I'll bring him some apples and he'll forgive me anything. Don't you worry 'bout him," he said, grinning now himself.

"Excellent, then I'll leave everything in your capable hands, Lieutenant Naal." And with that, he walked into his new home.

Chapter 5

Spies

It had been an exciting four days for Kalamar. In between hunting down all the occulari in the castle, he'd been pouring through all the books he'd purchased, meeting every noble in the barony who'd come to greet the new high wizard and setting up his third-floor home.

The legend of Jack Bennibauk spread to every corner of the land and no one talked about much else. Those who'd actually been there were the most sought-after dinner guests and couldn't keep up with all the invitations. His confidante, Cory, had more business than he could accept. And he'd just had a toast with his new friends, Garret and Mac.

They'd been his dinner companions during the welcoming ceremony and had met several times since. Garret was a lieutenant in the baron's army and wanted nothing more than to be a soldier and study war. Mac was a priest of Saa'Vey and he and Garret had been best friends since childhood.

He was on the fourth floor of the tower in a room the archmage had set aside as a workroom. On the table were the five occulari he'd found. His master had found them on the first day, but had given Kalamar the experience of locating, capturing and moving them here to be examined.

They'd traced the occulari back to their makers and learned who was doing the spying even if they had yet to know why. Four of the occulari were created by Pack 39 in Hoff[16] and the fifth by a mage named Adrienne in Torrence.[17]

Baron Terrance, Lord Malcolm and Ghan Teague entered the room together and after brief greetings, the archmage explained what they'd found and who the creators were. He even used illusions to make the occulari visible to non-caster eyes. The baron was incensed they were being spied on, especially the one found in his very bedchamber.

"It is not to be borne," Baron Terrance spat. "How dare they do such a thing?"

"They probably feel that's where the best secrets are to be learned," Ghan Teague replied. "Many men say things there, they don't say elsewhere."

The baron looked like he wanted to punch the high chaplain but mastered his temper and bit his tongue.

"And what are we to do? Now that we have discovered these," Lord Malcolm asked, directing the conversation elsewhere.

"We have done it," Ghan Teague replied. "We've discovered their actions and blocked them from continuing. What else can we do? We can't go to war and with what little evidence we have, we can't even send an envoy to complain as we don't know who ordered their creation. We haven't had contact with either barony in over twenty years."

"There is a bit more that we can do," Archmage Crow offered. "I know who they are and am watching them in return. They don't yet know they've lost them, so I'm waiting to see how they respond. It

---

[16] The barony of Hoff is to the north and east of Eddington. Other than a few independents or outlaws, all wizards there are forced into packs. Each pack is assigned specific areas of responsibility by the baron with the overall goal of training for war against their hated enemy, the barony of Torrence. When not fighting Torrence, they plot and scheme against each other for power and position inside a ridged hierarchy.

[17] The barony of Torrence is due east of Eddington. Wizards are not forced into packs like Hoff and retain their independence like any other member of the community. However, as a defensive measure against their longtime nemesis, Hoff, the barony does hire and train a special corps of wizards. Unfortunately, it is greatly diminished from its glory of yesteryear.

could be very telling as to what their intentions are. We should watch to see whether they are opportunistic or just curious."

"I see your reasoning, Archmage and it seems sound to me," the chancellor added. "A little patience could reveal a great deal about their plans, if any."

"Very well," the baron conceded. "Proceed as you see fit, but keep me informed of any progress or changes."

"Of course, my lord," replied the archmage.

"What will you do with the things?" the high priest asked.

"Destroy them."

"They are so crude." Everyone turned to Kalamar. He hadn't realized he spoke out loud and ducked his head, embarrassed that he'd interrupted.

Ghan Teague chuckled and said, "And you think you could do better, my boy?" To which, other than his master, they all smiled.

"Yes," he replied without hesitation.

"Well, prove it then" was the high priest's response. His retort had a bit of an edge. He didn't mind the accidental slip of the tongue as the young learn their place, but the last response seemed to be challenging his elders and he would nip it in the bud.

Kalamar, however, accepted the challenge and moved to the other end of the table. He cleared his thoughts and then cast a simple shielding spell over a small area of the table to work on and then a cleansing spell to remove any energetic debris. Here he paused again to organize his thoughts. He realized that the spells he needed were above his circle. He knew them of course, as he had a rare mind that remembered everything he saw, but casting them would be painful. He was a Third Circle Junior Journeyman. His last few weeks of training and study had confirmed it, but he needed two fourth-circle spells. Mages with talent and focus could cast spells of higher circles but the penalties were severe. The soul was not ready and it could weaken, damage or even kill the one who tried. He knew he could cast those spells individually but together, combined with all the others he needed? Exhaustion would be the best possibility, burning out his ability to cast magic was far more likely.

He was wasting his energy and knew it. He'd accepted the challenge; he knew he could do it; he knew he would pay a painful price and he would not back down now.

First, he needed a shell to contain the spells and give the occulari substance. This was the easy part and he quickly created a globe ridged enough to keep its form while he completed the project. He smiled as his master created the illusion of what he was doing so everyone in the room could see. He wasn't going to help, of course, but he was interested in the outcome.

The next spell needed was the first fourth-circle. He needed an energy source to power all the other spells. All spells draw their energy from somewhere and something like this needed to continue functioning without drawing from the mage himself. He saw the spell in his mind, but the runes did not burn clear for him like those he was able to properly use. They were cold like ashes that he had to fan to life. He whispered the words clearly and distinctly, using every technique he knew to get maximum power and focus. The energy poured from him in a torrent.

He nearly lost control and had to stop himself from shaking, but it had worked. He held on and the beating power source for his creation was there in the heart of the shell. He quickly linked it to the outer shell, like veins in the body. He would have been giddy with delight but was already tired and had much to complete before claiming success. He quickly added the spells for vision, hearing, and motion. He tied them into the heart and ensured that everything was working smoothly. He was exhausted and had a slight tremble in his hands but couldn't quit now.

Taking a deep breath, he pushed on. The last spell he needed was again fourth-circle. It had to be able to remember what it observed. Otherwise, it was only useful when the mage's senses were directly connected. Two of the occulari they found were like this but he was not going to settle at this point. His master's lessons on false pride appeared in his mind, but he banished them as distractions. Taking another deep breath, he again fought stone-cold runes and poured his will into the spell. His vision went dim; blackness was hovering around him but he did not lose the spell. He linked it to the senses he'd already given his creation. Rushing, he sent his senses through all the components, making sure all the links held and it worked the way it needed to. His last thought before passing out was victory.

Lord Malcolm stepped to the boy's aide but the archmage raised a hand to stop him. Crow had grabbed Kalamar magically and laid the boy gently on the floor. Malcolm shook his head at the odd sight, but remembering the banquet feast, he'd certainly seen stranger things.

"Why do you keep muttering that, Ghan? It's annoying," the baron said.

"It's not possible," the high priest said. "It's just not possible."

Malcolm looked from the boy to the boy's master and saw a slight smile on his face. He then turned to the priest and said with a laugh, "Obviously, it is possible."

"No, it's not possible," the high priest said even more emphatically.

"You just saw him do it, so of course, it's possible. Enough!" Baron Terrance declared.

"Why is it not possible?" asked Malcolm to cut the growing tension in the room. The Ghan was clearly troubled and the baron was in no mood for it.

The priest looked up from the table and glanced around at each of them. Realizing he wasn't making sense, he took a deep breath.

"All right," he said. "Let me start with these." He pointed to the five occulari on his side of the table. "Each of these was created by a master of at least Fourth Circle," he stated but looked to the archmage, who nodded in confirmation.

"Those two"—the archmage pointed—"were made by a full master. Fifth Circle."

"Just so, the best on the table were made by Fifth-Circle wizards. Men who have spent twenty or thirty years studying and using magic." The archmage nodded but said nothing, so he continued, "And to create these, they probably fasted, meditated, and cast spells over a week."

"Four days," the archmage interrupted.

"All right," Ghan Teague growled. "Four days." He pointed at the unconscious boy and said, "And he just created one in less than a half HOUR," raising his voice to make his point.

The room grew quiet as they considered the import of his words. Malcolm again looked at the archmage, who remained unconcerned and still had that small smile on his face, as if enjoying a secret only he knew.

"We have been repeatedly told the boy has talent," he finally offered. "It's quite clearly true." He shrugged as if that should settle it.

Ghan Teague looked fit to be tied but gamely continued on. "You're still not seeing the whole picture." He paused for thought. "All right, let me continue this way. You know how a sword is made." It was and wasn't a question. They knew quite well the work and effort that went into its crafting.

After seeing them nod, the priest continued. "Now, how would you compare Kurrellnah[18] to a regular blade?" he asked slyly. "That's the difference between Kalamar's work and these five masters' endeavors." He paused again and let the weight of his words fully settle.

"Now, to complete the picture, imagine that Kurrellnah was crafted by an apprentice who had never made a sword before." The high priest pronounced this last part like a religious edict, like one passing judgment on the damned.

Now Malcolm understood why the priest was so upset. When put that way, it really didn't seem possible.

"Is his work truly that much better?" Baron Terrance asked the archmage.

"It is," Archmage Angus Crow responded. "Kalamar has a talent for the craft that is exceptional. I have no doubt, he will be the greatest mage of his generation. Perhaps of all time. He has the gift and the heart to follow it."

---

[18] Kurrellnah was the name of the Eddington family sword. It was crafted by the blade-master, Rafer, who was widely acknowledged as the greatest sword maker of all time. There were only eleven known examples of his work and they were desperately sought after. Every smith would petition to hold or even see them in the hopes of gaining some clue to their construction. The first Eddington completed a heroic quest to gain his and seal his family name in legend.

Each of them was lost in their own thoughts and it was Ghan Teague who broke the silence. "As I understand it, no one becomes an archmage without extraordinary talent and skill. Only the finest minds reach that summit."

They all looked at the archmage and he responded, "It is true that very few ever reach the heights of Seventh Circle magic. Maybe one out of ten thousand mages. I can honestly say that I am the best of my generation. It is my humble prayer that I have lived and will continue to live up to the expectations of my teachers and be worthy of the gifts I've been given."

Malcolm was troubled by these words, as they all were; but with a flash of insight, he was able to pinpoint the disquiet in his heart. "What does it say," he began, "of the forebodings that we've been given that two of the most talented wizards alive are here? Now?"

That struck a nerve and they each looked to the other but no one offered an answer.

Chapter 6

School

Kalamar looked at each of the new students it was now his job to teach the Sarrik runes.[19] His master had dropped the entire burden on his shoulders when he'd awoken the day after passing out. It had been three days now, but at least the pounding in his skull had stopped.

He glanced around the pie-slice-shaped room he'd designated as the classroom. Each floor of the tower above the first had walls that cut the floor into four equal slices. They were on the second floor where the apprentices were assigned living quarters. Looking from left to right, he saw Farley, a miller's son; Kenny, a candle maker's son; and Bedelia, a lord's daughter. The students were sitting together in chairs at a table facing him.

Kellyn sat quietly in the back. She would be allowed to listen to his lectures and learn but he would not be teaching her any magic or revealing any of the Sarrik runes, as she was not an official student.

All three students already knew how to read and write as well as perform simple calculations with numbers. These three were the best

---

19 Runes were not just the sigils of power but the language used to cast a spell. There are many rune languages. And as languages, some were better in some areas and worse in others. Sarrik runes were some of the most tightly guarded and highly sought runes in the known world. They were very versatile but also more complicated. A Sarrik caster was assumed to be able to cast the same spell, but with more power. There was debate, however, about the reason. Was it the rune structure itself? Or was it the extensive training each Sarrik received?

of the applicants the archmage received after announcing he would be accepting students.

"You are each here," he began, "to learn the art of magic. But what is magic?"

Kenny started to speak but Kalamar quickly cut him off.

"You will only speak when called upon. If you have a question, you will raise your right hand and keep it raised until the presenter responds to you. Is that clear?"

They each started to mumble a response and he interrupted again.

"When you, as a class, are asked a question, you will respond together by saying 'Yes, Master' or 'No, Master.' If you are fortunate enough to be listening to the archmage, you will respond 'Yes, Archmage' or 'No, Archmage.' Is that clear?"

"Yes, Master," they responded mostly together.

"Better. Now, since I have not told you what magic is, it is not possible for you to answer that question yet. I was asking it rhetorically. To continue, magic is the direct manipulation of energy using will. Let me say that again to be clear. Magic is the direct manipulation of energy using will. Now, what do I mean by that?" He paused a moment to see if they understood his prior admonishing concerning when to respond. With their silence, he continued.

"As an example, suppose I want to move the vase on the stand to my right over to the stand that is on my left." There was a half column set up against the wall on both his right and left. The one to his right had a clay vase sitting on it and both had several vases on the floor around them. He proceeded to walk over to the right, picked up the vase and carried it over to the left. Setting it on the column, he walked back to the center before the table.

"Anyone, did I use magic to move it?" He waited for a response.

"No, Master," replied Farley, "you didn't."

"Why not? Wasn't it my will that the vase be on my left instead of my right? Anyone?"

"Master..." Kenny began but paused as if unsure to continue. Kalamar nodded, so Kenny finished, "You carried it."

"An insufficient answer," Kalamar responded. "Let's try another way."

He looked at Bedelia, who had not yet participated and said "Bedelia, move the vase back to the other column." When she seemed hesitant to respond, he barked "Now." She quickly left her seat and moved the vase as directed. Sitting back down, she was flushed and angry but wisely held her tongue.

He again addressed the class and asked, "Did I use magic to move the vase? This time I didn't physically touch the vase. Anyone?"

"No, Master, you didn't. Bedelia carried the vase," Farley said.

"True," he said, "but why wasn't that magic? Wasn't it my will that wanted it moved? Clearly, Bedelia didn't want to move the vase, so why did she? Kenny?"

"Because she had to," Kenny stumbled for a reply. Kalamar stared at Kenny until he added a hasty "Master."

"An insufficient answer."

"Did I use magic on you to make you move the vase, Bedelia?"

"No, Master. You didn't," she managed.

"Then why did you move it?" he asked.

"Because I swore that I would obey you and the archmage when he accepted me as his student, Master."

"Good. So, we can say that I used my will to manipulate you, through your oath in this case, but I didn't manipulate energy. Yes?"

"Yes, Master," they replied.

"All right. Let's try again." This time he reached out and drew upon etheric energy stored in the tower shields instead of his personal energy. He directed it to surround the vase and moved it across the room, setting it down on the left column. Their eyes were large with excitement and he had their complete attention at the first direct magic they'd experienced.

"Now," he asked again, "did I use magic to move the vase?"

"Yes, Master," they replied.

"Why was that magic? Anyone?"

"Because there was nothing between you and the vase but energy? Master," Bedelia responded.

"An insufficient answer. There was nothing in between me and the vase when you moved it for me either."

Farley hesitantly raised his hand.

"Yes, Farley?" Kalamar said.

"It was only your will and your energy. Nothing in between?" Farley's voice rose as if asking a question.

"Correct. But not complete," he replied with a smile. "If I made someone invisible and they moved it for me, it still wouldn't be magic making it move. Just magic hiding how it was moved. Now, let's try something a little bit different that will make it clearer. What if I want the vase to fall?" he said as he walked over to the column and picked up the vase. He walked back to the center of the room and opened his hand, dropping the vase. It shattered upon contact with the floor, causing the students to jump in their seats.

"Did I use magic to cause the vase to fall? Anyone?"

"No, Master," Farley explained. "The floor broke the vase."

"I wasn't talking about breaking the vase, just about making it fall. I didn't throw the vase. I simply opened my hand and it fell. Isn't that magic?" Kalamar asked.

"Master, wouldn't it fall by itself?" Kenny asked.

"Yes, and that is a good point. Whether I wished it or not, the vase would fall the moment I let go of it, but isn't that magic? Didn't I use energy, the energy of gravity to make it fall?"

It was clear he had stumped them. He waited a few more moments and then said, "So, I wanted it to fall. I know that gravity will make it fall. I used gravity to see that it fell. Why was that not magic? Let me recite the definition again. Magic is the direct manipulation of energy using will." He paused and let them think this through.

It was Bedelia who raised her hand to speak. Kalamar nodded, and she said, "You took advantage of gravity but you didn't directly manipulate it, Master."

"Exactly. Well done." Whatever anger she had from earlier was gone, replaced now with satisfaction.

"So, I used energy but not directly. I simply let it do what it was going to do anyway." He walked over to the left and picked up another vase and brought it back to the center. "Now," he continued, "if I wanted the vase to rise once I let go, I would actually have to fight gravity to do so." He suited action to words and drew again on the stored energy, this time causing the vase to float to the ceiling. He left it there for a few moments as they watched and then released the energy. The vase fell and shattered on the floor. The boys were grinning at the destruction as only boys would.

"So, it is important in life, and especially to a mage, to understand the natural energies in the world and how they will affect anything you want to do. Some can be harnessed to improve your spells and accomplish your goals. Some will oppose what you are doing and have to be overcome."

He looked back at Kellyn, who was fascinated. "Thank you, Kellyn. You may return to your duties," he said with a friendly smile.

"Yes, Master," she said and with a curtsy, left the room.

"Each of you have a small candle and holder that you will bring each day to class. The first cantrip[20] you will learn is to draw heat from your surroundings and concentrate it into a small brief flame. The runes are Char, Vestrum, Nash." As he spoke each rune, he also caused them to be drawn in both rune form and phonetically behind him on the wall in flames. He smiled at the awe on their faces.

"Char creates a container to hold something. Vestrum draws something in or pulls something to a fixed point. In this case, the magical container we created with the rune Char. Nash is heat or fire energy."

As he described each rune, the definitions were added to the illusions of the runes.

"So, we are creating a container and pulling heat into it, which at the end of the spell, the container collapses, releasing all of the combined energy in a single burst, creating a spark of flame." He summoned his own candle from the small writing desk behind him and kept it floating before him. He then clearly and distinctly pro-

---

[20] A cantrip is the smallest of spells. They have about one-fourth of the power of a first-circle spell. They are quick to cast but have extremely limited effect and duration.

nounced the spell. The candle wick flared into flame and he returned it to his desk.

"Each morning you will be given an opportunity to cast this spell and light your candle. On the day you do, you will be given the rest of the day off to go or stay as you will. Now, you could say those runes over and over every day of your life and probably never create a spark. That is because you don't understand them. You can't sense them. And you have not developed any will to direct the energy the spell needs to succeed. The greater your will, the greater the magic that you can call and control. Your will gives you authority over the runes. So let's get started."

*****

Kalamar was walking down the street, overwhelmed by frustration. He'd been teaching for over two months and none of his three students had yet lit their candle. He'd lit his in eight days. He knew they *could* do it. He could see and feel their growing strength, but they had yet to succeed. He'd left his master's study after being assured they were making progress and they were meeting the standard goals of a Sarrik student. Unfortunately, this didn't make him feel any better.

He turned left on Blackthorn Street and saw his destination in sight. The Sleeping Nag was a favorite watering hole for the common soldiers in the baron's employ. It was also the favorite place of his friends, Garret and Mac. Even though Garret's life ambition was to command soldiers in battle, he felt most at home with his soldiers instead of his fellow officers. The three of them had met here many times during the summer.

Kalamar walked in and was greeted by plenty of light, noise and friendly faces. He'd been made welcome even though he wasn't one of their own. The innkeeper greeted him warmly as he ordered his usual. He saw and waved to Mac as he made his way to an unoccupied table. By the time he took his seat, the prettiest serving girl, Lily, had brought him his wine with a plate of food. He received his customary friendly catcalls from the nearby tables over his choice of wine instead of ale. He responded with a silent salute and toast with his glass. He'd devoured half his plate when Garret and Mac dropped down at the table beside him.

"So," Garret began, "the high and mighty has decided to partake with the unwashed."

Kalamar laughed at this and replied, "Well, someone has to remind you that there are more important things than drinking and slapping pretty girl's behinds."

This was met with boos from the next table and Garret grinned.

"Well, well," Garret mocked. "That sounded like our oh-so-noble lord is questioning my honor. Wouldn't you say so, Ghan Mac?"

Mac drew himself up straight in his seat and declared, "It sounds like a challenge has been issued."

Cries of challenge went up from several of the tables as this had become something of an entertainment. Garret and Kalamar would arm wrestle. The problem was, Kalamar never lost. Since he was half as strong as Garret, it was known to all he must be cheating. The problem was, they couldn't see how. The entertainment came from watching their lieutenant strain and pull till blue in the face and not move Kalamar's arm at all. Several other strong men had tried and gotten the same results. Kalamar would talk, joke, laugh and even eat or drink while they all tried to move his arm to no avail.

Of course, Kalamar was cheating. He was using magic. But the men all thought he would need to be chanting or muttering incantations for a spell, so they kept looking for some tell that would give away the trick. With his food and glass moved to the side, Kalamar extended his arm to Garret and waited for Mac to start the game.

"Go!" Mac shouted and the contest was on. Kalamar had already opened his mind and begun drawing on the power to lock his arm before they began. As such, Garret pushed and yanked, but made no headway as usual.

Kalamar was just thinking of something funny to say when a low and sultry woman's voice whispered in his ear, "Hello, handsome." When he turned his head to see who it was, Lily kissed him on the lips. Not a little peck, but a full-on, take-your-breath-away kiss. His arm crashed to the table to the thunderous cheers of the crowd that he didn't hear. The kiss seemed to go on forever and ended impossibly soon as she pulled away and whispered, "We should do that again sometime."

She slowly stood up straight, giving him plenty of time to see all the beauty the gods had blessed her with. With a laugh she turned and flounced away into the crowd of cheering patrons.

Kalamar took a few moments to come back to his senses and realize what had happened. As he turned back to his laughing friends, he knew he was blushing furiously. Gaining control of himself, he stood and raised his hands for silence.

It came slowly, but he was finally able to say, "It seems that my friend here, Lieutenant Garret Walker, has finally discovered a way to beat me." A great cheer went up from the crowd and Garret waived benignly from his chair. Kalamar again called for quiet and finished. "However, no man, NO man, has ever enjoyed losing as much as I just did." To which another great cheer went up from the crowd. He grabbed his glass and turned to raise it in salute to Lily, whose turn it was to blush and laugh.

He plopped back down in his seat to much backslapping and good-natured jokes, realizing he felt much better than when he entered. His master was right, he thought. His students were growing stronger every day and it would not be much longer.

It took three weeks…

*****

Kalamar walked into the classroom. His students were there already. As required they were attentive and waiting for class to start. He nodded his head for Farley to begin. He randomly selected who would be the first to try the cantrip each morning. He watched as Farley closed then opened his eyes. He heard him clearly say, "Char, Vestrum, Nash," and in a rush of joy that surprised him, he saw the candle flicker and flame to life. The other students gasped and only then did Farley's face light up with joy at his accomplishment.

"Excellent," Kalamar said to him. "Bedelia, your turn."

She quickly pulled herself together, closed her eyes, and repeated, "Char, Vestrum, Nash." Her candle also burst into flame and she smiled in evident satisfaction.

"Excellent. Kenny." He nodded encouragingly.

Kenny's smile turned to a grin of excitement and he quickly followed with "Char, Vestrum, Nash." But in his case, the gathered energy was not enough and the candle did not light.

A stab of disappointment pierced Kalamar and he took a moment to gain control. He saw that Kenny's face had crumpled in disbelief and self-reproach that he'd failed where the others had succeeded.

"Farley and Bedelia, you are excused from the remainder of classes today. You may go where you wish within Stormlake but be back in your room by the first hour of evening. Remember, you represent the archmage and any poor actions on your part tarnish his honor and reputation. You will wear your school robes and maintain a proper attitude. Enjoy." Both quickly bowed their head in acknowledgment, grabbed their possessions and left the room.

Kalamar took a few minutes to reflect and was glad that Farley had been first. He was slow and steady, always taking his time. Kalamar had thought before he would have made an excellent priest, as his strongest quality was belief. Once he believed something, he never questioned it again. Now that he knew he could cast a spell, his progress would definitely accelerate. His deliberative manner, however, made him seem slow and stupid to his classmates. This would go a long way to changing that.

Bedelia was convinced she was smarter than the others. Being raised a noble child, she was also convinced that she was born better. These attitudes made her arrogant and inconsiderate, which were often fatal flaws in a mage. She was learning, as Kalamar was disabusing her of those notions with the training, but it would be good for her to reevaluate the situation with Farley.

Kalamar looked to Kenny and could see that he was barely holding back the tears. Of all three students, he had the most natural talent.

"Do you know why you didn't cast the spell correctly?"

"No, Master."

"It's because you are lazy," he said in total and brutal honesty. This was clearly not what Kenny expected to hear.

"You think that magic is a way for you to get something without doing any work for it. Waive your hand and coin and power will just appear out of nowhere. You could have cast that spell weeks ago. Did you know that? You've been bursting with the power and ability, but you just won't focus your energy and concentrate from the beginning of the spell through to the end. Even today you had it, but you rushed through the runes and didn't gather the maximum potential power to make the spell work. Do you understand what I am telling you?"

Kenny took his time with this, finally ducking his head and answering, "Yes, Master."

"Very well then. Today we are going to return to the question of why the element of fire is different from the other elements."

He'd originally been going to discuss Harbinn's Treaty of Accelerated Growth but there was no sense in covering new ground with the others gone. In addition, this was an area that Kenny was struggling with. All he said was, "Let's begin."

Chapter 7

sharp lessons

Kalamar walked up the stairs to the fifth floor with some trepidation. The gloomy overcast sky wasn't helping to settle his nerves. He was going to invite his master to a testing tomorrow that was… unusual for a mage, to say the least. The snows of winter had just started and he'd been training with Garret and Mac throughout the summer and fall to use soldier's weapons.

This had all been prompted by a question Garret asked him during their welcoming banquet, which seemed a lifetime ago. They'd been enjoying a spirited conversation about tactics and strategies when Garret asked, "What does a mage do when he runs out of energy to cast spells?" Kalamar had laughed and replied, "What does an archer do when he has no arrows?"

Everyone had enjoyed the quip, but on further consideration, he didn't really like the answer. To be left helpless was something he had no interest in experiencing. To that end, he'd sought out his new friends later that week and they'd spoken at great length.

He'd learned staff and dagger skills from his master but the training had always left him feeling incomplete. To his mind, it was cursory, so the three of them had decided to pursue a course of training for all of them. He would learn the sword in addition to further training with staff, dagger, crossbow and familiarity with everything else they could think of; and in return, he would show them how to fight a mage, what was possible and potential defenses they could employ.

They had met almost every morning the fifth hour of night in a glade northeast of Stormlake, away from prying eyes. While they

66

weren't actually breaking any rules, they didn't think it would be welcomed and wanted to discover its value before becoming the speculation of gossip.

It had proceeded remarkably well, however. They had each pushed their powers to the limits against each other and created many new tactics and strategies both offensive and defensive. When they combined their talents, they learned they could be quite deadly. Kalamar enjoyed the training and competition as much as he enjoyed teaching. In addition, their friendship had become an important part of his life.

As he stood outside the door to his master's parlor, he wondered how the archmage would respond. He quickly gave that up as a useless exercise. He would know soon enough as the door opened before him.

His master was sitting in his favorite yellow stuffed chair by the burning fire. It was a magic fire that required no fuel. Like everything else in the tower, it was powered by the energy stored in the shields the archmage created to protect this tower and its occupants. He'd summoned a second guardian for just this part of the castle.

The archmage motioned him to have a seat across from him, which Kalamar took.

"How goes the training?" the archmage asked.

It was going well and he informed his master so. It was exactly as his master had predicted. Once the students began casting spells, it was like going from crawling to running. The students now had real results to build on and proof for themselves they had it within. That made all the difference. Self-knowledge is far superior to anything external as his master always said.

With their growing confidence, however, had come arrogance. They'd begun casting spells on each other and tried to sneak them on him. It was quite normal and every teacher at this point in training modified his personal shield to reflect cantrips back on their caster with an extra gift for good measure. Students learned quickly and painfully not to provoke a master. As long as they kept it to themselves, if it was done on their personal time and was kept under control without getting personal, it was a good learning opportunity.

What was not acceptable in any form, however, was using their newfound power on anyone else. Both Kenny and Bedelia, for different reasons, had cast spells on the servants. They spent the next week cleaning out the castle middens by hand. The lesson was learned.

His master listened to his update. The archmage nodded approval or added the occasional observation as he felt warranted. When Kalamar was done, his master said, "I sense something else is on your mind this evening? Would it have anything to do with your early-morning errands with your friends?"

Kalamar smiled and nodded yes. He hadn't made any attempt to keep it from him and he'd learned long ago not to be surprised at his master's powers of observation.

"Master," he began, "I'm hoping that you will join us tomorrow morning, as I will be tested."

"Oh" was the reply. "And what are you being tested for?"

"Swordsmanship, Master." He then presented everything they had been doing and what he'd learned. His master sat silent and thoughtful, not interrupting.

"That certainly explains your calluses. May I ask why you didn't bring this to me in the beginning?"

"In the beginning, Master, we weren't sure of its value. Once we realized we were onto something, we decided to wait until we had something substantial."

His master considered this and then responded, "Very well. I accept. Will Ghan Teague and General Shay be joining us as well?"

Kalamar smiled and nodded. "They are being asked now as well, Master."

"Then I look forward to it."

*****

Kalamar had performed the martial forms well he thought, but now was the test he feared. Not that he would be hurt but that he would embarrass his friend and teacher. General Shay stood across from him in a relaxed, almost bored, manner. He'd asked if Kalamar was ready a full minute earlier and had proceeded to do nothing.

68

Kalamar knew, both from the archmage as well as Garret, to not react or rush in. Boredom and frustration were fatal mistakes.

It always fascinated Kalamar how fast Garret could move and General Shay seemed even faster. One moment he was waiting and not even a heartbeat later, he was deflecting a blow that would have removed his head from his body. His arms trembled with the effort. General Shay seemed to combine the speed of Garret with the raw power of Mac. Kalamar spent the next few minutes backpedaling furiously. Moment by moment his whole world condensed into just trying to keep his opponent's sword away.

Then a fraction of hesitation from the general. Kalamar now attacked without letup. The general now backpedaled, but he did so easily, casually. Without warning, it stopped and defense became offense. Kalamar didn't stop either. Every defense became an attack; every attack became a defense. He was in the void, so crucial to both magic and martial prowess.

He loved the freedom it provided. All thoughts, emotions, distractions were external. Here one simply existed. No past, present or future. Just being. Here nothing and everything mattered. Each breath was pure pleasure and irrelevant. He simply observed as his body was being exhausted, his breathing was becoming labored. His arms trembled as sweat poured out of his body and his steps were slowing. He would fail soon he noticed, but didn't care. The outcome was irrelevant.

Just as that inevitable arrived, General Shay took a full step back and raised his sword in salute. Kalamar saluted back and returned to the world with his familiar friends, Pain and Exhaustion, greeting him.

General Shay strode over to the archmage after having sheathed his sword and said, "I understand that the boy has talent for sorcery but he has a real gift for the sword. Give him to me and I can make him one of the greats. I've rarely seen such poise and calm from a student in such a short period of time."

Archmage Crow smiled and, after a moment, responded, "I agree. He shows real talent with the sword."

"You'll give him to me then?" General Shay responded eagerly.

"I think you should watch" was his reply as he walked into the field.

"Kalamar," he called, "I want you to use everything that you have. Do you understand?"

"Yes, Master," he replied.

The archmage took his time walking out into the glade. This was no doubt a courtesy to give Kalamar time to catch his breath. Instead of the six paces General Shay had started from, Archmage Crow came to a stop thirty paces from him. This was how wizards dueled.

"When you are ready, Journeyman," Angus Crow called.

"I am ready, Archmage," Kalamar replied.

Both mages began at the same time. The traditional strategy was to first cast a fixed shield[21] and then attack.[22] Both raised shields. At this point, they had a choice, begin a weaker, quicker attack, hoping that the other's shield was not strong or fully prepared; or begin a longer, more powerful attack to overwhelm the other's shield or at least weaken it so a quick follow-up could finish them off.

If the shields remained strong, then it became a matter of whose collapsed under the barrage first. Given the disparities in level and power, it was inevitable Kalamar's would fail before the archmage's.

After raising a fixed shield, Kalamar cast a delayed series of firebolts. This meant the spell was cast and would spread the firebolts

---

[21] There are generally two types of shields. Fixed or static shields are much like a stone wall, solid and fixed in place. You create them and then can ignore them as they do the job they're designed for—blocking. They require no further concentration or thought until they fail. The caster can repair or rebuild by releasing or bleeding energy into it. A dynamic or personal shield, however, moves with the caster. It also can be repaired by draining power directly from the mage. With a dynamic shield, however, each blow is felt it a limited sense, and this makes it very difficult for most to maintain as they can't concentrate on multiple spells at the same time.

[22] In wizards' duels, sometimes a mage will go for a fast attack, especially if they can maintain a personal shield. If they attack fast enough, they can disrupt their oppositions shielding spell and quickly finish off their opponent. It's a high-risk maneuver. Most play it "safe" or "smart," depending on perspective and shield first then attack.

out over twenty seconds or so instead of all at once in a massive attack. This allowed him to keep the archmage honest and remember his shielding while he cast his first surprise.

As a student of Sarrik who was not trained at the academy, Kalamar could never teach the Sarrik runes without direct permission from a "true" Sarrik. During his six months of training with his friends, he'd designed his own set of runes, a set created with battle in mind. These runes allowed him to combine some spell runes into a shorter/quicker form he called Cluster Spells. It allowed almost instant casting of spells that would normally take up to a full minute to cast. There was a price, of course. To pull that much power through the caster so quickly was physically draining and required a high level of stamina. The training he'd been putting himself through with his friends had been just what he needed. In quick succession, he cast a second-circle acid attack and a third-circle fireball. The effects were immediate and spectacular.

His master's strategy was more traditional; he'd gone for the slower but more powerful first attack, believing his student would not make a simple mistake in casting his shield.

So, as Kalamar's fireball engulfed his master, the archmage's lightning strike shattered his shield. Kalamar had anticipated this and removed himself from the shield letting it collapse. When he leaped from its crumbling remains, he cast a simple illusion, causing not one of him but three to go racing across the distance to his master while the archmage couldn't see from the smoke and debris of Kalamar's fireball.

His master wasn't fooled and casually shattered the illusions one at a time, but Kalamar had one last trick up his sleeve to play. He leaped high in the air with sword drawn in an attempt to shatter his master's shield with a physical attack, but at the same time dropped his last creation he called a Seed Spell.[23] As he went up, the seed hit the shield and released a shock shadow. He'd created the shadow

---

[23] A seed spell is actually two spells. The first creates a shell or seed pod that holds all the power of the second for instant release. It's like a spell scroll, but the spell is already cast and ready. It's extremely delicate and dangerous because the slightest error will release the second spell prematurely.

specifically to reach through a wizard's shield, delivering a powerful electric shock, which could cause him to drop his shield.

As Kalamar and his sword came down on his master's shield, the shock shadow did what it was supposed to do. It uncurled from the seed and took on a vaguely defined shape with red glowing eyes. It also generated the shock that would reach through the shield to its creator. That's when everything fell apart.

Kalamar found himself on the verge of unconsciousness, pinned to a tree on the other side of the glade. He could barely breathe and struggled to even see what was happening. His master had him pinned ten feet off the ground by a giant magical fist. The archmage had also frozen the shock shadow in place and was walking around it, studying it.

"Do you yield?" his master called across the distance.

"I do," gasped Kalamar, who was unceremoniously dropped to the ground. Clearing his head, he used the tree to get up and slowly walked across the distance to his master.

"What do you call this thing?" his master asked when he was by his side.

"A Shock Shadow, Master."

"Ingenious, very clever indeed and what do you call the shell?"

"A seed spell, Master. I am preparing a Vetae Mashtu[24] on each of them and should have it ready for you by midwinter."

"That is very generous. Thank you." Normally, a mage never gave spells to others as they were the most precious secrets they had. In this case, Kalamar simply felt he was repaying his master for all the access to higher-level spells that a normal master would have never given without compensation.

"Where did you get the idea for these, may I ask?"

---

[24] A Vetae Mashtu is a detailed schematic or compendium with detailed drawings breaking down a spell, how it is cast, the explanation of each rune used and the spells proper usage. Generally, when a mage finds a new spell he hasn't seen or one in a rune set he isn't familiar with, he will have to spend time meditating and casting magical sensing spells to follow its energetic properties and learn its proper purpose, function and activation. A proper Vetae Mashtu makes this unnecessary.

"The shock shadow just came to me as I was trying to find a way around or through a shield. It is also very effective against anyone wearing or holding any metals, especially metal armor. As for the seed spell, I remembered the story of the mage battles from the kingdom's founding and the poetic verses of laying the ground with spells like seeds. In addition, there is a picture that shows a mage scattering what looks like seeds on the ground before the battle."

"The same picture where you got the cut of your robes from?" his master shrewdly asked.

"Yes, Master. The same."

"I also noticed," the archmage continued, "that the spells you cast were not Sarrik or any runes I've heard of. How do you explain that?"

"I created them, Master," he responded simply.

The archmage studied his student for a long time and said, "And why would you do that?"

"The first is, I will not be able to pass on the Sarrik runes without getting permission from an official Sarrik. In all honesty, this rankles. I don't blame you for that, it's just a rule I understand but don't agree with. Since I don't feel that the other runes I'm familiar with are nearly as good as Sarrik, I needed my own. The second is that I wanted something that works better in battle. The Sarrik runes are the most versatile and comprehensive of any I know, but my Four Element runes allow me to concentrate power quicker."

The others had walked over during the conversation, and the archmage asked, "Do you still think I should ask him to give up magic to pursue life as a swordsman, General Shay?"

"No, I don't," the general replied with respect. "I've never seen such a display. He will be pure destruction on any field of battle. These two are telling me they can't beat him unless they team up and even then, it's not certain. I would not have believed it if I hadn't seen it for myself. What say you, Ghan?"

"I say these three have changed warfare as we know it and we need to learn everything we can about those changes. Dangerous times are coming and we need to be prepared," Teague replied.

"Hear, hear!" Shay affirmed. "Now to the matters at hand," he continued. "Kalamar Sylvicheld, your name will be added to our scroll, and you are welcome to train in our house whenever you wish. Welcome." Then he turned to Garret and said, "You, however, are another matter. You have been training a student without my permission. I notice, however, that you did not teach him any of our special techniques. Was that your idea?"

"No, Master," Garret replied.

"I thought not. Yours?" He turned to Mac.

"No, General," Mac replied.

"So you thought of that to spare your friend, I suppose?" He turned to Kalamar.

"Yes, General," Kalamar responded.

"I see, so you did not break your vow and reveal any of our hidden knowledge."

Shay continued, "I understand why you did not come to me and ask. I would have refused for many reasons. All of them wrong. This does not invalidate your bending the rules, but I must consider the circumstances in this case. It is clear you must be punished, so you will endure the following.

"First, you will be responsible for Kalamar's initiation this evening and the party afterward. I will be checking in myself to make sure it is legendary. Second, after the party this evening and you will not cut it short, you will find me and spend all night explaining every thought in your skull on what you have discovered here and every tactic you think might be possible concerning these new strategies. Third and finally, there is a batch of newbies that were to begin training today in our school. In a display of my famous generosity, I will give them the day off and have them begin their training tomorrow. Since you think you are capable of teaching, I am putting them entirely in your hands. You will be solely responsible for them and I expect my customary standards of excellence to be met.

"Now, have I been crystal clear in my expectations?"

"Yes, Master. I understand and am honored."

General Shay laughed out at this. "I dump on you enough work to kill an ox and you think it's a promotion. Very well, you have done well here considering. It is time to see if you are ready for more."

"I will not fail you, Master," Garret replied.

"Then be off with you and get to work." Shay shooed him away and Garret bolted back to Stormlake.

The general then turned and addressed the high priest and archmage. "I would be honored if you two would attend this evening. I would also, going forward, appreciate hearing your thoughts and impressions on this. It seems that I need to learn a bit more concerning sorcery."

Both responded that they would be delighted and then the archmage turned to Kalamar.

"Since you will no doubt be useless after the party and I've been looking for an opportunity to extensively test your charges, I think I will begin today. I will not let the general's claim to generosity pass unchallenged and I have no doubt that your students will welcome the opportunity to be vigorously examined on their progress thus far. I think a three-day holiday for you will be in order. Make sure to keep yourself otherwise occupied until I've finished."

"Yes, Master," Kalamar replied.

During the general's speech, he'd been both delighted for his friend's promotion and concerned at the amount of work he knew was just dumped on him. His master's words to him, however, filled him with no small dread. The only contact his students had with the archmage to this point had been as a wise and kindly old man. They were about to be overwhelmed with grueling questioning, testing and demonstrations that would require perfection. He'd gone through it and knew his master was scrupulously fair, but it was tougher than anything he'd put them through.

The three elders simply grinned as they began their return while Kalamar and Mac exchanged a long sorrowful glance.

Chapter 8

a noble fool

To say Kalamar had the best night of his life just didn't seem to do it justice, as he thought back through the events.

He'd spent most of the day discussing strategy with General Shay and Ghan Teague, trying to condense, analysis and summarize their training and discoveries of what strategies worked and what didn't. Ghan Mac was there for most of it and Lieutenant Garret would join when available. The challenge of it was fun and exciting as they verbally jousted while the day quickly disappeared. He occasionally would wonder how his students were progressing but knew the archmage was far more qualified than he and would proceed in their best interest, even if they didn't agree.

The initiation was short, simple and led straight to what they called a bar crawl. Since the object was to have a drink at every establishment in town the name made perfect sense. He and his "guardians" were quite a hit as they traversed the town. He had no idea if they actually visited them all, but since everyone had a great time, nobody cared.

As a mage, he wouldn't let himself get too drunk, but he certainly had his fair share by the time his "best friends in the whole world" escorted him home. He couldn't get why they kept giving each other sly grins they thought he couldn't see. Until that is, leaving them at his door, he walked into his bedroom. Several candles were lit and as his foggy mind tried to puzzle the reason why, he heard from his bed, "Hello, handsome."

He'd spun just a bit too quickly and saw Lily wearing that same grin she'd given him all those months ago in the bar. A grin and nothing else, he mused.

*****

It was a night he would never forget and as he looked down on her sleeping form next to him, he knew he could never repay her. It wasn't love, of course, that would be foolish; but it was a pleasure and happiness he'd never felt. It was early in the morning yet and she was still asleep, with only a gentle moan or murmur as she shifted from time to time.

He leaned down close to her ear and whispered, "What would make you happy, my dear?"

She smiled as some thought passed through her dreams and whispered, "Hal."

Rage surged in Kalamar so quickly that he found it hard to breathe. His hand was trembling so forcefully he had to clench it into a fist to bring some measure of control. He fought the viciousness of his anger and bludgeoned his mind back into control. His breathing slowly eased and the trembling stopped as he regained his equilibrium. With a final quiet laugh, he banished the petty emotions that had just tried to consume him.

He'd just the moment earlier told himself he wasn't in love; and the moment he thought there might be someone else, jealousy reared out of nowhere, seizing almost total control. His father had once told him that jealousy could make the most solid of men do the most unstable things and he'd just gotten his first taste of it. He hoped it was his last but shook his head in doubt.

He looked down again on her sleeping form and saw that she had not moved. His inner battle hadn't disturbed her in the least. She was every bit as beautiful as she'd been just moments earlier but his feelings had changed significantly, if subtly. Instead of possessive, they now felt protective. Who was this Hal? He didn't know any and didn't recall hearing the name before.

He leaned over again and whispered, "Who's Hal?"

"Mervin's son." As she said this, a frown flowed over her face as her thoughts turned darker.

He didn't want her to wake, so he quickly whispered back, "Everything will be okay."

This seemed enough to banish whatever storm cloud occurred in her thoughts and she rolled over with a sigh of contentment.

He quickly, but carefully slid out from the blankets, got up and dressed. He still didn't know who Hal was but could quickly guess the problem. Hal was probably from a family that had high expectations for their son. The kind that wouldn't allow for a barmaid. His parents would obviously expect him to marry up the social ladder and not down. Hal's love for her, if he even did, would be irrelevant. Even if he was a younger son, he would still be expected to marry into a name that could improve the families' standing.

Kalamar didn't like those expectations, but understood it was how everything worked. Family obligations were a matter of honor and the idea of marrying for love was only in romances or adventures like Raghnall the Red Fox.

He found himself pacing and quickly realized why. He saw the issue as a problem and he was trying to solve it. He didn't know how, but as he looked over at her sleeping face, he knew that he would. The idea itself was ludicrous but he didn't care. The first thing he needed was information and he was already out the door and racing down the stairs in search of it.

*****

Cory Dresden had seen, heard and experienced a great deal in his life. He'd fled his home at a young age, after getting into a dispute between families. He'd run into every type of person and trouble imaginable as he'd crossed the known world to make a new life for himself. None of that had prepared him as he sat, dumbfounded, listening to his lord's story. Of course he knew who Hal was. A dutiful son from a good family. He also knew the marriage would never be allowed. His mother, Shannen, in particular, was ambitious and wanted greater status for them all. She, being a commoner herself, would never allow her boys to marry one.

Kalamar had finished and was sitting patiently. There was no expression on his face that indicated he knew how impossible this was or even how much trouble it could cause. He realized with his last thought that he'd already found a solution to the problem, but it would be expensive in more ways than one. He also didn't know if his lord was fully prepared to accept the consequences. His duty to his patron required that he provide the solution. His duty to his patron required that he protect him even if from himself. He laughed in his own mind as he realized the delicious irony of it all.

Kalamar waited patiently. He'd seen the disbelief and incredulity on Cory's face as he told his story. He'd also watched as Cory argued within his own mind over what to say and do. He knew full well Cory had a solution and he knew full well he hated that solution. Something about that solution caused him fear and Kalamar found himself fascinated with how this particular drama would play out.

Cory cleared his throat. Then he did so again. "My lord," he began, "it is clear to me that you are quite serious about this but I must respectfully ask if you have considered the enemies you will make? Many noble families will take affront with your pursuit of this course. I understand that you may not see the harm in this generous behavior, but I can assure you several will be incensed and respond accordingly."

It was at this point that Cory's wife, Alana, came in and gave Kalamar a big motherly hug. She was a kind woman and a great cook, as he'd learned over several of their evening meals. "Cory is right, lad." She rarely addressed him as anything else unless in public. "It is the most romantic thing I've ever heard. Straight out of a story, but there will be many powerful people who will hate you for this kindness."

Kalamar considered for a few moments and finally responded, "You are correct that I had not considered this to be such a cause for concern. While I have not yet heard your proposed solution, I can now make some guesses about its direction from your words so far.

Without knowing the proposal, is it possible to mitigate this danger? Is there a way to allow me to pursue this while undercutting the concerns of these nobles?"

He watched as Cory considered this and responded, "I believe there is a way to lessen the damage and perhaps win a few to your side. Ma has provided us the answer. If this is presented as youthful exuberance, if you are made out to be a hopeless romantic, overcome by the unrequited love of these two, then perhaps. This will, however, make you appear a bit foolish or gullible. It won't appease all, but it might be enough. Are you prepared to live with that?"

Now it was Kalamar's turn to pause and consider. Did he really want to pursue this that badly? He could leave now, give her some gift or token and be done. No one would think lessor of him for it. But if he pursued this path, was he willing to be thought a lovestruck fool? Someone who had so easily been taken advantage of? Just to make some grand gesture?

He did not need to know the specifics of Cory's idea to understand that any action he took to raise Lily enough to convince Hal's parents would be seen as a diminishment of the nobility. It was also clear that Hal's father must be of noble blood or at least a knight to be causing this much fear in Cory. If noble stature could be bought, *which it frequently was,* he thought ironically, then it was a cheap commodity; and the very basis of social order could be questioned. Wealthy merchants and craftsmen would want it and would not be content with something less.

This was an extreme reading but Kalamar knew that several nobles would deliberately see it this way and they would cause problems. Could he cause burdens to his master from this gesture? What harmful consequences could or would occur?

He looked over from the window back to Cory and Alana and said, "All right. It is clear I had not considered it from that perspective. As such, my duty requires me to bring this to my master before I move forward. I cannot, in good conscience, knowingly cause his reputation harm, so I will make you this deal. Let me hear your plan. I will consider it and discuss it with my master to get his approval before proceeding. Will this relieve some of your concerns?"

Kalamar needn't have asked the question since the look on Cory's face was awash with relief at the mention of going to his master first. It seemed he was convinced the archmage would squash this mad plan.

Cory agreed it would and proceeded to share his idea—an idea that involved large sums of his money to purchase a small property on the farthest eastern edge of the barony. A forty-acre hunting cottage actually, abandoned years ago, had come on the market when the children inherited. It was too remote to effect repairs without great expense and their main estate had come upon hard times.

*****

Kalamar waited for his master to speak. He'd told him his thoughts, Cory's plan and Cory's concerns with the consequences. His master had listened without comment as he always did. No expression crossed his face as he'd simply absorbed the details. Now, however, he broke into a great grin and, with a rueful chuckle, sighed.

"Ah, to be so young again. What a true romantic fool you are." He chuckled again and continued, "There will be several nobles who will hate the idea but I believe that most will be amused. I also don't believe your reputation will be damaged as such. Proceed as you wish as it will not bother me either way. Your students are cursing my name but holding up so far. Have this all wrapped up by tomorrow so you may return to your duties."

"Thank you, Master, I will," he said as he stood up and left.

*****

Lord Malcolm Cherrheld had been mildly curious when his assistant entered his office with a visit request from Sir Kalamar Sylvicheld and Master Tailor Cory Dresden. He knew that Kalamar had become a patron to Cory, but he couldn't think of a reason why both would need to see him.

He found himself feeling sunstruck as he listened to the story of a barmaid and a knight's son in love and Kalamar wanting to make

Lily his ward and buy her the Black Forest Hunting cottage so they could be together. Not with Kalamar, but with Hal. He kept looking from Kalamar to Cory who, while maintaining a straight face, had eyes alive with laughter. If this was some kind of joke, there was going to be hell to pay.

He hadn't realized he'd said that out loud until Kalamar responded. "Lord Malcolm, this is not a joke. I am interested in purchasing Black Forest Cottage for fifteen pounds and need papers drawn up making me the executor but establishing the property in Lily's name."

"The cottage is worth fifty pounds if it's a penny but that is beside the point. Master Tailor, what exactly is your interest in this affair?" Malcolm demanded.

"My lord, I am here to see what my face looked like when I first heard the tale," Cory responded gravely while trying to keep from laughing.

"That is too bold, Master Tailor. Perhaps an evening in the cells would help you remember your place?" he said with a growl.

"Of course," Cory replied. "It would be worth it, my lord."

He needed to remember to have the tailor flogged for some reason later. He realized he couldn't wrap his head around what he was hearing. It was just too damned insane, so he tried reason.

He lowered his voice like he would use with a child and said, "Kalamar, surely you must think about what you are saying. How this must sound. No man in his right mind would do this. There can be no circumstance that occurred last night that would require you to make this kind of gesture. You didn't swear an oath did you?" He asked this so gently like speaking to an addled child.

"My lord Malcolm, I did not make an oath. I can assure you that I am in full possession of my wits. I know that what I am saying may not make sense to you, but I ask that you respect my wishes and sell me the cottage for fifteen pounds. I can assure you it is in terrible repair and that offer is quite fair. Would you like to see it?"

He said yes before he thought through how cleverly he'd been redirected. His curiosity won out, however, so he didn't interrupt. Kalamar simply began chanting under his breath and as he watched, a silvery cloud formed in a perfect circle to the right of his desk. As it became denser he began to see colors. It then congealed into a perfect picture of a broken-down shack surrounded by forest. He was amazed at how clear it looked. He felt he was actually there, thirty yards in front of the cottage. The image then began to move, like someone walking. They went through the door, which was disconcerting, then around the structure. The walls were mostly sound, but the roof was caved in on one side and it was clear the elements had been hard at work destroying the place.

A bit in awe, he whispered, "Can you show me anywhere?"

"Where would you like to see my lord? There are limits and rules but I can certainly find anywhere in the barony."

"Can you show me my estates at Bandon?"

A map quickly replaced the image, but not like any map he'd ever seen. It showed the barony, but as if the gods were looking down from the sky. The detail was breathtaking.

"Where is Bandon, my lord?" Kalamar asked.

Malcolm pointed to the spot and replied, "Just east by north of Green Craig."

The image showed the ground rushing up to meet them as if a hawk was diving on some prey. Where he had pointed became the focus as the road heading east from Green Craig was now in the vision. They raced east up the road faster than any horse could run and he shouted, "Stop."

The image did and he said, "You just missed the lane on the left."

The image seemed to turn. Slower now, they went west until they saw the lane. This they took at a slower pace and in a few moments, the image before him was his home Cherrheld. He was stunned at how real it was. Snow covered the fields and he saw smoke rising from the chimneys.

They watched as someone came out the front door. It only took a moment to recognize his eldest son, Allen, dressed against the cold. He was clearly taking the path to the stables. He wanted to shout to him but realized he wouldn't be heard and it would probably startle him if he did. He wondered where he needed to go in such weather. He would have to remember to ask in the spring as the snows were beginning to shut down any travel.

He felt strangely lighthearted at seeing such a simple, comforting sight and said, "Thank you."

"You're welcome, my lord," Kalamar replied and the image faded from view. Disappeared as if it never was.

"Can you do that anytime?" Malcolm asked.

Kalamar grinned as he replied, "I'm sure we could come to some type of arrangement, my lord."

Malcolm laughed in spite of himself. "What a devilishly cunning rascal you are, sir. I will have to watch you much closer in the future." He finished with a smile.

"Why, thank you, my lord. I will take that as a compliment," Kalamar replied while nodding his head. "Does that mean we have an agreement on my request?"

He shook his head and sighed. "You know this is addled. But"—he laughed—"it's your coin. It is also clear that the property is far more damaged than Lord Daire described. I will have the papers drawn up by this afternoon. I assume that you wish to move quickly as the snows are getting too heavy for travel?"

"I do, my lord. I mean to leave immediately to meet with Hal's family and make the arrangements. Cory is going to hire a carpenter willing to head out today and begin the repairs. I need to see them married by tomorrow so that I can return to my duties for the archmage."

Malcolm nodded and said, "Sir Melvin is in service to Lord Treavor of Northspring. He is a friend and if you will give me about an hour, I will accompany you and make the introductions."

"I am honored, my lord. That is very gracious," Kalamar replied.

"Gracious has nothing to do with it. I wish to see their expressions as you explain it to them." He laughed and said, "And I'm going to inform the Lord Baron right now." He turned to Cory and further declared, "Master Tailor, you aren't the only one who can enjoy a spectacle."

All three laughed at that.

*****

Lord Treavor was delighted with his unexpected guests. He was also intrigued with the somewhat-mysterious nature of the visit. He'd sent for Sir Mervin; his wife, Shannen; and his youngest son, Hal, with piqued curiosity. He was assured that no matter of honor was involved and not to worry on that account. He'd met Sir Kalamar over dinner during a trip to Stormlake this last summer and everything he knew and saw suggested he was honorable, diligent and intelligent. He admired quick wit and rather enjoyed the conversation during the wait for those summoned to arrive.

While he would never admit it, he loved personal drama and intrigue; and as Kalamar made his presentation to Hal and the family, he'd relished every moment and expression. Sir Kalamar had left out of the story why the barmaid had become his ward and he made a mental note to dig into this at a later time.

Hal's face lit up at news over the woman he obviously loved. Mervin had grown quiet, but it was Shannen who'd gone cold. It was clear she wanted nothing to do with this and the idea of her son marrying a barmaid was unthinkable, no matter how much property she had. Treavor wanted to rub his hands with glee at the spectacle he was witnessing. Kalamar had finished and now sat, patiently waiting for a response. He'd been calm and poised throughout, but it was clear he was watching carefully himself.

It was Sir Mervin who broke the silence first and said, "I don't understand several things in this story." He cleared his throat and continued, "Why did you make her your ward?"

Kalamar nodded as if expecting this and replied, "That is my affair and doesn't really matter. What is important is that she has shared with me she is in love with your son. She also claims that he feels the same way and they wish to be married. I have taken her story to heart and decided to help if I can."

"Nonsense," Shannen replied. "My son has no interest in a barmaid and you have wasted our time with this foolishness." She declared this as a final verdict and stood as if to end the conversation and leave.

"Sit down, Shannen," Mervin said, causing her to her pause shocked. "It is not as simple as that."

She did sit down but immediately responded, "Merv, you can't be seriously entertaining this. How could he possibly be involved in any way? It's nonsense pure and simple."

It was Malcolm who stepped into the story at this point and said, "Before coming here, I spoke with our liege on this matter. He and his wife are quite taken with the notion. It is a romance straight out of a bard's tale. They have offered to allow the wedding to take place in their private chapel. Additionally, to show their support, they've agreed to host a banquet in the couple's honor tomorrow after the ceremony."

It was clear Kalamar didn't know this and he bowed his head deeply to Lord Malcolm in thanks.

"See, Shannen," Mervin added, "how could we possibly object when even the baron is in support of this?"

"I object," she replied with real venom, "because I will not have our son marry beneath him. We have not worked so hard—"

It was here Kalamar interrupted brusquely and said, "Enough. I have heard and seen enough. I will not have Lily slandered in this way. I have no doubt that when I announce her dowry, she will have suitors fighting for her hand. While she may have some temporary heartbreak, it will quickly pass as she settles into her new life as mistress of Black Forrest Cottage."

"How dare you so quickly declare our love dead. She loves me and I love her," Hal spoke for the first time as he stood before Kalamar with fists clenched as if for a fight.

Everyone moved. Shannen covered her mouth with her hand in disbelief. Everyone moved, that is, except Sir Kalamar. He'd remained calm and only after a deliberate pause did he raise his head and say to Hal, "Do not stand so to challenge me, boy, for I am not the enemy. I came here to see if you are worthy of her and willing to fight for her. If you mean to prove those words you just spoke, then you need to challenge your actual opponent."

The room was very quiet as the words sunk in. While the idea of a similarly aged Kalamar calling the hulking giant "boy" normally might have seemed strange, the poise with which he said it left no doubt as to who was the senior in the conversation. Hal's face, previously flushed with anger, now went pale with understanding. He took a deep breath, nodded to Kalamar and turned to his mother.

"Sir Kalamar is right, Mother. If I'm to be worthy of her, I need to stand up and fight for her."

"Stop this, Hal. She is not worthy of you. You are not marrying a barmaid who obviously whored herself out to Sir Kalamar."

"STOP IT, MOTHER!" Hal shouted. "If she is a whore, it is because I made her one. She gave herself to me and lost any chance for a future because she loves me."

"THAT'S NO REASON TO RUIN YOUR LIFE!" Shannen shouted back.

"Being with the woman I love is not ruining my life. We've been praying to the gods for a way to be together and now that one has been provided, you think I'm going to throw it away? Whatever she's done has been for us to be together. I will not spurn her for following a path that I forced her to take. I will accept whatever conditions Sir Kalamar requires to make this happen. With or WITHOUT your blessing."

Shannen's face was pale and drawn as her husband drew her away to a corner and began urgently whispering to her. Everyone else was still, unwilling to interrupt the drama before them. When they returned, it was Shannen who wore a smile of victory as her husband said, "I assume that once the marriage is complete, the property will be put in my son's name, as is customary?"

"No," Kalamar replied. "I've not gone through all this effort to see her dream come true so that she can be discarded at the first opportunity and left in the cold. I will remain the executor of her estate for as long as necessary. I will not have a lovers quarrel or 'family' dispute leaving her in the streets."

Shannen's face turned sour and it was clear to everyone that was exactly what she had in mind.

Kalamar continued, "I need an answer and have no more time to waste discussing it."

It was a rude demand, but under the circumstance, no one ventured a critique.

"Yes, I accept, my lord," Hal said as he turned from his mother's rage to Kalamar. "I can never thank you enough or repay the kindness you have shown us."

"Very well," Kalamar returned. "Upon my return, I will let her know. I've sent a carpenter ahead to the property to begin repairs. Chancellor, what time has the baron asked that we have the wedding?"

"Since he understands that they need to get ahead of the weather, it is the third hour of morning," Malcolm responded.

"Excellent," Kalamar said and then turned to Hal. "If you wish to see her tonight, she will be staying with Master Tailor Cory, who is making her dress. If not, we will see you at the chapel in the morning."

Treavor continued to watch as Hal assured him he would be there and then the family began a heated discussion. He was quite impressed with how calm Kalamar had remained in the face of such insults and how he'd anticipated the attempt to take the property. His initial impressions were confirmed.

"If you don't mind waiting a bit, my lords," Treavor began, "I and my wife would like to accompany you back to the capital. Would it be possible for us to attend tomorrow?"

It was Malcolm who answered, "The chapel is small and will only hold direct family members but you are most welcome to attend the banquet."

"Excellent," he responded. "Let me fetch my wife, and we'll join you."

*****

Kalamar rode behind the new couple's cart as they made their way through the streets of Stormlake. It was a grand procession as the entire town wanted to see the happy couple off. The snow was falling and the weather getting cold but that didn't stop anyone from shouting their well-wishes and bearing witness. She was one of their own and they couldn't be prouder.

The wedding had been simple and beautiful. Lily had shone in a cream-colored dress with golden thread. While many nobles had already returned to their estates for the winter, those closest had all answered the baron's call and attended the banquet. The cart was laden with gifts that would help them through the winter. The cart also included a young girl as lady-in-waiting to help her learn her new role. The townsfolk shouted so often for her to stand and show the dress she remained upright until they left the eastern gate.

Cory watched his lord as the crowd that had cheered the new couple now turned to Kalamar once the gate was closed. It wasn't simply shouting and cheers; it was almost a reverence and respect for what he had given Lily and, by extension, to them all. He watched the startled expression on Kal's face and just shook his head. *He had much to learn yet*, he thought.

His bemusement was short-lived, however, as he caught sight of several men serving Lords Clearwater and Greenheld at the edge of the crowd. Their abrupt gestures and angry faces made clear how they and their masters felt. He watched them disperse after Kalamar had passed and wondered what mischief their lords would yet cause.

Chapter 9

consequences

K alamar was sulking and he knew it. It made him angry he was sulking but that didn't stop the sulking. The irony of the entire situation was that he had made every decision leading to this point, knowing that it would bring him here and he'd made them anyway. He had absolutely no one to blame but himself.

He got up from his desk and walked across his study to look out the window. What he saw was uninspiring, to say the least. From the second floor of his house, he could see the entirety of Hayden Hamlet. He was now lord of Hayden Hamlet and all its surrounding domain. It was a tiny place about three quarters a mile east of Stormlake but it might as well be one thousand miles.

He was basically banished from civilization as Hayden's six hundred citizens were the absolute poorest of the poor. Their homes were mostly mud and thatch. A hundred hovels lined two streets smashed up against Stormlake. Barter was the primary method of transaction as no one really had any coin. A few rare individuals worked menial jobs in Stormlake, but the rest scratched out a living either in rickety boats fishing or trying to get the poor local soil to produce. Other than his own house, the only other building of significance was the inn across the street. It wasn't any better made than the others; it was just larger, in the design of a longhouse from ancient days.

There was supposed to be a hand-over ceremony today but Baron Eddington had canceled for some vague emergency and the local assistant exchequer had handed him the documents deeding his ownership and change of status. On paper, he was now a wealthy, propertied lord with five square miles of land. In addition, he was allowed to keep all the taxes that were due the baron as well as due him.

Since there was nothing to collect and what little was collected consisted of a few fish or vegetables, this was considered no great loss to the barony. Of the poor souls dwelling here, over two hundred were villeins who owed him work in exchange for living on his property. Most of the rest rented from him and only eighteen families actually owned their own land in his domain. He had yet to meet any of them. As he gazed out the window, he thought of the events that led him to this sorry existence.

He'd not known at the time, but with the new spring and the nobles' return from their estates to Stormlake, a campaign had begun to have him removed from the castle and his post as protégé. The stated line of attack was actually very clever. They never directed anything against him at all. What they wanted was one of their own as protégé. When they asked the archmage, his response was simply, "Would you like me telling you how to run your estates, my lord?" That quickly ended the conversation.

What they did next was to hound the baron and every one of his other officials to make one of the soon to graduate students the new protégé, as a sign of unity and a brighter future, of course.

With the archmage rightfully not budging, Baron Eddington demanded that his high chancellor find a way to make the problem go away. This led him to come begging Kalamar for help, offering land, title, a refurbished house with furnishings, and a free hand to run it as he saw fit. He also offered both his and the baron's enduring gratitude. *The baron's had already evaporated*, he thought darkly.

When he discussed the offer with his master, the archmage was irked they'd gone around him but wasn't surprised, only saddened the baron was so easily manipulated.

"Kalamar," he'd said. "You and I have spoken several times about students needing to leave their masters, to experience the world and seek their own path. You are certainly both capable and ready to do this. I just want you to be sure about why you are doing this. I will support you in this decision whatever you decide and if you do choose to leave and give the baron a way out from standing up to his nobles, then I hope you at least wring as much out of him as possible." He'd added the last with a grimace.

After a great deal of reflection, Kalamar had agreed to leave and began the preparations for his students to pass their final exams. It was an exciting phase for them as well as himself. The graduation ceremony was as emotional for him as the students, no, not students but fully capable, Sarrik-qualified, Initiate First Circle mages.

Bedelia had scored the highest and was the best overall of the class. As such, she was offered the protégé post. Farley and Kenny had been sponsored by the barony and would be working for ten years to repay the debt. They would also be living in the castle and serve at the direction of the archmage.

The standard fee for an apprenticeship was one hundred pounds per year per student. His master had given him most of this fee in addition to his salary to begin his new life. It was extremely generous, and he was most grateful for it. His new property could not even support itself at its current level without massive new taxes and he was not about to do that. These people barely had enough as it was and any new burden would be a crushing blow. With his almost three hundred pounds sterling, he could eke out a living for a few decades maintaining the property and grounds as they were, but that was a distasteful option.

A third option was to find or create new revenues. The problem here was the nearness of Stormlake and its abundant supply. They had what they needed and his own people were too poor to afford anything new. That meant pouring his limited wealth into new industries wasn't likely to pan out either. As such, short of discovering some mineral wealth in the poor soil, he was pretty well boxed in. Since he had known this before accepting the deal, he had no one to blame but himself, hence his sulking.

It had rained the last couple of days and there was a dry stream filled with the runoff from Stormlake that ran right through Hayden. The runoff ditch also collected any debris from the town and washed it here before dumping into Stormlake proper. As this was a known issue, the nobles that made no pretense of their dislike for him were having parties for throwing out the trash. It was petty and childish, but that's who they were. Most of the townsfolk inside Stormlake called the people of Hayden outsiders or just siders and now Kalamar was outside too.

He was watching a few people walking the street when he saw an elderly woman scramble into the water-filled ditch for something. She shook the water off her prize and scurried away with a burst of speed to get home. Kalamar had caught a glimpse of it before she left. A cabbage, he noted and felt a deep shame. His people were digging through trash to make due and he was enraged over personal slights.

It only took a few moments for that shame to turn on himself instead. That cabbage was an unexpected gift and she was going to make the most of it. He, on the other hand, was whining about how unfair his own life was and how he was cut off from Stormlake. How dare he complain when they had so little? He rushed out the room, down the stairs and out the front door. He walked across the street and entered the tavern.

His eyes quickly adjusted to the dimness inside and he noticed maybe a dozen patrons in the table-filled room. Kalamar smiled as the inn keep came around the bar to welcome him. It seemed to him all innkeepers came in two sizes—tall and whip thin or short and rotund. This one was the second.

"My lord, welcome, welcome," the innkeeper said, "Please come this way." He directed him to a table on the far side of the inn. He slashed his cleaning rag against the tabletop a couple of times to resettle the dust and then introduced himself. "Parlan's my name and welcome to The Scupper. What can I get for yuz?"

"Whatever food or drink you might have handy," Kalamar replied and watched Parlan disappear through a door behind the bar. The conversations had grown louder with his entrance but now seemed to dissolve into whispers as he scanned the room, noting faces. The clothes seemed to be the same worn and patched uniform rags, but he noticed that the faces and hands didn't match. He would have expected gaunt and haggard, but there didn't seem to be anyone starving or missing too many meals. He took that as a hopeful sign.

Parlan came back with a serving girl to deliver the food, and Kalamar asked, "Master Parlan, if you have some time, could you tell me a bit about Hayden and those who dwell here?"

Parlan was delighted at the request, took up a chair and promptly started making introductions of those present and describing those not. Kalamar choked down the food in between greetings and listened to the colorful stories about the residents. Parlan was a good storyteller and kept even the locals interested in a fun, playful manner.

Kalamar had long finished his meal and was nursing his honey ale when he interrupted the narrative. Parlan had said his eldest son, Lars, would be back tomorrow from getting supplies in town to which Kalamar asked, "Why would he stay overnight in Stormlake?"

Parlan replied with a laugh, "Not Stormlake, my lord. He went to Glendmere, just to the east."

Kalamar's mind started racing with an idea. While he suspected he knew the answer, he asked anyway, "Why would he go five miles east for supplies when Stormlake is so close?"

"Why, the prices, my lord. It would cost me three times in Stormlake and the quality's no better."

Kalamar nodded in confirmation and replied, "I ran into the same thing as we were coming from the west. Prices continued to rise the closer we got to the capital."

"Just so, my lord, just so. 'Tis always seems to be that way. Cost more to live in the big city. Always has, always will." He pronounced with finality, as many of the patrons murmured and nodded agreement.

"Master Parlan, is there some young lad who could take a message into Stormlake for me?"

"Of course, my lord." The inn had been filling up as word spread the new Lord of Hayden was inside. Parlan pointed to a young lad about eight and said, "Yuz, Orville, Lord Sylvicheld needs a message sent to the Storm."

Once Orville had rushed over, Kalamar said, "I need you to invite Master Tailor Cory Dresden, his wife, and youngest son, Nevan, on Burnt Oak Road to join me for dinner this evening. Bring me back their reply. Got that?"

"Yes, my lord." Orville bolted out the door.

"Parlan," Kalamar turned back and addressed, "is there someone who could prepare a dinner for me and my guests this evening?"

It was Anna, the serving girl, who spoke up, "My grandma used to cook for Lady Aislinn, my lord. She could do it."

Kalamar looked to Parlan who nodded and then he said, "Please ask your grandmother if she can and get with Kellyn at my house for anything she needs. Thank you."

He turned back to Parlan as the girl took off. "I hope this isn't too disruptive to your business, Master Parlan?"

"Not at all, my lord. We can manage for the time it takes her."

"Thank you. Now, if you would do me a small favor." Kalamar pulled out a single gold coin and handed it to the innkeeper while continuing, "Please see that everyone in Hayden has a drink on me and if that runs out, let's settle up in the morning, okay?"

"That is no favor at all my lord. 'Tis most generous and will be my pleasure," Parlan said as the room erupted in cheers at free drinks.

*****

Lord Malcolm Cherrheld, High Chancellor of Eddington, was in a foul mood. The last two weeks had been insufferable because of certain lords' disgusting and dishonorable behaviors. The last few nights of Throwing out the Trash banquets had been despicable. The worst had been his liege lord's refusal to see what was going on. He simply could not understand the viciousness and pettiness being shown by some of the nobles.

The noble code of honor required them to set the standard, not engage in this type of gutter behavior. How had they fallen so low? And worse, where would it stop? His thoughts were interrupted by a knock on his office door, followed by his first assistant, Monahan, entering the room.

"My lord, I apologize for the interruption but Lord Sylvicheld is most insistent on seeing you first thing this morning."

Gods above, Malcolm thought. The one person who could make him feel worse wanted to see him. No doubt to register a complaint about the ignoble behavior of certain Lords.

He sighed and said, "I don't suppose he has that damnably clever Tailor with him?" His question was hopeful, but his tone was not.

"Actually, my lord, he does. Shall I send them in?"

Malcolm's mood brightened instantly. Those two caused trouble and he was feeling rebellious. "Yes, send them right in."

He rose up to greet his guests. He noticed there was no anger or bitterness in their expressions. Everyone was seated and the pleasantries were soon exchanged.

"So, my lord, how can I be of service this morning?" Malcolm asked.

"I need several legal documents drawn up as soon as possible, my lord chancellor. The first is forming a business partnership between myself and Nevan Dresdon on a sixty-forty split, with Nevan being the managing partner. The name will be Blue Rose Shipping. Second, I will need a document creating Hayden Orderly with Nevan as the proprietor. Third, I will need multiple documents creating separate agreements with multiple merchants agreeing to work with Blue Rose shipping on a sixty-twenty-twenty split."

"My lord Kalamar," Malcolm began cautiously, "I must admit to being at a bit of a loss concerning the exact nature of what you are asking for. Could you please clarify?" He then sat back to a delightful tale. With a growing lightness in his heart and a smile on his face, he listened to the incredible plan.

Kalamar was going to build a shipping business through every town and village in the barony. He was going to sign agreements with a local merchant in each town to act as an agent for Blue Rose, placing and transacting business based on orders from the other agents in each municipality. Anyone could ship anything through the agents. Each wagon would be driven to the next village and then continue with different drivers for the next leg of the trip depending on the cargo. It would take a wagon only seven days to go from Stormlake to Nellis once everything was in place and a steady volume reached. Even smaller villages would receive shipments on a regular basis even if it wasn't daily, all based on their cargo traffic needs.

Malcolm sat back, stunned by the implications. It would connect the barony in a way only great cities were now. Currently, every town and village produced what it needed, with only the occasional purchase for hard to acquire or expensive items. Only nobles traveled between the towns and even that was limited. This would all change.

A craftsman in Nellis could produce for the market here in Stormlake and still make a profit because of cost differences. A Stormlake merchant could expand his operations to produce more cheaply and sell to a larger clientele. The increased volume of crafts would make prices drop, allowing more people to afford better-made necessities. Tax collection would increase as more sales generated value and more value generated a larger taxable base.

Additionally, each wagon passing in and out of a town or village generated a wagon tax; the payment of which was split between the barony and the locality. Official pronouncements and local events would be spread more quickly. This was incr—

"My lord," Kalamar interrupted. "I can see that you are open to the possibilities this makes possible for everyone, but I'm sure you realize there will be several interested parties that would like this enterprise stopped if I don't get it up and running before they figure out what I'm doing."

Malcolm knew exactly the no goods he was speaking about and said with a growl, "Certain noble lords who have a personal dislike for you!"

"There are those, of course, my lord, but there will also be certain craftsmen and merchants who will not want to lose their restricted markets and won't want to change how they do business. They will be forced to compete with other tradesmen and will not appreciate the loss of their monopolies," Kalamar finished.

"Your point is well taken, my lord. And I'm thinking that we must be prepared to deal with them when they do. I believe you're right. If you can get up and running quickly, everyone will see and feel the benefits.

"Now, you're going to need lots of horses and wagons. Lord Treavor owes me several favors. Tell him to use two of them for what you need. He will also be able to point you in the right direction for drivers. There's a man you can find at the Frisky Fish Tavern on Broad Street who would be a great trainer for your guards. I'm assuming you want to hire out of Hayden first but he can find others you need as well. If you need any loans to cover anything you let me know and I will provide those personally. It will be kept quiet between the three of us and I'm sure you understand why. Now do you have a list of possible agents?"

Both Kalamar and Cory were taken aback by the unexpected candor and the generous help. It was Cory who spoke first, saying, "My lord, you could cause yourself trouble for the help you have just offered. Why would you put yourself in such a position?"

Malcolm paused for a moment before responding, "Because it is the right thing to do. Kalamar has been treated unfairly and I hope my help can start to balance the scales. I also know that this enterprise will benefit the baron and all the citizens in these lands, including those who will hate him for it. It is appalling to me that our nobles have fallen so low in their conduct and it is past time to oppose such behavior and restore proper leadership and etiquette."

Kalamar replied gravely, "I am touched by your words and your faith in me, my lord. And I swear I will not disappoint or take for granted your trust." He bowed his head in acknowledgment.

Malcolm said, "It is you, Lord Kalamar, that has shown the very highest qualities of nobility and it is our shame that we don't all recognize them. Let us together reset the standard." Malcolm returned the bow.

Malcolm then listened to the list of possible agents and only suggested one change. The merchant in question had recently become indebted to Lord Clearwater and that could become an issue. He didn't say why and Kalamar didn't ask. Malcolm refused the 20 percent commission for finding an agent saying he wanted no connections, official or otherwise. They accepted that and he escorted his visitors to his door in a far better mood than he'd been in a long time. It was a much brighter future he envisioned as they said their goodbyes.

*****

It was midafternoon as Kalamar, astride Shadow, rode east out of Hayden, leading a single wagon filled with goods Nevan purchased that morning. He smiled as he thought of the tale already being told that he was taking a wagon of goods to his ward, the Lady of Black Forest Cottage. He smiled because this was true, but not the whole story by a long shot.

The wagon of goods would make the journey with stops at every village along the way, but as soon as he was out of sight, he was going to race ahead and set up agents in each of those villages. He was then going northwest to Northspring and arranging for horses and wagons to be sent to Hayden and Blue Rose Shipping. From Northspring, he would head west, setting up agents and getting supply lists for purchases to ship both ways, sending the orders back to Nevan magically.

This would allow them to get the shipments up and running before anyone was aware of their plans. He laughed at the sky as he spurred Shadow into a gallop and the wind sang in his ears. He thought about being trapped in the tower with his responsibilities to oversee three new mages and continued laughing. His enemies had no idea what they had set in motion.

Chapter 10

unexpected attack

Kalamar looked up from the latest ledger Nevan had prepared concerning the Blue Rose Shipping's finances. With over forty wagons making almost daily runs during workable weather, it would take nearly five years to get back all the funds he'd so far invested in the enterprise. That was a long time to wait and a significant reason nobody had tried something of this kind before.

He smiled briefly as he thought of the two nobles who were trying to set up competing businesses and thereby keep him out. They were already losing money and would fold as soon as their treasury couldn't take the pressure from their pride. He wasn't doing it to make a fortune. It was the indirect benefits that it brought. He'd brought jobs and new money into Hayden and that provided more jobs, more money and even taxes to provide for his people.

He had to stop himself from laughing as he didn't want to wake Theresa. She'd been his almost constant companion in the two months since his move to Hayden. She was beautiful and curious about everything and he'd grown quite attached to her company.

He rose from his desk in the study and looked out the window. It was the fourth hour of night and far too early to see anything. His years with the archmage had taught him to appreciate the early morning quiet and the amount of work he could get done before the rest of the world awoke. The harvest was over and the days were starting to shrink into winter's darkness. He'd dedicated his lands to the gods[25] of goodness and they had poured their blessings on his people and their work. The new prosperity, the best harvest anyone could remember? Even the lake was providing an abundance of fish. It was as if…

A disturbance in the night air pulled Kalamar out of his thoughts. Something was wrong and he extended his senses to discover the problem. He turned and walked out of his study and across his bedroom to a northern window. His gaze was drawn to the northwest, where his instincts told him something was off.

He drew on his power and sent a call to the archmage. It was a simple spell sending a brief message. It would be stopped by the shield around the castle, but his master would sense it and respond as needed. It was but a few heartbeats before his master replied. Not with a message but a request to speak mind to mind. He recognized his master's specific call and opened the shield around his house to allow the link.[26] He was quickly seeing the images from the occulari his master was sending north of Stormlake.

The images raced over the ground with the crescent moon providing some light. It quickly reached the tree line northeast of

---

25 Lands could be dedicated to a god or goddess who would act as a patron. This created a bond between the people and their gods with responsibilities and obligations from both parties. The gods would provide their blessing and protection while the people would worship and honor them. These agreements gave the priests of those gods the legal authority to question the leadership among the ruling class and even oppose those rulers when they didn't live up to their responsibilities. It was for this last reason many lands did not have patron gods. Most rulers didn't want to give up power and authority. They certainly didn't want to give anyone the right to question their decisions. Sandar was the patron god of Calledon and all parts of it were supposed to be under his care. However, the duke of Genevieve had used a technicality in the treaty of Bourdou to allow Calledon lords south of the Nantukk mountains the freedom to choose on their own. All of them, including the duke, had chosen to abandon the gods.

26 A mind-link spell allows the initiator to create a psychic link between two cooperating minds. This facilitates the sharing of images and surface thoughts. The link is not deep within the mind as that could permit attacks but is more akin to a projection on the surface, where it is controlled by all the participants. It takes time to learn to pass useful information in a clear and concise manner.

Stormlake. Passing through the trees, it stopped at the same clearing Kalamar and his friends used for training last year. In it, however, was a very different sight than he last remembered.

A large magic shield bristling with energy encompassed an area large enough for over a dozen people and even more horses. Guards were stationed inside at the four quarters of the shield edges. Several servants waited on the eastern side with the horses. It was the people in the center around the large bonfire that drew his attention and focus. There were four wizards in a circle, chanting around a fifth. This fifth was clearly acting as the heart of the spells they were working. Even as he watched, the leader raised his voice in a shout while thrusting his staff to the south. A large globe of red-orange fire tore out of the bonfire to hover briefly above the shield's apex before racing south. Kalamar shifted his main focus back to his own eyes as he watched the globe of destruction streak out of the woods, over the fields and strike the castle shield with a thunderous crack, like ice breaking on a frozen pond.

The archmage's response was immediate. Lightning streaked back from the castle and smashed into the attackers' shield, exploding in static bursts going every direction. Kalamar watched through the occulari as those inside jumped and shrieked in panic at the counterattack. Only the wizards maintained some composure and responded with another attack of their own.

Kalamar's mind raced as he considered the situation and what needed to be done. He also cursed the shortsighted privy council for insisting that he not create any occulari of his own within the barony. He was blind to any other forces that could be moving even now against his own people.

He quickly cast a vision spell and sent it flying in ever-widening arcs around Hayden. The archmage, at the same time, left the guardian Tor, to respond to the attackers and released several more occulari in multiple directions to also spot any other forces around the capital. It was a bit disorienting at first, seeing so many images within images through the rapidly growing network of occulari, but he quickly adjusted.

By the time the wizards launched their third attack, he and his master had discovered no other obvious forces within the immediate area. Kalamar released his vision spell and proposed a strategy to Archmage Crow. When his master agreed, he turned from the window and rushed across the room to wake Theresa.

"Theresa, wake up! You must wake up quickly!" he insisted as he reached out to shake her from sleep.

"Huh, what is it, Kal? What's the matter?" she responded groggily. At that moment, there was another distant crack as another attack struck the castle shield.

She jumped. "What was that?"

"The castle is under attack, my dear. I have to lead a force to take out the attackers and I need you to dress and gather the people together here or in the shipping yard where they will be protected under the shields," he responded in a rush. Time was wasting and he needed to hurry.

It was clearly too much, too fast, as she responded, "What, wait, you can't leave me. What are you talking about?"

Another crack sounded from the castle and Kalamar had to firmly unwrap her hands from his arm. He reached up to hold her face and slowly and clearly said, "The castle is under attack. It will be okay but I need to go and help. I need you to gather the people of Hayden either here in this house or at the Blue Rose Shipping building so they will be safe under the shields." It was at this time Kellyn knocked on the door.

"Master, something is not right," Kellyn said. "There is something going on at the castle."

Kalamar opened the door and replied, "You're right. The castle is under attack. I'm going now to see to the defense. Please take Theresa downstairs with you and then gather everyone under the shield here or at the Blue Rose. I'm heading there next to gather the men."

"Yes, Master" was her reply as he rushed downstairs. He grabbed his sword off the hook by the door and headed out. The servants had already gathered but he ignored them as he heard Kellyn explaining what was going on and what needed to be done. He was comforted knowing she would handle things and see they were accomplished. The fact that she was eleven rushed through his mind, but he dismissed it for more immediate concerns.

As he made the gate in front of his house, the hamlet was already awake and watching the night sky light up with fire and lightning. It actually made his job much easier.

He used an amplification spell so his voice would carry without shouting.

"Everyone," he called, "listen to me. I need you to remain calm and attend my instruction."

All eyes were on him as he continued, "The castle is under attack. There doesn't seem to be any indication they will come this way but I want to be prepared. As you know, there are shields around both my house and the Blue Rose Shipping Yard. It will be a tight fit but I need all the women and children to gather under both of those shields. I need the men to gather around those shields, forming a circle. I don't believe it will be necessary but it is better to prepare for the worst than hope for the best. I also need volunteers to join me for a strike against those attacking. It is a small group and the archmage and I have a plan to end this."

While his words first caused gasps of alarm, the mood of his people soon turned to purposeful action. He had a plan; he was calm and certain, so they quickly began following his instructions. They were used to working together in diversity and while there hadn't been an attack in living memory, there had certainly been fires and floods that required quick action and teamwork.

All freemen of property were required to have arms and armor. They must be ready to respond when called by their lord for the common defense. He soon had forty-eight fathers and sons before him, awaiting instruction. In addition, the guards working for Blue Rose Shipping were also there, giving him a precious fourteen more men with actual training if not experience.

He addressed them all and said, "All right, I need two groups. The attackers are in a glade northwest of here about a mile and a half. I need a group who can run that distance with me and be ready to fight at the end. The second group, I need to take up guard positions around the town within sight of the man to either side. You must be ready to shout the alarm with everyone running to him to form up and defend the town. Leverett, I'm leaving you in charge of this second group. Defend the townsfolk until I get back."

The grizzled old fighter nodded before calling off those in the second group and setting up the defense. This left him eleven young men in mismatched weapons and armor.

"Now for the fun part," he said to them, receiving grins and chuckles in reply. They were young enough and inexperienced enough to actually believe him. He shook his head as he thought that some of them might not make it back. What he said, though, was, "Let's go." He turned to the glade and began a slow run northwest to battle.

*****

Running over fields at night was not as easy as it sounds, Kalamar decided. It had taken them a half hour to get to the glade. The attacks hadn't stopped but instead intensified. He'd retained his link with the archmage. He knew his master was making the castle shield appear weaker and ready to fall to encourage the intruders to pour more of their energy into their strikes. This, in turn, would mean less energy to put into their defense when Kalamar struck.

Kalamar gathered his men just out of sight and explained the plan. "There are four guards at the cardinal points in the glade," he said as more lightning from the castle struck the shield ahead. The counterattacks were also getting weaker to reinforce the deception. "I need each of you to pair up and attack those guards when I launch my lightning attack. Understood?" He looked at each to make sure they heard and understood. "When I cast my spell, the shield will go down. I will shout 'Charge' and rush in. That is your signal to do the same.

"Now, this is the most important part. There are five mages inside the circle. If any of them try to speak, you must kill them. Don't hesitate and don't try to wound them. Their spells will kill, so don't give them the chance. Do you understand?" Again, he looked to each one to make sure they were with him.

"Good," he said. "Now, follow me as I walk around their shield, looking for the best spot to strike. When I find it, I will stop and signal you. Keep your eyes down to the ground until I shout for the attack to begin. This will help you keep your eyesight once the spells are cast."

He turned then and made his way slowly through the last few trees to the glade. He stayed behind the last row and worked his way around to the left, looking for the best spot to launch his counterattack.

The enemies' attacks were even faster as they thought they sensed the imminent collapse of the castle shield. *They looked exhausted,* Kalamar thought with satisfaction. He was almost due west from the glade when he found what he sought. Their shield was developing cracks under the strain of assault and they were so focused on the castle they hadn't noticed. He signaled the men and they fanned out behind him.

The runes burned in his mind as he gathered himself and tapped into his power. He used the Sarrik runes since the archmage was timing his counterattack with Kalamar's spell through the link established earlier.

The spell drew power and light into his hands until they were lit up like a star. As he reached the maximum he could hold, he shouted the release rune and lightning stabbed out into the night, reaching through the cracks in the enemies' shielding and blasting into the center mage. The five mages were thrown about from the concussive force. At the same time, the archmage launched a massive strike of his own that shattered their shield and deafened with the thunderous concussion that followed.

"CHARGE!" Kalamar shouted as he drew his sword from his back and ran into the clearing. He headed directly for the wizards, leaving the guards for his men. Only two mages were even slightly upright. He cut down one, and his backswing caught the second flat blade against the skull, knocking him or her to the ground, unmoving. He turned to the group of mages down on the ground and cast a sleep spell over them in case any were pretending. Only then did he notice that one had been cast half into the bonfire and was burning. The stench was horrible as he continued to scan the encampment for anyone left willing to fight.

The servants were cowering near the horses, no doubt with ears ringing from the sudden onslaught of their counterraid. His men had all the guards he could see down, so he headed past the servants to check on the last pair behind the horses.

As he strode past, the lead servant reached into his boot and threw a small blade. Kalamar caught this from the corner of his eye and reacted by spinning left, bringing his blade from right to left, adding his left hand to increase his strength in the blow. Even as he turned, he knew he was too late. The servant and his blade moved incredibly fast, almost blurring in the flickering flames of the bonfire.

The moment slowed in his mind. He watched the thrower smile as they both knew the dagger would strike first. It was a perfect strike to the chest. Perfect, except Kalamar had his personal shield that blocked the blade and it bounced down to the dirt at his feet. The grin of victory only had time to change to confusion as Kalamar's blade took out the assailant's throat. The knife thrower toppled over, hands reaching to his neck as he tried to staunch his life from pouring out. A few spasms and the battle for his life was lost.

Kalamar looked down on the now still form in a moment of déjà vu. While he still regretted the necessity, he was not overwhelmed with guilt. The man at his feet deserved nothing less. His eyes were drawn to his feet and the knife that had almost slipped between his ribs and punctured his lungs. As he reached down to retrieve it for a closer look, one of the servant girls shouted, "Don't! It's poisoned!"

Kalamar stayed his hand but sent his senses and power out. Indeed, the entire knife, blade and handle, reeked of a poison he had not felt before. He looked up to the servant who might have just saved his life. On her knees, hand outstretched to him, it was her face that told her story. While less than twenty years, it looked like she'd lived with nothing but horror and misery. Ears bleeding, face bruised and maybe some fingers grown crooked from being broken long ago, she was the picture of abuse and sorrow.

Heartbreak was the closest Kalamar could apply to the emotions now whirling through him. Reminding himself that he still had duties to perform, he stood back up and looked around. The men he was going to check on had come to him, dragging the captured guards with them. The wizards had not moved and the servants were huddled where they'd been the entire time. It was over.

He looked back to the woman who'd warned him. She was frozen still, as if afraid to move. The others also cowered in fear at what was to come next. One horror had ended for them, but they had no hope that another hadn't found them.

"You have nothing to fear from us," Kalamar began. "You will be well treated if you provide no threat to my people. We will certainly want to speak with you to learn what you know of this attack, but you will not be harmed." He walked over and reached down to the woman with his hand outstretched, offering to help her up. "Thank you for warning me. I will not forget it," he said. "Please, all of you, stand up. We will pack up this camp and head to the capital. Your wounds will be tended there and we will then decide what your futures hold."

It didn't take long to pack, as they'd been prepared to flee if things went badly and needed a quick escape. They tied the dead and unconscious mages to their horses and formed a train with all the horses tied to the one in front. Kalamar made several circuits of the clearing looking to make sure nothing was left.

On the last circuit he looked out and his senses told him he was being watched from the north. He did not pause or give alarm but sent the thought to his master, who replied he was aware of the watcher and for Kalamar to proceed with his plans to return. A Stormlake company of soldiers, led by Bedelia, would meet them.

*****

Grand Master Ormand Starcaller had watched the events of the night with great interest, carefully considering what he learned. It had been only recently he'd compromised the Eighth[27] in Pack 38.

---

[27] Pack members were simply addressed by numbers: First, Second, Third, etc. Each person's position changed so often with the infighting it was simply easier to address wizards by numbers representing their position than to keep learning new names.

In doing so, he'd learned that someone claiming to be a Sarrik archmage was living in Eddington. With Stormlake being so insignificant, his first thought was of a pretender fooling the ignorant locals, who wouldn't know any better. He no longer shared that opinion as he watched those dead from their failed attack hauled off before his eyes.

The power and skill displayed from the castle proper were undeniable. The Sarrik had easily led the pack to exhaust its energies, thinking the castle shield would quickly fall. That massive counterattack could only have been accomplished by a wizard of at least the Sixth Circle.

Why a Sarrik archmage would waste his time in such a backwater was an interesting question all on its own. What the barony of Eddington would do in response to this attack was another. He'd never wasted any time on this region and was at a disadvantage because of that. Since he hated being in such a weak position, he was going to change that quickly.

It had been idle curiosity prompting him to teleport out here. He'd decided to evaluate the skills of Pack 38 and sell that information to a certain noble lord he occasionally worked for. He now had something far more valuable and his mind raced down new paths to determine how best to profit from it.

He watched the young lord finish sweeping the clearing for any stray items. Clearly satisfied, he then led his men and the prisoners south. Ormand's position to the northeast of the clearing and the distance he kept from it, had not allowed him to see them gather for the attack. He had seen, however, the speed and skill used to take down the pack wizards. He had also witnessed ripping the throat out of one of the servants, no doubt to quell any thoughts of disobedience. He could not overhear what was said, but after the display he just witnessed, he was too experienced to risk casting a spell to enhance his hearing.

The party had long departed the clearing but still he waited. Patience was a cruel teacher but a necessary one for those who wished to enjoy a long life. He smiled at the thought, realizing he had reached his answer to the question of whom to sell this information to. No one. He would watch and wait. He would learn what he could both from here in Eddington and by watching how Pack 38 reacted to its leadership's failure to return.

The Eighth had insisted this was an unauthorized attack and no evidence as to what they intended was left behind to cause problems for the First when he returned. Succeed, and the First would have valuable information and bragging rights. Fail, and he could kill any followers he brought with him and blame it all on them. Dead, Ormand added to himself and the problem was no longer his concern.

Finally judging the situation clear, Ormand began the first spells to safely pass through the shields protecting his official residence in Alberton.

*****

Bedelia led them to the temple of Saa'Vey, where the high priest quickly took charge of the prisoners. The center of the temple of warriors was obviously a training hall. Since it was the largest part of the temple, this was where they laid out all the mages, both dead and unconscious, next to their possessions. The servants were being tended to by the acolytes of the goddess of healing, Mallynne.

He attempted to tell the lead ghan about the poisoned blade but was interrupted with a "We know what we are about, my lord." He nodded his head and backed up. Other than the rude remark, they did indeed seem to have everything well in hand. They were meticulously going through all the persons and personal effects to discover any clues as to their identity and motives for the attack.

He watched as they examined the knife thrower in particular. He observed as the ghan he'd addressed cast a spell locating the poison blade in the boot, where Kalamar had returned it for the ride home. He also watched as he reached into the boot and extracted it. The priest dropped it with a shout, clutching his hand and backing away as he swayed on his feet. It appeared that Kalamar wasn't the only one watching closely as High Chaplain Ghan Teague was quickly at the priest's side, raising his hand and shouting, "Stop!"

Everyone remained motionless after turning to Ghan Teague, who continued, "This dagger is covered in a deadly poison." He announced to the entire hall, "Any who touch it should die. The reason our prideful fool, Ghan Houston, is not yet dead is because our ever-wise Lord Saa'Vey has a lesson he wants to teach." Ghan Houston was staring in horror and pain as he listened to the head of his order while continuing to hold his hand in agony.

"Ghan Houston's arrogance," Teague continued, "caused him to dismiss out of hand the warning that Lordmage Sylvicheld tried to deliver. This priest's jealousy of the victory that the lordmage won today is eating at his soul. The lesson therefore is this, the poison will not kill as it would have already done, but the pain will not stop until Ghan Houston has learned humility and respect. You will not be excused from any of your duties, now get back to work."

With that abrupt announcement, Ghan Teague and everyone else went back to their tasks. Ghan Houston, for a moment bewildered, glanced over to Kalamar, looked back down to his hand and, with a deep breath, seemed to gather himself and return to the knife and his duties with agony etched in his every gesture.

Kalamar was still admiring Houston's courage and dedication when Baron Eddington entered the sanctuary with several of the council, including Archmage Angus Crow. Concern and anger were the emotions most on display but it shocked him that the archmage was in a rage. It was only in a glance that he caught it and anyone who didn't know the archmage well would never have gotten even that much. He headed over to the group as they walked up to the high priest for an update.

"High Chaplain," Lord Terence demanded, "what have you discovered?"

"My lord," Ghan Teague began, "as best we can determine, they came here because they didn't believe the archmage was a Sarrik and they wanted to prove it by murdering him."

Several people gasped as that statement sank in. Angus's expression didn't change.

"Now let me explain what we know," he continued. "They did not come here with official orders. This appeared to be an impromptu outing orchestrated by the late First of Pack 38. His underlings were not told his reasons. The slaves and remaining guard only knew rumors. They did, however, really fear that man"—Teague pointed to the knife thrower—"and called him a Forcer. It's probably short for enforcer, as he was the one ordered to mete out punishments for any displeasure the wizards marked. The knife he tried to kill Lordmage Sylvicheld with was poisoned not only on the blade but also on the handle. It is a poison called Widowmaker from the Koreth flower. The only profession I know of that would develop an immunity to poison and coat the entire weapon is an assassin.

"I just don't know why he would have stayed in camp during the attack if he was here to kill. His best opportunity would have been during the attack, so maybe he was simply hired for protection or maybe it's possible the attackers didn't know his true profession." He shrugged with the last statement.

"This is an outrage, my lord," Lord Dugan began. "Assassins and murderous bands of mages. We must demand justice. We must take this all the way to the duke of Genevieve!"

"And what exactly are we going to take to them?" asked Lord Ferguson. "We have the word of some slaves and a guard. We have no evidence to present and no proof that we could even link them to the Hoff Baron at all. They came without orders, so he would just deny it or say they went off on their own."

"I must reluctantly agree with Lord Ferguson, my lord," Lord Willem added. "We know that the duke will never give us justice on so little evidence and we also know that we are no match for Hoff if we tried to use force to make demands. We haven't even had contact with them in over thirty years, so it's unlikely we could find anyone in Hoff who would be sympathetic to our plea."

"So we are to be denied justice?" General Shay asked. "Is that your counsel?"

"Justice has already been done," the archmage responded. "Those who attempted this deed are dead. None of our people were hurt. We are now aware, whether through lax standards or devious plots, we need to strengthen our guard against such marauders and stand a closer watch on our borders."

"Here, here!" added Lord Malcolm. "We boost our defenses. Watch our borders for any further treachery and gather further proof until we have a case that the duke would accept. Perhaps, Archmage, you could begin spying on them, since we know they certainly have no problems spying on us?"

"You are quite right, Lord Malcolm," Lord Terrence remarked. "I have not forgotten those damnable spying spells we discovered in the castle or the constant attempts the good archmage has fought off since to replace them.

"We are not in any shape to go to war to see our rights honored in this, but that doesn't mean we can't respond in kind and better prepare against the next attack. Lord Dugan, call the council together so that we may discuss the best course to see to the defense of these lands."

Lord Dugan nodded and headed out of the temple as the high chaplain spoke. "My Lord, I suggest that we allow the archmage to continue the investigation that I've begun here. He may have additional ways of getting information. As I recall, our agreements with him explicitly state that anything of a magical nature would be turned over to him and be his responsibility to oversee. There are still three mages alive that also need to be dealt with. Now, in this case, Lord Sylvicheld was instrumental in the counterattack and defense of your lands and people, so he should share in any possessions from the attackers."

Kalamar quickly spoke up, saying, "I defer to the archmage's judgment in this matter."

Lord Angus nodded in acceptance of the statement and compliment.

"You are right, Ghan." Baron Terrance turned to the archmage. "This is your area of expertise and it is right that you should carry out the investigation and see to the spoils. Please update me on any progress and let me know of any assistance you need."

"My lord," Angus said as he nodded in acknowledgment. "I will keep you apprised of any developments. As to the spoils, I would offer the high chaplain the first pick of four of the horses and gear in celebration of this victory today. I would offer the baron the next four horses of his choice as a gift." Each man nodded in acceptance.

"Lord Kalamar, I would ask a favor. As the tower is no place for it, I ask that you take charge of the guard and slaves and find a way to incorporate them into a new life here. It is obviously not possible to simply return them home. In payment of this, take whatever remains of the horses and gear." It was Kalamar's turn to nod in acceptance of the charge and gift.

Angus continued, "I will take the sorcerers with me to further study and interrogate. They will not be allowed to cause any trouble and will be dealt with appropriately when I'm finished." There was steel in his voice as he finished speaking.

"I approve," the baron stated. "Now let us be about it." Suiting deed to word, he walked over to the horses with Teague.

Kalamar walked over to the prisoners and said, "You have been turned over to my custody. It is not possible to return you to your homes. If you are willing to obey our laws, however, you will be allowed to live among us in peace. I will help you find new lives here, if you are willing to do so. Slavery is against the will of the gods and is not allowed here. Whatever your old roles were are done and forgotten. Your life begins anew."

The former slaves, servants and guard all bowed low and murmured their thanks and loyalty. It was a bit much, but they would quickly adjust, Kalamar was sure. He turned to the priest of Mallynne and said, "In thanks of the healing you have performed this day, I would ask that you also choose four horses as a gift in gratitude for your goddess' blessings on my people."

The ghan nodded in acceptance and thanks.

Kalamar turned at the excited murmurs from behind him and saw the archmage using magic to lift the sorcerers and their possessions up in the air and seemingly make them vanish. In fact, he was placing them in a holding box created in the ethereal plane so he could transport them back to the tower for study.

He turned again as a ghan of Saa'Vey came over to him and said, "My lord, we will bury the dead and when finished bring all the remaining horses and items to your house."

"That is very generous. Thank you," Kalamar replied with a nod.

He looked over to his people both old and new. "It's been a long night, so let's go home, shall we?"

*****

Kalamar waited in his study for the archmage. In all the excitement, it was clear that work was the last thing on anyone's mind, so he'd declared a holiday. A great feast was being ordered with everyone in Hayden invited. He was making preparations when he'd received the message from his master, asking to meet privately. It was late afternoon as he watched the archmage appear before him through the gate he allowed in the shield around his home. Angus took the proffered seat and then the glass of chilled wine Kalamar knew he liked.

He sat down in the padded chair across from his master as Angus said, "I want to thank you for your help today. You and your people performed well and are to be commended. I am just sorry to say that is the only thanks you will get. The council"—the emphasis placed on this word made it seem distasteful—"has decided they don't want to provoke Hoff with undue celebrations, so there will be no official recognition of your deeds. It is both unnecessary and cowardly, but there it is.

"This I am only telling you and Ghan Teague. I have tested[28] the wizards and one has passed. Her name is now Amanda and I will release her south of Eastcove. She will stay out in the wilds a week or so, adjusting to what she has learned and then make her way north to discover us. She is third circle of the Seven Royals runes. She has confirmed what Teague discovered. She has also provided much detail into the pit of evil that was Pack 38.

"I used the word 'was' deliberately." Angus paused. "I am only sharing this with you. It burned to the ground this morning. All but

---

[28] The archmage tested the sorcerer's with a spell that allows him to invade and control their dreams. At his level of expertise, it can allow for weeks or even months to be experienced in only a few minutes of actual time. Things learned can be remembered by the recipient. Spells can be taught this way but the dreamer must spend time getting the body to handle the skills and power the mind thought it had already mastered in the dream.

a few servants were killed in the blaze that seemed to be caused by a fire elemental that got loose from its imprisonment."

Kalamar said nothing as there really wasn't anything to say.

"We do, however, have another problem," the archmage continued. "The watcher that you sensed is a grand master and not part of Pack 38. He is what Hoff considers an independent wizard.[29] He is patient, talented and powerful. Hoff independents don't survive that long without being clever. I will show you who he is when you next scry.

"Speaking of scrying, I am removing the foolish prohibition of you creating and using occulari or any other devices. Any aide you provide will be welcome. While the baron has agreed to increase patrols, I am not confident he will continue them indefinitely or that they will be of sufficient size and scope to make an adequate defense."

His master paused momentarily, then sighed and shook his head. "It is clear to me that the baron is not his father. He does not lead or stand on principles but instead is led by the council majority in most issues. This has not served him well and has allowed interests other than honor and duty to rule these lands." It was a bit of a shock to see his master seem dispirited. It didn't suit him. "But," he continued returning to his usual self, "that just means I will have to take a more active role in council decision-making. Now, to more important matters. Are you still thinking of building a university?"

Kalamar took a moment to gather his thoughts and said, "I am. However, it will be two years before I have the finances to begin. If things continue as they are with my current plans, I can begin with a small group after fall harvest in 1413."

---

[29] All sorcerers are conscripted into the packs of Hoff with two exceptions. The first would be to acquire an exemption from the baron. These exemptions were almost never given to the wizard directly but given to a noble lord who could then procure a court wizard. That wizard was then in the service of his lord and could teach a single apprentice at any given time. Occasionally, one could be bought, but the price was extraordinary. The second occurred when an unaffiliated wizard was discovered and they demanded the right of challenge. If they succeeded in dueling to the death, a pack wizard of the next higher circle there were given a pendent confirming their independence.

"I see," Angus mused. "And what if you had almost five thousand pounds sterling, a library of several thousand books, dozens of assorted desks, tables, and other equipment. The only reason I mention this"—his master paused for effect—"is before Pack 38 burned to the ground, I removed everything of any value. In addition, I saved all the slaves, servants and two apprentices that were not wholly corrupted and might yet be turned into mages of some worth." The archmage pulled a small box seemingly from the air and set it on the arm of the chair Kalamar used. It was six inches square and intricately carved with crows.

Kalamar's breath caught as he stared down on his master's ethereal dimension box. He'd seen it several times and knew it could indeed contain all that his master just described.

"I don't know what to say" was all Kalamar could think to speak as his mind whirled at the new paths and opportunities available.

"You don't need to say anything. In addition, I've included all the belongings of those who attacked us today. I would like to peruse the library for anything of interest once it is open for use."

Kalamar could only stare as Angus continued, "Build your university, Kal, and don't let any of the noble halfwits stand in your way. And don't let any thoughts of possible trouble for me hinder you either. I welcome the opportunity to put these provincial idiots in their place." Lord Crow was grinning by the end of his little vent and was clearly in much higher spirits for it.

Kal laughed as his master raised his glass in a toast and they both drank to the future. Their noble adversaries wouldn't know what hit them.

*****

The archmage left and Kalamar managed to resist the impulse to open the box and sort through the treasure it contained. Instead, he reminded himself he had a party to attend with his people. He rushed downstairs, calling for Theresa as he went. She loved being the center of attention and he was in quite the mood to oblige.

As he reached the main floor, he was met by his cook, Gammie. She had stayed on from that first night and insisted that everyone call her Gammie. The look on her face, however, warned him that something was wrong.

"What is it, Gammie?" he asked while slowing to a stop before her.

"My lord, you will not find Theresa here," she replied.

"Why not? Is she unwell?" he asked with growing concern.

"No, my lord. She is well, but she will not be around any longer," Gammie replied softly.

"I don't understand, Gammie. Whatever could be the matter?" he queried.

"When you ran out this morning to do your duty, Theresa realized that she cannot handle that kind of life." Gammie quickly saw she wasn't getting through and he was getting both confused and angry. "My lord, please be patient with old Gammie as she tries to answer. Some women can wait while their man goes off to war and danger. But some cannot. It eats at their insides and causes rot to take hold. I'm sorry, my lord, but Theresa learned today that she cannot."

Gammie stopped then and waited. Kalamar understood the words, but they didn't make sense. Not at first. As they sank in, his earlier euphoria changed to confusion and now was becoming anger. *This was outrageous*, he thought. She didn't want to stay. Fine. There were certainly plenty of others who would appreciate the life he could provide and the company he offered.

He knew these thoughts were unworthy and he also knew that he didn't have time to deal with them. He had a party to honor the men who risked their lives this morning. He took a deep breath and then another. Reaching deep inside, he managed to find some control and balance while banishing this part of him to a room in his mind to be dealt with later. Nodding to Gammie, he turned and walked out the door. His people needed him and he had a new world to build. There was just too much to do for him to be stopped by this.

Gammie had watched the emotions race across her lord's face—anger, loss, rage and so many others that she knew but had no name for. He was a good man but he had a young man's passions and she worried about what that would lead him to. She said a prayer to every god she knew on behalf of the young lord she now served. The man who gave so much to everyone else now needed something himself. She prayed that he would find it.

Chapter 11

going home

Kalamar spent the last three weeks visiting every town and village from Firstlook in the east to Nellis in the west. Almost every noble and merchant with means wanted to sign their children up for the first semester of university the following fall. He was already creating a wait list even though he had tripled the size of the first class to sixty. Even with the wealth and furnishings the archmage had given, he simply couldn't construct the buildings large enough or fast enough. Winter was closing in fast and light snows were already falling most evenings.

From Nellis however, he did not head east for Hayden. Instead, he went west, retracing the first leg of his journey with his master, heading back to Briar Patch Farm, his home. He passed through the collection of farms where Riordan's spy had lived. He'd even stopped by and introduced himself. That life seemed so long ago.

At Wilson's farm, he learned of the first changes to the place of his birth. His parents were no longer living on their farm. His father was now sheriff and leader of the homesteads out here. The area itself had taken the name of Wildwood Shire and began trading with Nellis the same fall Kalamar left for Stormlake. His oldest brother, Glen, had taken over Briar Patch; and his other brother, Merv, was making a farm of the archmage's cottage, now called Mage Field. So instead of continuing west by north, he headed almost due north to the gathering.[30]

---

[30] The gathering is the name given by the locals to a clearing they would meet, celebrate or mourn as a community. It made the ideal place to begin building a center for Wildwood Shire.

The changes as he arrived on this cold and overcast day were obvious. There were now four buildings just west of the patch-worn center: two log cabins, a large storage barn, and a chapel to Telmar. It was the second cabin that drew his attention, or more exactly the large man that walked out, heading for him.

Shadow, he'd quickly learned, loved being the center of attention and didn't like being led meekly to meet the hulk of a man heading their way. Greer had always seemed a giant to him and despite Kalamar now standing over six feet, he was still four or five inches shorter. Nothing seemed to have changed. His gait was just as steady, there was no additional grey in his black hair or beard and his eyes were the same dark blue that didn't miss anything.

"Dad," he said as he was engulfed in a bear hug. It was impossible to sort out all the emotions running wild inside and he didn't bother to try.

"God's above, boy!" his father said as he grabbed him by the shoulders to look him up and down. "It's damn good to see you. You look as well as we've heard." He added the last with a laugh.

He hadn't seen her, but without warning, his mom was in his arms, crying with joy. His dad stumbled back from being shoved aside and grinned. It was every bit a homecoming as he could wish for as he was practically dragged into the house for good food and a barrage of questions.

*****

The bonfires blazed in the night as the party continued late into the evening. His homecoming had turned into an excuse to celebrate and every farm was represented. He'd spent the afternoon and early evening telling and retelling all the stories of life in the capital and his adventures. Apparently, he was quite a topic of discussion in Nellis and with regular trade opened up, they knew more about his life than he did.

The only tragedy he'd learned was his sister, Mekenna, had gotten married after he left but her husband had fallen in a sinkhole shortly after and been killed. There seemed to Kalamar something disconcerting about missing both the wedding and funeral. There were a few other changes, but he found it easy to slip back into the community he remembered.

Kalamar found himself on the north side of the clearing, outside the fire's light, staring into the forest. He quickly realized someone was watching from the foliage.

His father quietly stole up beside him and asked, "What is it, son?"

He extended his senses into the trees and with a pleasant shock, he said clearly enough to carry that far, "We have guests, Father."

At that moment, four cloaked figures appeared out of the forest edge, walking toward them. They were small and thin. The tallest was maybe five feet high. His father drew a deep breath as the waxing, almost full moon shone through a break in the clouds on the strangers. Delicate features with large, almond-shaped eyes were obvious under the moon's light and Kalamar knew that ears with points on top would be under their full heads of hair.

Stepping forward, Greer said, "Muranan to Leatha obreeness arthonis," while extending both arms away from his sides, with palms forward.

Kalamar was surprised his father knew the traditional elven greeting. This had never come up during stories of mercenary days before meeting his mother.

The leader of the elves stepped forward with a large grin and responded in kind with a melodic, feminine voice. She then continued in Calledonian, "This is a night of many welcome surprises for us. We were traveling to the west when we heard your celebration. It isn't often that we are detected when we wish to remain hidden. And to be greeted in our own tongue in such an out-of-the-way place by humans." She laughed lightly and said, "Surely the gods smile on this visit."

"I would surely agree with that. We are celebrating the unexpected homecoming of my youngest son, long gone from us. Having elves from legend join us, if you're willing, will sear this night in all our memories. The fare is simple as is the company, but you are most welcome to join us."

"I am Surane'tha. This is my brother, Panetheyy, my son, Freth, and daughter, Truce. We are delighted to accept your offer of hospitality," she said.

"I am Greer, and this is my youngest son, Kalamar. I will introduce you to the rest once we join the others." He extended his arm to her as he finished and led them back to the bonfires, followed by the two children, with Kalamar and Panetheyy bringing up the rear. His father, always loving a good story, made quite the dramatic entrance to the surprise and delight of the community. Soon, however, the party was once again in full swing as the elves joined in the revelry.

"Where did you learn so much about our people?" Surane'tha asked during a break in the dancing.

"My master, Archmage Crow, was a thorough teacher. He was insistent that I have a well-rounded education. He once said, 'You will never understand the elves if you don't learn the three classic dances.'" Kalamar noticed just the slightest change in expression when he'd mentioned his master's name. It would be rude in elven custom to pry, so he said nothing.

Surane'tha laughed gaily at this and said, "Did he teach you the three classics?"

"Of course," Kalamar continued with a smile. "As I said, he believed in being very thorough."

"And do you have a favorite?" she asked with growing interest.

"TuWatha neim Veheeliss" was his reply.

She now studied him very intently and asked, "Why is that your favorite? Most humans don't care for it."

"It has a gravity, a solemnity that I didn't find much in my elven studies. I found it deeply moving, personally."

She withdrew into herself for a time but finally replied, "And why are you so interested in studying the elves?" There was a forced lightness now in her voice.

Hoping to brighten her thoughts, he responded, "I'm young enough to want to know everything about everything." He also added his most innocent grin.

Her laugh was musical and her mood shifted once more. She responded, "I think I'd like to see that."

"And will you be my partner?"

"We don't really have the instruments to perform it properly." He was surprised by the dodge.

"Let me take care of that." He walked out to the center of the dance area and announced his intentions.

When most people think of glamours or illusions, they think of sight, but the most successful illusions include all the senses. So as the crowd grew quiet and moved back to give him room, he cast a glamour spell from his memory, a spell repeating the sounds that his master had created for him as he had learned the dance.

He took his place in the center, with left hand extended, as if waiting for a partner to join him. Releasing the activation rune, he began the dance. Graceful and intricate steps he made, always with left hand extended, calling to a partner. The crowd oohed and aahed as the music seemed to come from the sky above.

Instruments played they had never heard and would probably never hear in person. The sadness of that seemed a perfect complement to the haunting strings and low wind instruments. After his first circuit, dancing slowly, sunwise with hand extended, Surane'tha stepped into the dance. Her steps mirrored his but at a faster pace as she appeared to be racing in larger circles to catch him. Pulled by the current of his lonely pattern at the center, her circles were slowly tightening to his until, right on cue, the music's tempo accelerated as she clasped his hand and two became one.

Their circle now expanded out to the edge of the dance area. With each circuit they made, Kalamar created the illusion of an elven couple joining them, pulled along as if in their wake. The richer the music became, the more illusions of couples he added. Soon the dance area was filled with elaborately dressed elves, not just Sylvan but Grey and Gold as well.

One became two, two became many. But nothing lasts forever and pair by pair the couples would dance to the edge and disappear in a shower of bright-colored sparks. The music also slowed as each couple left; the high energy of before seemed to drain away, leaving melancholy in its path.

After a time, it was down to two but even that did not last. His partner broke off, drifting away, slowly falling behind and away until she stepped out of the dance, leaving just one—one with hand outstretched, reaching for the other needed to complete.

As with his magic and martial training, Kalamar had stepped into the void for his performance. Only there would he have the wherewithal to execute such complicated tasks. In this dance, everyone was supposed to end the dance at the exact spot they began it. As the last note faded away into the cheering gathering, Kalamar smiled, realizing he had done just that.

Panetheyy quickly took up the melody on his flute while the elvish children tried to teach a large group of eager young people the steps.

Surane'tha pulled him aside and said in awe, "That was masterfully done!" Her tone changed once again, deeper, huskier, almost a whisper. "I have never seen anyone make such a display. The skills required to produce such beauty." As she said this, she reached out and ran her hands along the outside of Kalamar's arms, ending by holding his hands and slowly pulling them up as if to examine them.

He did not have a chance to respond as, at that moment, his mother grabbed him by the arm and started pulling him away, saying, "Kalamar, excuse me, dear, I need your help with something."

Kalamar looked from his mom to Surane'tha, who raised her hand to her mouth and hid a smile. He grinned at her and then turned to his mom still tugging on his arm and said, "Of course, Mom," as he followed her back to the group.

His mother didn't really need help with anything. It had just been an excuse to separate them. She kept a sharp lookout the rest of the evening and it almost became a game for Kalamar to move closer to Surane'tha and watch his mother break off whatever she was doing and head over to him. His father soon caught on and would just laugh and shake his head at Kalamar when their eyes would meet.

While elves were said to party for days, most humans could manage about one. In this case, as everyone had work tending farms and animals in the morning, it was pretty well over by the last hour of evening. Many had either already left or just grabbed space in the houses, barn or chapel as convenient spots for a few hours rest before dawn.

Kalamar's mother was adamant not to rest until his father swept her into his arms and carried her to the house. She started to insist that she wanted to stay but Greer whispered something to her and she became strangely quiet. He winked to his son as they disappeared inside the house.

After they were gone, Surane'tha walked over to him and said, "If I didn't know better, I'd say you were tormenting your mother this evening."

"Tormenting is such a harsh word," he responded. "I would never do something like that." He laughed.

She smiled back and said, "Would you walk with me?"

"Of course."

They headed north from the glade on a track he remembered would lead to a pile of stones he'd sometimes played on as a kid. Their best guess had been, it was from a tower fallen over centuries before. The supply of rocks had been used by everyone as building material and was substantially reduced at this point. They found a couple of stones too large to easily move and sat down opposite each other.

"Why didn't you ask me, when you saw I recognized the name of your master?" Surane'tha asked. The moon had sunk low in the western sky and the stars blazed in the heavens.

"It would be rude in your culture to do so," he replied.

"That's true. I appreciate the gesture." She smiled a sad, wistful smile and paused. Looking away, she started again. "I was just a child when our community was overrun by goblins from the mountains." She hesitated once more as she was reliving those memories. "We had been on the run for two days when we reached the brook. A solitary figure hooded and cloaked, staff in hand, was waiting for us on the western side of the stream. Our elders approached with caution, speaking quietly with the stranger.

"When they returned to us, they sent three warriors to the stranger who led them north along the stream to the mountains. We had been heading east but now turned south, walking in the stream to mask our trail. Four days we headed south as fast as we could travel. All during that time, I would look back north, especially during the night. I swore I could see fell lights against the stars. We had escaped, but it seemed that the cost was our warriors and the stranger who led them off our trail.

"The fifth morning dawned and the stranger reappeared, with two of our warriors carrying the third. He had been killed, but they would not leave his body as so many had been left at our home. The stranger left without a word, but the warriors told the tale. A tale of powers they hadn't conceived possible. Even among our Grey elven brothers, who devote themselves to magical studies, I've never heard the equal. The five thousand who overran our home were driving us into an equal number just the other side of the brook. All ten thousand converged on the brook, following the trail and scent going north. It seemed the goblin gods themselves had sworn our destruction.

"Time and again, our saviors slowed to be caught, keeping the focus on them. Time and again, the stranger would kill hundreds before they escaped to head north again. They followed the waters high into the mountains until they reached a summit that leads in multiple directions. Only here, with many possible places for our people to disappear, did they themselves teleport to safety and return to us."

She stopped speaking, and Kalamar remained quiet. His master had indeed mentioned a battle almost a century ago to save some elves at a brook but nothing on the scale or detail such as this. It had been a dry note in the story of the larger topic, why elves were scarce in this part of the world.

"The stranger had called himself Crow, and his staff was carved with many of them among runes of power. When I saw your skill during the dance, I knew that your master must be the same Crow who saved us. That kind of skill, especially in one so young, is not found by accident. It must be nurtured and passed down."

"I indeed know that staff," Kalamar said. He created a simple illusion, not just of the staff but his master holding it while wearing his favorite green cloak.

Her intake of breath was all the confirmation he needed and after a moment, he released the image.

"My people made it to the safety of our kin living in the southern forest he told us of. We have lived there ever since. We are leaving that home now and traveling west to our great forest kingdom near the Rusaurmontellis Mountains. War is coming to these lands and we will be washed away if we stay.

"The goblins have been driven back into their mountain by your kind, so I wanted to show my children the land of my birth before we left. I almost wish I hadn't though. There is nothing left. The forest is gone and in its place are fields of grain overseen by men who beat their own kind to gather it. The goblins may be gone, but their evil remains."

Kalamar again said nothing so as not to intrude on her private grief. He knew full well the evil that thrived in Hoff. He had calculated the rough location of her childhood home from both hers and Crow's descriptions. It enraged him that this evil was allowed in a kingdom dedicated to good by the greed of power hungry men. So desperate for it, they would willingly allow the subjugation of their own kind to further their petty desires.

"It is nights like tonight, however, that remind me all is not lost. It is a balm for me and my family to see love, community and respect still alive and well among your people. We will not forget the kindness you have shown us this evening."

"It is what I have devoted my life to. Protecting people like this from the horrors evil would show them. Someone must take a stand and it seems I'm suited to that task." He now turned outward to the night, examining the truth of the words he'd just spoken.

They sat, lost in their own thoughts for some time, before she got up, came over to Kalamar and sat in his lap, wrapping her arms around his neck, saying, "Is this rude in your culture?"

Kalamar wrapped his own arms around her waist, pulling her in closer, saying "I won't tell Mother if you won't."

It was early morning and Kalamar gazed into the forest that had swallowed the elven family as if they never existed. It was a custom among the Sylvan to gaze long after parting company in a farewell gift. They were miles west of here by now. His father, understanding the custom, had waited with him. He now said, "I understand your sister is going to live with you in Hayden?"

"Yes," he replied. "I'm hopeful the change will help her make peace with the past. There is much to do and see. She can make a new life there as I have."

"I think you're right. Even in our new home, there are ghosts here for her. Come," he said, putting his arm around Kalamar, "we need to get you both on your way and there is much yet to do."

Kalamar and his father walked back to the house as snow began to fall. It seemed fitting to Kalamar as he began the day.

Chapter 12

an unexpected teacher

ayden smeared away the sweat rolling into his eyes. His rotting, rank-smelling garments were tattered and soiled. Even though it was early spring, the late afternoon sun was boiling down on the trash-strewn alley he camped out in. The smell would be gagging if he wasn't used to it after all these years. Food so rotted the rats wouldn't touch it. Stale ale and vomit from too many drinks at the seedy inn across the alley, but the worst, the worst was the unwashed drunkards who wriggled like worms caught in the sun in this forgotten, run-down neighborhood.

Here he was, along with the rest of these forgotten souls, baking in the hot, windless air. There was a difference, however, between him and the other poor souls wasting away. He was here by choice. He had been here the last two days, watching the comings and goings of people through the rather-unimpressive building across the street. He briefly wondered whether that made him mentally unstable. The others here had very little choice. He would have laughed, but that would be out of character for his disguise.

He thought back over his own life and revised his earlier thought. Maybe he had no choice either. This was how he made a living, learning things of value before others. It gave him a leg up on his competitors sometimes and that could mean the difference between a full or empty belly. His master had died unexpectedly before his apprenticeship was complete. Every day since then he'd had to scramble to keep the old shop going and the few customers they'd had coming back.

If he'd only been…

Vayden froze as he felt the hairs on the back of his neck stand up. The sweat running down his back suddenly chilled like ice. Slowly he turned his head backward, just enough to shift his vision to cover the interior of the alley he sat slumped against the wall in.

A portal! There was a full magical portal open in the back of this lice-infested alley. He stared in disbelief as a young man stepped through into the filthy street. Young, handsome, well dressed and well made. He couldn't imagine someone like that here. But that wasn't the most extraordinary part. There was a magical aura around the man radiating more power than Vayden had ever seen. Where most auras around casters seem to shift and flow, even flare from time to time, this young man's aura was like a physical shield around his body. It appeared as solid and steady as a physical object.

Vayden could only gape in awe as a second man appeared behind the first. Where the first was young, this one was ancient. He could barely see his physical features, however, because this man's aura blazed like the sun itself. His mind could only grasp a single coherent thought. An archmage, he was seeing an archmage—those nearly godlike beings atop the pinnacle of the magical firmament.

The gate closed and the pair began walking toward Vayden and the larger intersection. The expressions on both were so ordinary he wondered if he were sunstruck and imagining the entire thing. The older man reached the intersection and, turning right, casually walked down the street. The younger however, walked straight up to Vayden, bent down and held out a coin. Vayden took the coin by route as he'd spent decades in this disguise, but his mind was a confused mess and he couldn't seem to gather his thoughts.

"I'd like to visit you later if that is all right," a pleasant voice whispered from the apparition in front of him.

"Su-sure," Vayden managed to stutter.

With that, the young man stood and hurried after his older companion. Vayden watched in disbelief as the fools walking around the two were oblivious to what they were. No one noticed anything and the two quickly disappeared in the crowd.

*****

131

Vayden glanced for the thousandth time around his shop, looking for anything out of place. He'd completely abandoned his earlier surveillance and made his way home as rapidly as possible without completely giving away his disguise. The possibilities from a meeting with the incredibly powerful young man who was clearly associated with an archmage outweighed any benefit from tracking down the rumor of a secret business meeting at the Tanner Street Hall.

The reasons were simple. While he was a shopkeeper who specialized in acquiring unusual or difficult to obtain items, he was also a failed sorcerer's apprentice. He hadn't failed because he couldn't complete the training; he'd failed because his teacher had died. He died and Vayden couldn't find another. There were several master wizards in the city, but none taught the obscure rune style his master trained him in—the Blood Skull runes.

It wasn't that he hadn't successfully acquired other grimoires from different styles and tried to learn them. He had Seven Royals, Five Kings and even Three Star rune tomes. He even had a Sha Zang spell scroll. It's just they never worked for him. Or worked badly. Their structure was so different they were impossible for him to properly cast. He did have a few first-circle spells of his own, but despite repeatedly tearing the shop and house apart, had never found his master's old grimoires to learn more.

Vayden jumped from the knock at the door. He quickly walked to the door and peered out the cracked glass window. It was after sundown but between the broken panes and the simple lit door lamp, he could discern the young sorcerer from earlier. He took a moment to try and settle his nerves only to realize how much he was expecting of this meeting. He still had no idea why the stranger wanted to see him. It could be for any number of reasons that had nothing to do with magic.

"Good evening," he said after finally opening the door. "Won't you please come in."

"Thank you" was the pleasant reply and the stranger stepped into the shop.

"Would you care to join me in my office?" Vayden asked.

"Certainly." The young man followed him into the only properly furnished room of the house. This was where he conducted his meetings with clients. As they were generally noble or certainly well connected, they expected to be treated to a higher standard for everything. And that included the furnishings they were asked to use. While everything here was old and dated, both he and his master before him had fanatically maintained and cared for it.

"Can I get you anything to drink? Perhaps something to eat?" he asked politely.

"No, but thank you. I'm fine."

Seating himself on a cushioned chair opposite his guest, he asked, "So, how can I help you?"

He watched as his still-unnamed guest took a moment to look around the room. Vayden had no doubt he was seeing far more than just the furnishings and walls.

"I must confess," the young man began, "to not knowing quite why I approached you on the street this afternoon. It was an impulsive gesture that I'm only now beginning to understand."

Vayden said nothing. It was an odd statement and he wasn't certain how to respond to such a casual confession of personal indecision.

"When I saw you on the street, it was clear to me your training had been interrupted. Now that I'm here, it's clear you lost your master at an early stage of that training." He paused, but just for a moment. "It's also clear you've continually tried to expand your personal power but you keep running into blocks. No doubt, the alternate rune structures you try keep falling apart. Like trying to hold water in your hands, it just slips away from your grasp."

Vayden was startled that a stranger could read him so easily. He was also getting angry that this boy could so casually speak aloud the most personal and private failures of his life. How dare he come into his home and make such embarrassing declarations?

With a portion of his anger bleeding through, he said, "How could you possibly know these things? How can you know what I've tried and how it works? Are you reading my mind?" He drew in a breath and added, "How could you even know who I am and where I live?"

He was standing now and his embarrassment and anger were getting the best of him. He'd quietly fought his magical failings for decades and now some child was going to lecture him about them as if discussing the weather.

The stranger, still calmly seated, raised his palms outward in a placating gesture. "I meant no offense," he began. "I've actually come to offer my help but if you are not interested, I can certainly leave." Suiting actions to words, he stood up and began walking toward the door.

"No!" Vayden shouted. He hadn't meant to, but the words were pulled from his throat as a chance to fix himself was escaping.

"No, please don't go," he said, somewhat calmer. "I didn't mean to get so animated earlier and I apologize for any offense I've caused. It's just that I've wrestled with this problem for so long my frustration is clearly getting the better of me." He clamped his teeth together to keep anything else from spilling out. He needed to calm down if this was a genuine offer. Nothing was free, he'd been repeatedly taught that lesson his entire life but he was willing to pay almost anything to become the sorcerer he knew he was always meant to be.

"I understand," the stranger said and returned to his seat. "And I apologize for speaking so casually of what is clearly a personal issue. It was rude and I ask your forgiveness." He finished with what appeared to be genuine regret and humility.

Vayden returned to his own seat and the young man continued, "As to your questions earlier. I'm not reading your mind. I know where you live because I marked the coin I gave you. As for your name and what you do, I simply asked some of your neighbors. As to the important questions of your training, I can clearly see your aura and the disruptions in it are usually a sign of stunted magical development.

"The spells used around this house are clearly Blood Skull runes and they are more powerful than you are capable of casting. So, I suspect they were cast by your master. They were created long ago, which means you have worked hard to maintain them as best you can over the decades. The shielding spells on this house are starting to separate, so you must not know how to repair them.

"Since the Blood Skull runes work in an almost opposite fashion to the popular runes systems like the Seven Royals or the Three Stars, you probably aren't having much success. If you had, you would have replaced your master's spells with your own and wouldn't have the distortions in your aura."

Vayden could only guess he looked like a fish out of water, gaping in disbelief at the stranger's accuracy in reading his deepest failings and fears.

Finally, he whispered in shame, "Are my failings so easy to read?"

"No," the strange boy replied. "At least not to most."

He continued, "I have some small talent with magic, which makes it a bit easier for me than others."

"Can you help me?" He knew it had come out like a child's pleading and he didn't care anymore.

"I can," he replied. "The question is, will you agree to my terms?" he added with a friendly smile.

"What terms?" he said without pause.

"I require you to reject evil," he said. "I require you to do your best to be a good person."

Whatever Vayden thought he'd ask, this wasn't it. Money, possessions, servitude, these would have been things he could understand.

"What does that even mean?" he asked, confused.

"A good person is someone who does what is right. Even when that costs them personally. A good person not only considers what is best for themselves but also takes into consideration what is best for all those around them. If you wanted to put it into simple rules. A good rule to start would be: a good person doesn't lie, cheat, steal, beat, break, bribe, slave, rape or murder. That's a simple formula but a straightforward way to start.

"You see, I do my best to be a good person. I certainly make my share of mistakes, but I own up to my failures and do what is necessary to mitigate the damage. I am offering you a great deal of power. As such, everything you do will reflect on me. I cannot, in good conscience, give you that power if you are going to use it to add to the evil of this world. I'm sure you can understand that?" he asked.

Vayden considered his words for some time. Finally, he responded, "I have done many bad things in my life. My best friend is a member of one of the local thieves guilds. I don't see how I can meet your conditions." This last part was said with a lump in his throat. The idea of finding and then losing a teacher at the same time was physically painful.

The young man's eyes bore into his and he could not look away. "You've had a difficult life and had to make some hard decisions, but I see no stain of evil on your soul. As for your friend"—he paused with a small smile—"a best friend is a treasure not to be cast aside lightly. While I expect my requirements could create some measure of change in your friendship, I suspect if you both try you could find a way to continue it."

Again, Vayden sat for some time, considering what he'd heard. What he'd seen of "good" people in his life was nothing like what he'd just been told. They were usually hypocritical, arrogant and constantly condemning others for their flaws. He saw none of those things in the quiet stranger in front of him. He seemed sincere, quiet and most astonishing for the power he clearly wielded, humble. He seemed like a man worthy of emulation. Vayden found he very much wanted to be like the person before him.

"Very well," he said slowly. "I don't know where your rules will take me. I don't even see how I can stay in business that way, but I will try. I will do my best and trust that my efforts will lead me to where you clearly are," he finished calmly.

"Fair enough," the stranger said, still smiling. "We will begin this journey together and see where it leads." He paused. "It is not an easy path to follow, but I can assure you the rewards far out way the price. Are you ready to begin?"

"Now?" Vayden replied, taken aback.

"Do you have something better to do?" he retorted.

"No, Master," he replied with a smile. "Nothing at all."

Chapter 13

the more enemies, the merrier

Lord Malcolm was growing ever more tired of the bickering done by certain council members. Once again, the Lordmage Sylvicheld was the cause of the complaint. Malcolm was now convinced there was an orchestrated plot against Kalamar. He just didn't have proof and while he knew some of the members, he didn't know who was leading them. Until he gained one or the other, he had to be content with observing and undoing the damage such foolishness caused as much as possible.

The current rallying cry was unfortunately too large to ignore. Over the winter, Kalamar had summoned a seventy-foot-high obsidian tower overlooking Hayden. He had also summoned a lecture hall for his university. Malcolm used the word summoned because, by every account, one day they weren't there and the next morning they were. If that wasn't enough, he had grown a high dirt wall around the entirety of Hayden and the new university he was opening in the fall, leaving openings for gates that were being installed by less controversial means even as they argued.

To add economic insult to injury, he'd created magical shields allowing all the masons and workmen he hired last fall to work through the winter, building a dormitory, teacher and staff living quarters and administrative buildings. By summer's end, just in time for the students' first year, he would have the beautiful campus finished.

And that, he surmised, was the problem. Kalamar's enemies wanted him to fail and he refused. The university was a boon to the

barony and themselves and they hated him for it. Malcolm grudg-
ingly refocused his attention as Lord Amergin decried buildings just
showing up, unexpected all over the barony.

Lord Crow showed remarkable patience as he said, "As I've
told you before, he can't just drop buildings from the sky all over
the land. He spent all winter crafting the spells necessary to construct those buildings. And"—he held up his hand to forestall the
next verbal assault—"at no time was anyone in danger from those
spells. I had full access to the shielding he created in case there
had been the slightest issue. WHICH THERE WASN'T." The archmage
didn't shout exactly but the force of his last words seemed to pierce
the soul.

Malcolm stepped in at this point, saying, "Guild Master Kelvin,
you mentioned earlier that these plans were not approved or known
beforehand but that is not the case. As you well recall, this council
voted to separate Hayden from Stormlake after the request was made
to extend the city's defenses to protect them from possible attack.
That decision gave the lordmage the same independence to build on
his lands, as every noble throughout the barony has. Are you suggest-
ing that we restrict what our nobles can build on their lands?" This
certainly grabbed their attention, as no noble would support such a
move. It made the Bakers guild master, Kelvin, shift in his seat.

"I am certainly not making such a suggestion and I do recall that
this council did vote to separate Hayden from Stormlake proper." His
special emphasis on "this" was a clear attempt to shift the blame from
him back to the council at large. He did not want to make enemies
of the nobles.

Malcolm picked back up the conversation and replied, "I'm
sure we are all glad to hear that. In addition, when Lord Sylvicheld
was invited to take up the administration of Hayden, he provided me
sketches and drawings for the college and received official permission for construction as would have been required were his lands still
part of Stormlake. We also all knew of his plans for the university.
He went from east to west throughout Eddington last fall, telling
everyone he was building the university and asking for any interested
student to apply for entry. Clearly, this is not a surprise."

The Craftsman guild mistress, Aileen, chimed in at this point, "I have questions on what he is actually teaching. He is charging fifty pounds each year and for what? He claims to be offering degrees in history, language, economics, and engineering. Has he demonstrated any qualifications in these? What are his actual competencies and certifications to be charging such a ransom?"

"RANSOM!" General Shay exploded. "How dare you accuse an honorable man like the lordmage of ransom?"

Archmage Crow's voice came out like bitter, biting ice as he reentered the conversation. "I find the accusations you are raising quite disgusting, Guild Mistress. So let me address your spurious charge quite frankly so that all is made clear. I can assure you that the lordmage is quite competent in each of those four areas of study. I can also assure you that any students that successfully complete the course of study will possess a degree that will withstand the highest scrutiny. The REASON I can assure you of this is because I am the one who taught him these disciplines and tested him to the highest standards.

"You might be asking yourselves," he continued almost conversationally but no one was buying it, "'Well, what are your qualifications to justify such lofty rhetoric?' So, let me answer that. I myself have eighteen degrees achieved over decades of study from The Royal Institute, Calledon University and Mallburg University. You might have heard of them since they are the greatest institutes of learning in all of Calledon! In addition to my personal degrees, I am a certified master instructor from all three, in addition, I am Loparn Mutarue[31] of The Royal Institute and honorary chancellor of both Calledon University and Mallburg University.

"As such, Kalamar has earned and holds Royal Institute degrees in history, language, economics, engineering and nonhuman cultures. In addition to the eight rune languages he has mastered, he is fluent in Elven, Dwarven and Goblin. I will be sure to suggest to him

---

[31] Loparn Murarue is a title given to the most dedicated and qualified scholars of at least three separate disciplines. It allows the receiver full rights and privileges to bestow degrees on qualified students they themselves train and certify.

that he post his degrees and certifications for your edification, Guild Mistress." His last emphasis on her title was sharp enough to cause her to flinch. Everyone else was stunned.

"Oh, and I almost forgot"—the sarcasm had a razor's edge as he continued—"you raised a complaint on the price charged for a year of study. The current rate at the Royal Institute is six hundred pounds sterling per school year. Fifty pounds sterling seems quite a bargain, all things considered."

Each man and woman around the chamber absorbed in silence these new revelations. His long list of personal titles and degrees also reminded them he was a member of the royal family.

It was Malcolm who finally broke the silence, "Lord Crow, I'm sure no one here meant to question either the lordmage's or your qualifications in this or any other matter. You have both proven yourselves to be men of high honor and accomplishment. Your words of wisdom are greatly appreciated by all."

This was followed by several calls of affirmation and the archmage nodded in recognition of them.

It was at this point that Lord Amergin spoke again, "I do feel compelled, however, to bring up another issue. The manor of his selecting students is troubling to me."

"Whatever do you mean?" the high chaplain asked in evident surprise. "It seems he is being scrupulously fair in accepting students on a first-to-pay basis. Those not enrolled this year are applying for next."

"But that is exactly the problem. My son was not accepted in this year, but others"—he paused here a moment, carefully choosing his next words—"less worthy were," Amergin stated.

"What do you mean by 'less worthy'?" It was Merchant Guild Master Shawn who responded this time. His daughter was attending this year.

Everyone on the council knew what his objection was and waited for him to make it. Amergin realized he'd said the wrong thing but couldn't get out of the corner he'd backed himself into. He gathered himself and blurted out, "My son is of noble birth and nobles should be first!"

The room exploded in shouts. It was the baron who brought order back by banging his dagger hilt on the table.

"Enough!" he shouted. "That is enough!" He glared around the table. "Lord Amergin, I am quite frankly shocked at your words. We work hard, *every single day*, to ensure ALL live in peace with each other and our places in society. ALL are given justice in a fair and impartial manner. That kind of talking and thinking will set us back centuries as a people and I WILL NOT HAVE IT! I also have personal knowledge that you turned Lordmage Sylvicheld down when he first raised the issue with you last fall. It is no one's fault but your own that someone else stepped up with the funds to enroll their child. It would certainly be churlish for the lordmage to renege on that agreement to accommodate your fickleness in this matter. This university is an absolute blessing to MY lands and I will not tolerate any obstacles being thrown in its way. Do I make myself clear!" The baron stood as he said this. When he received the appropriate response, he continued. "This council is dismissed," he commanded and walked out of the chamber.

*****

Grand Master Ormand Starcaller had received word from one of his many spies that Pack 70 was planning something major against Stormlake. This spy was not highly placed, so Ormand had done additional research and learned they indeed intended to launch a magical attack at midnight. He now knew what and when, but he could find no answers to how and why. The laws of magic dictated that a physical attack on a magic shield required close proximity. The greater the power, the further the distance.

When Pack 38 had attacked with five sorcerers, they had been at the extreme edge of their spells' effectiveness, not even a mile. Pack 70 was launching the attack from over eighty miles. While the pack had over one hundred members, they would need ten thousand to launch an effective attack from that range. Unless, of course, they had discovered some powerful artifact or new spell that overcame the obstacle of distance. Such a discovery would change the rules and make someone both wealthy and powerful, hence his interest.

He'd just finished setting up two scrying mirrors. One was fixed on Pack 70 and the other was fixed, from a distance, on Stormlake. This last part caused him to grind his teeth in frustration. He'd completely failed to insert a single occulari anywhere within the town of Stormlake. They were destroyed within moments of being teleported in place. He'd given up by the thirty-first attempt and hated it.

The archmage must have some type of artifact, giving him the advantage. He was reduced to indirect scrying and even that could only be for a limited time before his spell was disrupted. This was why his second mirror was attuned at a distance. He had to be outside the border, which was miles away. His plan was to witness the attacking spells and follow them in to observe their effect.

He had time, so he paced the floor, considering what he had learned over the last year.

First, sometime around the disastrous attack by Pack 38 on Stormlake, a fire elemental had destroyed that pack, with only a few terrified servants making it to safety. The damage had been total, with nothing salvageable. That was the official version. He was convinced a Sarrik archmage could have easily broken the shields to slip in and get revenge for the attack on his life. He had no proof, so he kept that to himself.

Second, the young lord that led the ground assault that night was also a master of magic and a personal student of the archmage. He had lands of his own just east of Stormlake.

Third, during the winter, a sorcerous tower had appeared and the young lord and master wizard had taken up residence. Everyone agreed the tower had just appeared during the night. All he knew was it hadn't been there at the time of the attack last harvest but was there in spring when he first began scrying. Its size and construction materials were quite different from anything around Stormlake, so he couldn't wholly discount the incredible idea.

Adding these to Eddington's ability to stop his spying, it was clear to him there were interesting challenges available there. And challenges meant opportunity. He stopped his pacing and moved over to his first mirror, the one focused on Pack 70.

The wizards were all gathered in the central courtyard and had begun casting. The powers from each wizard were combined into a single point above the group and, at maximum power, released in a single bar of etheric energy. While the raw power was impressive on its own, he knew, just from observation, it wouldn't be enough. The power was released like an arrow from a bow, streaking across the sky west, southwest toward Stormlake. He moved his gaze to the second mirror but the spell didn't even make it to the Eddington border.

As he returned to the first mirror, he saw the pack's First was already exhorting them to greater efforts for a second attempt. This casting also failed. The third was better and did make it into range of his second scrying spell. It was diffused and had no real power but it was visible, like a heat mirage against the stars.

He saw no reaction from Stormlake and watched as Pack 70 raised the energy for a fourth and probably final attempt. The weaker members of the pack were already collapsing from the attempts. *It did seem to be more powerful,* he thought as the spell raced out of the first mirror's sight.

A few moments later it raced into view of the second mirror and he followed as it flew past. He did not know if intended or not, but it didn't make it to Stormlake, instead striking Hayden Hamlet. It was weak and scattered through the night sky and reached Hayden with all the power of a whisper's echo. Like water against a shore, it seemed to rise up against the shield protecting the village while disintegrating in a spray of colored sparks. He brought his occulari to just outside the shields near the eastern gate. He quickly glanced back to the first mirror and confirmed there were no more attempts. His gaze returned to the second mirror, looking for any type of response.

He was about to end his spells when first one then several buildings within the Hamlet lit up with a silverish hue, bright in the evening darkness. On closer examination, it wasn't the buildings but individual shields around the buildings. He quickly counted five shielded buildings around the tower where the lordmage made his home. Their shields grew to a much-brighter intensity.

The tower shield now lit up with its own glow gradually growing in strength. When its intensity matched that of the five other buildings, a beam of light shot out from each of the smaller shields, connecting them to the pinnacle of the tower. Each smaller shield faded as its power was absorbed by the tower, which kept growing brighter and brighter.

Fascinated, he watched the smaller shields flare out and go dark while the light around the tower shield was slowly drawn up to the highest point on the tower roof. All the energy was collecting there in what he could now see was a fist-sized crystal. Burning like a star in the sky, it pulsed brighter with the light it drew up from below in shrinking waves. The closest description he could imagine was a stage curtain being drawn up for the opening act. The curtain was the light, being drawn up to the crystal.

It pulsed several times, three, four, five… On the seventh pulse, it shot into the night, heading back to Pack 70. A comet racing to return the favor. He quickly shifted his gaze from the second mirror back to the first. He didn't have long to wait. After a few moments the same comet of light appeared. Not diffused and degraded but just as it had left Hayden.

In less than a heartbeat, it struck Pack 70's shield with a sound like iron shattering stone. With a blinding flare of light, the shield around the pack splintered and disintegrated before his eyes and the concussive force of its destruction threw the assembled wizards to the ground. Dust and dirt were thrown up in the night, obscuring all below.

He raced his occulari into the courtyard to observe the aftermath of an event that he wouldn't have believed if he hadn't seen it himself. The dust slowly settled. Dirt and blood-covered forms rolled and groaned over the ground. Ormand watched as some began to pull themselves up. First on knees and slowly a few to unsteady feet. Those with staffs used them. Some, he observed, would never get up. The First was unsteady as he looked around in understandable confusion.

"TRAITOR!" a robed figure shouted, pointing to the First. "This is all your fault!"

Ormand quickly realized it wasn't the Second making a move for leadership but the Third. The expression on the First's face said it all.

He knew there were no words that would get him out of this disaster. Someone had to be blamed and he was the likely candidate. He had no defense, as he had no idea what had actually occurred. Whether he was a traitor or not really didn't matter anymore. He would die either way. Shouting runes, the First vanished in a cloud of dust.

"After him," the Third called. "He must be in his chambers, preparing an escape." With shouts like braying dogs, the Third led everyone who could move into the manse. No one wanted to be seen siding with the losing side of this power struggle.

The courtyard quickly cleared of all not dead or incapacitated. All, that is, except one. The Second stood breathing heavily and his expression made his thoughts obvious. He had waited too long and the Third had taken the initiative. The Third would become the leader and the Second would be charged with conspiring with the First in this debacle. Evidence or innocence was irrelevant to justice in Hoff. Only power and perception meant anything.

The Second quickly came to the conclusion that the only way he lived, if only for a few more moments, was to flee and he headed to what appeared to be stables. Ormand's glance was distracted by a flash of light in the second mirror. He focused his vision and realized that the First had not bolted to some hideout but had teleported to Hayden instead. He watched as the First pounded on the shut gate and listened as he demanded entrance, claiming asylum. The door opened and out walked the lord he had seen that night of the attack last year.

"Please," the First begged, "spare my life and I will tell you everything. I know much that you will find useful. Please!" He'd gotten on his knees to plead.

The young lordmage looked down on the pitiful creature at his feet and replied, "We shall see." He held out his left arm in a gesture to enter the gate. As the First scrambled to his feet to race inside, the young master looked directly to the occulari, looking as if he could see the grand master on the other side of the mirror. With a smile and almost courteous nod, the lordmage made a twisting gesture with his right hand and the occulari was destroyed, causing the mirror to go dark.

Ormand did not have time to ponder the meaning of that display as he saw an opportunity and was not about to waste it. He quickly but carefully cast the spell for teleportation. He'd successfully learned to rush this spell as his life had depended on quick exits numerous times. He was soon walking through the stable doors in search of the Second before he fled for his life.

He found him pulling a horse out of a stall and said, "Why do you flee?"

The Second jerked around, looking at the grand master in fear and panic.

"Who are you? I don't know what you're talking about. I'm on important business, so you better not interrupt." The words spewed out of the Second far too fast and far too high-pitched to be believed.

"No," the grand master replied calmly, "You are fleeing for your life because the Third reacted faster than you and will have you killed once he consolidates his leadership." He held up his hand to forestall any argument. "I, however, offer you a different choice. Do as I say, and you will lead this pack."

"And what do you ask in return?" the Second breathed, a bit of hope in his voice.

"Loyalty!" the grand master replied. "You will pass on to me anything of value that you learn. In return, I will help you advance and gain further power."

It didn't take the Second long to realize that he didn't really have any options. "All right, how can you make me First?"

"You must act quickly. The Third is wasting time trying to hunt down the First when he has already fled to Hayden, asking for sanctuary."

"How do you know this?" the second demanded.

"You're running out of time. Are you going to listen and obey or die when the Third realizes his mistake?"

"Sorry, I'm listening."

"You need to go to the Third and those taking his orders and tell them to leave off tracking down the First in his chambers as he has already fled. They will ask how you know this and you will tell them you used a simple location spell and scried his location."

"I don't know a location spell," the Second confessed.

"Idiots," Ormand whispered and drew the spell on the ground. "Can you cast that spell?"

The Second stared down for a few moments and then nodded. "Yes, yes," he said. "It is simple enough. I can cast this!"

"Now, listen very carefully. The pack is vulnerable to its enemies and it's shield is shattered. You must redirect everyone to restoring the shield. This is what a leader would do. Protect his people first. The older wizards will see this and agree," the grand master continued.

"But what of the Third? He will not just give up," the Second objected.

"No, he won't. You must send him to warn your leaders of the First's traitorous actions."

"He will use the opportunity to destroy me!" the Second objected again.

"He will try, but he won't be able to resist and that will be his undoing. You must also ask him to take someone he chooses with him as confirmation. He is a fool and will take his closest ally in support. This will mean you won't have to deal with his most loyal spy here.

"As I was saying, he will try to make himself seem the rightful claimant but what your leaders will discover is that you ordered the shield restored and acted the true leader while every self-serving declaration he makes will tie him tighter in his own shroud."

"Yes, I see! You're right."

"No, don't get too excited. You must act firm and with purpose. Now go. You are running out of time. And if you try to break our deal, there is no place you can go that I can't find you." The grand master added this last with murder in his eyes and violence in his voice.

"I, I understand. You have kept your part and I will keep mine." The Second bowed and walked out into the night.

Ormand stayed in the stable thinking about his next move. He sent his occulari to follow the Second to observe how things turned out. He was soon nodding to himself as the Second managed to pull it off. He'd found them outside the First's chambers trying to break in. The Third couldn't resist the opportunity to be the one reporting the events and was even now heading to the stables to begin his journey. That was his signal to leave. He was gone by the time the Third arrived none the wiser.

Ormand did not stay home once he returned. There was still one last move to make this night. He changed his cloak for something simpler and made his way quickly to the servant's entrance of the only great lord in Hoff he had any respect for. The others were fools, powerful but brutish and unimaginative. He'd never found the opportunity to introduce himself, but his patience, it seemed, had finally paid off.

Lord Godfrey's palace was on the outer edge of the noble's district. The servant's entrance was actually in the scribe's and servant's district which made it much easier to slip different classes of guests in and out unnoticed. He had once done a small job for Godfrey's chancellor Wendell and that is how he had a passphrase that allowed him through the guards standing outside in the guard shack. The small room he entered had two exits farther into the palace. An additional pair of guards waited here and a neatly dressed servant was sitting behind a desk, making tally marks against another list.

He walked over to the desk and said, "I need to see Chancellor Wendell immediately."

The servant lifted his eyes from his work and stared intensely at Ormand. It was almost the first hour of night. He had never before seen Ormand, but this stranger was asking him to wake the second most powerful person in the palace. Ormand didn't flinch under the scrutiny and stared back. He and the servant both knew that if he woke the chancellor for no good reason, they would both be killed for it.

"Very well." The servant's voice was soft and high pitched, almost a woman's voice. "Wait through the door behind you." He then returned to his sheets. As Ormand turned and made for the door, one of the guards went through the other door.

The room he entered had no furnishing but did have three doors, including the one he entered. He did not wait long before Chancellor Wendell and two personal guards arrived. He was fully dressed in rich brown robes with intricate stitching of birds and flowers. He appeared fresh and in no way looked like he'd just been woken.

Wendell remembered him and wasted no time saying, "What is this about, Ormand?"

Ormand bowed politely and responded, "Pack 70 launched an attack on Stormlake. Stormlake retaliated and shattered the pack's shielding. The First fled for his life and has requested sanctuary in Stormlake."

It is the mark of a professional not to make unnecessary outbursts or exclamations. Wendell simply absorbed the information and kept his thoughts to himself. Ormand could have been discussing the weather for all the reactions it caused outwardly. He also knew that the chancellor was deciding if he could trust this information or if this was some type of trick or trap for him or his lord. Whatever judgments he made in his mind they didn't take long. He turned to one of the guards and whispered some instructions. To Ormand he said, "Follow me," and turned, exiting the way he came, fully expecting to be obeyed. He was.

Ormand was led through a curious route, the purpose of which seemed to be delay. He understood the reason for the delay when they finally arrived at their destination. It was a comfortably apportioned drawing room, designed to be cozy and intimate. There were several plush chairs, which he was not invited to sit in. Lord Godfrey of Frostburg was already there. He was wearing a bright-blue sleeping jacket as if coming from his bedroom, but he was fully awake, watching as they entered much as a hawk watched a hare in the field—imperious, but not missing anything. Ormand bowed lower this time after entering.

"Tell me what you know of this evening's events." Godfrey's voice was deep, rich and full of command. Here was someone used to getting exactly what he asked for when he asked for it.

"Yes, my lord." Wasting no time, Ormand quickly and succinctly went through the events of the evening, leaving out only his activities with the Second.

Like his chancellor, Godfrey wasted no time with silly outbursts but said, "How did you know about the ritual?"

"I have an acquaintance in the village. He didn't know what was going on but knew it was important. He notified me. With some research, I was able to put together what they intended and when, my lord," Ormand answered matter-of-factly.

While Godfrey absorbed this information, someone entered the room from another entrance behind a screen to the left. Ormand instantly recognized him as a wizard, master level. He had stitching in his robes that matched the chancellors as well as the Frostburg emblem, so he must be the court wizard.

The wizard went straight to Lord Godfrey and, with a slight bow, began, "My lord. The details are as yet sketchy but the general description I was given appears to be true. The Third of Pack 70 is being interrogated with one other at Helligg Ruk. My contact there says his story has changed significantly as both of them have been questioned separately.

"The basic story is, the First launched the attack to see if they could discover the secret for Stormlake's uncanny ability to find and destroy all their occulari and prevent their attempts at scrying. Apparently, they have been almost completely unsuccessful at getting much information out of Eddington. The rumor is, the court wizard there is claiming to be an archmage. Given the trouble they've been having, it's a possible explanation."

Ormand had listened to this and admitted it was a clever idea to discover if some new type of shield was around Stormlake. Obviously, the First had known that no strike of theirs would affect anything, but it might have reacted as it struck other magics in the sky above the city. He also admitted to himself, he felt better that no one else had yet succeeded where he also had failed in defeating their detection spells for scrying.

Godfrey turned from the master spell caster to Ormand and said, "What do you know of the wizard living in Stormlake?"

"There are several, my lord. Two of especial importance. The court wizard is not only an archmage but he is Sarrik. The other is his student, both a local lord and master of magic."

At the word Sarrik, the court wizard drew a deep breath but said nothing.

"Sarrik," Godfrey began and looked at each of the others in the room. "That would be the school of magic from the Calledon capitol? The school that every wizard in our lands both hates and envies? That Sarrik?" He ended by looking at his wizard.

"Yes, my lord. They, who claim to be the greatest in the world. The stories of legend. There has been no rumor of one south of Nantukk for a century."

"And now one is in Eddington." Godfrey turned his gaze to Ormand. "How do you know this?"

"I have witnessed his skill and power directly. I watched as he destroyed Pack 38's leaders last year when they foolishly tried to attack Stormlake."

Wendell spoke up and said, "Pack 38 was destroyed in a fire. Caused by a spell gone bad or so the story is told."

Ormand replied, "Two weeks, or there about, before that fire, five sorcerers including the First launched an expedition to Stormlake to confront what they thought was a pretender, claiming to be a Sarrik. I learned of their attempt from the Eighth before they left. On the night of the attack, I teleported to just outside their camp to observe.

"The ease with which they were led to overextend themselves and then be crushed was appalling. The archmage's student, the lord-mage, led the ground assault that finished them off and he carried their corpses back to Stormlake on their own horses. The *fire*"—he put emphasis on that word—"occurred sometime shortly after that night. It conveniently destroyed everything."

None of the room's occupants spoke for some time as they considered the possible implications. Finally, the chancellor said, "My lord, it is clear that there is more to this than has been disclosed to the baron's council. In addition, the possibility of a Sarrik archmage could be a serious cause for concern."

"I agree," said Lord Godfrey. "We need to take a greater interest in the packs and in Eddington." He turned to Ormand and said, "Grand Master, I appreciate you bringing this serious matter to my attention. You will be rewarded. A thought has just struck me, however, that perhaps you could answer."

"I'm at your service, my lord," Ormand answered with a bow.

"As I understood before tonight, the distances between Pack 70 and Stormlake would have made it impossible for Eddington to retaliate as they did. Am I misinformed?"

"No, my lord. Before tonight, I would have said the same thing. The laws of magic, short of a powerful artifact, should have prevented them from attacking, much less so easily destroying the shield surrounding Pack 70."

"That is troubling indeed, very troubling," Lord Godfrey replied.

Chapter 14

betrayal everywhere

Captain Garret Walker was finding it more and more difficult to still his rage with the young Lord Allen, son of Lord Angus of Greenspring. They'd been on patrol along the southeastern border of Eddington for the last three weeks and his disgust had begun the moment they met. At that moment, the young lord and tyrant had handed him an order from the baron's council, turning complete control of the patrol and its mission to Lord Allen.

This was simply unheard of. As young lords grew into manhood, they would be assigned to these patrols to continue their education in leading men and tactics. As such, the experienced soldiers of the Baron's army were always left in command. Apparently, Lord Angus used his influence to change that. His son had taken command with a vengeance, ordering the men about like toy soldiers.

He refused to allow even the most reasonable of suggestions for the men's well-being. Holding them at attention for hours, needless inspections, marching in zigzag patterns until they were ready to drop—it was enough to cause a mutiny. Garret had suffered the worst of it because he insisted on resisting those orders. Using every ounce of his patience, he had tried to protect the men and teach Allen the right orders to give and proper military instruction. It was to no avail. The young fool only became more obstinate and more erratic in his commands. Even his best friend, Ghan Mac, couldn't get the boy to see reason. It was also the only…

A flight of arrows flew out of the sky into his men. Garret turned to the right and looked up the hill they were marching beneath as a second flight shot down in their ranks. Men cried out and the few horses of Allen and his minders whinnied and screamed in alarm.

"RETREAT!" shouted Lord Allen, and he and his protectors fled on horseback.

"CHARGE!" shouted Garret as he rushed up the embankment, knowing the only chance they had to survive was to close with the enemy, whoever it was. Fortunately, his men rallied to him and charged up the step bank to find a sight they had only heard in stories.

Orcs. It was a small party of orcs. Ignoring his shock, Garret continued his charge into them with all his strength and speed. Ghan Mac was at his side, his massive ax hewing everything in his way. His men overcome their initial shock and ran to join them. It was soon over. There were only five orc archers and they all lay dead.

The men started to cheer but he quickly silenced them. This party was just the western guard of a larger encampment charging even as they stood, looking around. Garret's mind raced as he considered their options and all were grim. Retreat was death. The orcs had a larger force by double and would be upon them in moments. He shouted for a shield wall to form against the charge and looked to his best friend, nodding.

Mac understood and took a small object out of his pocket, setting it on a stone near his foot. Raising his boot, Mac crushed the small object. As he turned his gaze back to the wall his men had just formed, he let his mind seek the void against the barking orc battle cries as they crashed into his men and battle was rejoined.

It was a short vicious brawl and he had been too directly involved to issue any commands to his men. They knew their training and it had served them well enough. They won the field, but at a hideous cost. He cleaned and sheathed his blade as he gave orders to separate the wounded of his men from the orcs. The dead orcs were quickly thrown into a makeshift wall as defense against further attack.

He had started the day with fifty-eight men. Including himself, eleven were standing. Almost two out of three were wounded and he hoped could be saved.

Garret spun around as one of his men shouted. His alarm turned to relief as he realized it was Kalamar. The lordmage had brought several priests of Mallynne, a most precious gift.

The lordmage looked around the chaotic battlefield. His gaze appeared to miss nothing as he strode through the camp to confront Garret. The healing priest immediately went to the wounded pulled aside and began organizing those standing to help as assistants.

"I received your message. Report" was all Kalamar said.

Garret did as ordered. As the ranking lord, Kalamar had command of the field. He gave a brief description of the battle and how it started. It was Ghan Mac who explained the nightmare they had been under over these weeks and the cowardliness of the future lord of Greenspring. Kalamar's face had gone from grave to livid as he heard the tale.

"You have this order?" he demanded.

Garret pulled it from his tunic and handed it over. Kalamar studied it briefly and nodded to himself.

"I did a quick scan after I found you. I didn't see any orcs within the vicinity. Until you are given others, your orders are to see to your men. If other dangers arise, use your own discretion to fight or flee. I will be returning to Stormlake with the worst of the injured. I have already informed the archmage and the baron has called an emergency council meeting. I will make my report and then order wagons from East Cove here to assist with the wounded. You've done exceedingly well under terrible circumstances Captain. You and your men should be proud as I'm sure all of Stormlake will be proud of your courage and honor." With that, Kalamar hurried over to the priest, who had separated the worst cases. The head priest discussed something too low to be overheard while making a few gestures. Kalamar nodded and walked over to three men barely alive. He knelt down, so that he could keep contact with all three. A few moments later, he and the men were gone.

Garret saw that the priest had the situation with the wounded in hand, so he turned his focus to his men and their defense. His heart was lightened more than he would admit by his friend's words. That recognition, along with the immediacy of direct action, had removed the galling weight of the past three weeks. He set about with new fire and vigor to give the men the leadership they deserved.

*****

Lord Malcolm, along with the rest of the council, listened in horror as the lordmage made his report. It was hard to know what was worse—orcs in the barony for the first time in over fifty years or the cowardly behavior of young Allen.

It was Lord Willem who spoke first and said, "I don't understand how Captain Walker could have so failed in carrying out the most rudimentary of soldiering. Why weren't scouts out before the company? How could they be taken so unaware? What was he thinking?"

Before anyone could respond to the shocking but necessary questions, Kalamar responded, "I'm glad you've asked that question, my lord, because it was this council that ordered him not to have scouts out to protect his men and the young Lord Allen."

The council erupted in shouts and insults hurled at this accusation. It was the baron's dagger, banging on the table that restored order. Malcolm observed how gravely calm the baron was as he heard him quietly say, "I'd like to hear his explanation for that remark."

"Thank you, my Lord Baron." Kalamar bowed and began, "Lord Allen was in possession of an order drafted by this council giving him complete and utter command of the patrol." Kalamar paused for effect and then continued, "He used that order from the minute the patrol began to override and ignore every command that Captain Walker tried to give. He also used it to keep the men at attention for hours, have inspections up to ten times each day, have them march all day in parade-ground formations and every other type of nonsense imaginable."

The council again erupted in shouting but it was General Shay's voice who cut through the din. "Who would write such an order!" he shouted. "Those rules exist for the safety of all. Young noble brats don't have the experience to be in command and give the necessary orders. They are there to learn, not humiliate dedicated and loyal soldiers with decades of experience. It is outrageous and I demand we get to the bottom of this."

"I concur with General Shay!" Ghan Teague added. "There must be an accounting for this betrayal."

"Now, just wait a minute!" Lord Amergin chimed in. "Just what proof do we have of any of this? For all we know, Captain Walker is making this up to save his own skin."

Several counselors murmured their agreement to this.

It was Kalamar who again drew everyone's attention as he pulled a scroll from his sleeve. His face was stone and his voice ice as he said, "I did not say that Captain Walker made these accusations against Lord Allen. Those were made by the priest of Saa'Vey, Ghan Mac. Now, if you wish to challenge his word and integrity in this matter, you are certainly welcome." His words caused several indrawn breaths as the priest would be utterly destroyed by his god for making up such an accusation. His word would be unimpeachable proof as to the deeds just told.

Kalamar had finished unrolling the scroll and began reading it. "It is the will of the Council of Eddington, with full knowledge of the Baron, that Lord Allen, son of Greenspring, be given complete authority over this patrol and all orders he issues are as if the Baron himself issued them. It is signed this second day, eighth month, 1412th year of the founding. Counselor Kelvin, guild master of Bakers, Stormlake."

A terrible, deafening silence settled on the room like a shroud. All eyes turned to the guild master.

Kelvin had the deathly pale look of a corpse. His eyes were lowered, fixed it seemed on his hands clutching the table in a death grip.

In a shocked whisper, Malcolm asked, "What do you have to say for this?"

Kelvin's eyes were pleading for understanding as he breathed, "It was only supposed to be for an emergency. He wasn't supposed to actually use it."

"An emergency," Teague shot back, "is exactly the time an untrained boy is not supposed to be issuing orders. That's why this tradition has been in place for centuries! Why would you issue such an order? How did you issue it? All orders have to be recorded by the chamberlain's office!"

Lord Dugan Highcliff, High Chamberlain of Eddington, quickly spoke up, "I can assure you that no such order was issued with my knowledge and there is no such copy in my office."

All eyes turned back to Kelvin and he said, "The lord of Greenspring promised me a favor if I wrote out the order. I used that favor to settle a property dispute in Chandrom. As for how, I simply used the stamp an additional time when I was last in the chamberlain's office on council business."

Lord Willem spoke again, "So that is why the lord of Greenspring spoke up on behalf of your friend, Mackenzie."

All eyes turned back to Kelvin as he defiantly stated, "Don't you dare judge me. I'm not doing anything different than every other counselor here!" More indrawn breaths met this declaration and he continued, "I have personally seen the orders drawn up by you, Lord Amergin and you, Guild Mistress Aileen"—he pointed to each of them as he said their names—"and heard of others, so don't you dare accuse me when you do it too."

"Can this be true?" the high justice, Lord Owen Greenfields, asked in his deep, rumbling voice.

There was no point in lying, as everyone knew the high chaplain would be using his god-given magic to ensure he knew the truth of their words. Both alternated between livid and terrified as Lord Amergin answered first, "I have settled a few small matters with something along those lines, but nothing of any importance and certainly nothing that caused the death of the baron's soldiers."

Guild Mistress Aileen said nothing and just stared down at the table, refusing to meet anyone's eyes. Malcolm was stunned, truly horrified at the outright corruption that had infiltrated the council. How many private affairs had been wrongly decided by such treasonous methods? How much ill will had the baron earned by his squabbling counselors currying favor? He was disgusted. It had taken an invasion by orcs to rip open the petty, treacherous behaviors of those who claimed to serve Eddington.

"My lord Baron," began Owen, "today is a black day in many ways it seems. It began with cowardliness and conduct unbecoming and has grown into perversion of justice, corruption and treachery. And this says nothing about being invaded by creatures from long past. When we should be at our strongest united together, we are ripped apart by petty evil and self-serving vanity and greed. What are we to do?"

"Archmage," said Baron Terrence, "do you have anything further of import to add?"

"I do, my lord," the archmage began. "As you know, I've been scrying the battlefield and its surroundings from the moment Lord Kalamar passed on the warning. In doing so, I've followed the young Allen as he's ridden his horses into the ground, fleeing north. I was puzzled at first when he didn't stop at East Cove, as that was the closest community to reach, but now know why.

"He is currently at Storm Reach, telling the lord there his story. He didn't stop in East Cove because they once insulted his father several years ago. He's telling Storm Reach that he and his men are the only survivors of an ambush after he valiantly tried saving the men. He claims to have personally slain dozens of soldiers from the raiding party before fleeing to raise the alarm. He's demanding replacements for his lame horses so he can carry the warning to Stormlake. The fact that he is claiming it was a raiding party of men and not orcs tells us how quickly he fled, deserting his men at the first sign of trouble. As for the orcs, I see no others within the vicinity but will keep looking."

The baron looked out, seeing something only he could know as the archmage finished his update. "So much gone wrong," he whispered to himself. Malcolm wondered if he even knew he spoke aloud. "First, General Shay, draw up a battle plan sending as many of our troops southeast as you can spare in case there are more. Second, Lord Justice, have young Allen arrested for cowardliness and desertion. I want him brought back here for trial immediately and executed when the nobles arrive. Third, Lord Willem, send out an order to all nobles summoning them and all their arms here to march within the week. Fourth, Lord Amergin, Guild Mistress Aileen, and Guild Master Kelvin. You have betrayed my trust and your duty to

Eddington. You have violated the honor of this council. You will confess to each time you have issued these illegal orders and everyone that was involved. You are immediately stripped of all rank, titles, property and positions and will be held pending trial to be set at a later date. How cooperative you are will determine any further punishments." The three were pale but silent as they knew further protest was useless. "We have enemies without and corruption within. I will not tolerate either. We have work to do. Dismissed."

Everyone hurried out but the prisoners...

*****

Stormlake erupted in activity as the baron's orders were carried out. As the summons to war swept through the land, every noble, knight and freeman poured first into Stormlake and then south to what was now being called Traitors Hill.[32] Kalamar, expecting the summons, had his men ready for the orders to muster[33] in defense of the land. He was informed however, that he was among a group of eight lords, strategically chosen by location, to remain behind to protect the barony from unexpected directions.

---

[32] Traitors Hill was named after young Lord Allen, who fled at the first sign of danger. The baron of Eddington marshaled his forces to repel any further orc invasion there. Lord Allen was executed before the week was out on conduct unbecoming and cowardliness.

[33] The obligations of duty and service were quite specific to a lord in all things, but most especially in matters of war. Each freeman, knight and lord were required to stand at a moment's notice, ready for battle. Each must have the equipment of war as befits their station and knowledge of their use. Land ownership was an additional multiplier and for every thousand souls living or working on your property, you were required to also provide one knight, one squire and ten men at arms fully outfitted and properly trained. These men would be separate from any personnel the property owner maintained that acted as guards, personal or otherwise. The militia was an additional but completely separate force. Every able-bodied man was required to present themselves four days each summer for training, and the local lord was required to keep light armor, sword and shield available in strategically placed armories for their usage in case of defensive emergencies.

With good grace, he accepted the charge and instead toasted each lord on their way south. With the dust settling from Lord Nellis's troops marching to war, he realized every noble in the land was going but himself. Determined to resolve the issue, he made a visit to Monahan, Lord Malcolm's first assistant.

"My lord, what a pleasant surprise! How can I be of service?" Monahan politely inquired.

"I was informed that Sylvicheld was joining seven other Lords strategically placed in defense of the lands. However, with the departure this afternoon of Lord Nellis, I have counted every lord and knight in Eddington. Where is my error?" Kalamar asked evenly.

"Ah, my lord," Monahan began with a slightly embarrassed look on his countenance, "I understand your confusion."

"Confusion?" Kalamar asked with a tinge of anger. "The conversation seemed fairly clear to me!"

"My lord, please." Raising his hands in a gesture of peace, palms out, he continued, "No one has lied about the other lords. There are indeed seven others who were not called. I'd actually be surprised if you knew of them, as they were effectively banished years and even decades ago."

"Banished? There are lords who have been banished? Why? Where are they? And why would they be included in the strategically placed category with Sylvicheld?"

Monahan got up from his desk and started looking through scrolls against the far-left wall.

"Ahh, here it is," Monahan said, extracting a scroll and returning to his desk. "Perhaps, I should start from the beginning, hmm?" Kalamar nodded and Monahan continued. "Banishment is probably too harsh a word. Let's just say that the noble families in question ran afoul of political considerations and were sent to remote locations within Eddington under instruction to not return to Stormlake unless a strategic or significant threat emerged. That is where the phrase in your orders comes from. As to where they are…" At this point, he unrolled the scroll on his desk to show Kalamar.

Kalamar got up from his chair and moved to stand over the desk. What he saw was a map of the barony unlike any other. It showed Stormlake and the surrounding area, some of the original settlements but none in the last fifty years or so, except the seven noble families and their locations. The scroll itself was very old, but the writing on it was in different scripts. Obviously, it was updated from time to time. The oldest, Ardara, had been banished in 1349, only twenty-one years after the creation of Eddington. The last was Fellate in 1399, thirteen years ago.

He'd always wondered why the population was concentrated above the Stonewash River and now had a partial answer. Five of the families were centered in the southern middle of Eddington. The last two had been sent to the northernmost edge. Kalamar was appalled at the callous disregard.

"Is any contact made with them? Are they forbidden from having contact with the rest of the barony?" Kalamar asked.

"Every ten years, a quiet delegation is sent to collect their taxes. As I understand it, they have contact with their nearby banished neighbors. At this point, I think it is more that they have been forgotten, not that they are forbidden to have contact with anyone else," Monahan replied.

"And what of those illegal counsel edicts? Were any of them banished as a result of those?"

At this Monahan got a very thoughtful look on his face. "Lord Owen, the high justice, is having difficulty unraveling those particular knots. Each illegal edict has led to another ten decisions that were tainted from the first. Some of the easiest have been settled with recompense and fines to the injuring parties."

The investigation demonstrated these declarations went back decades. It was all too plain to see in hindsight how they had been used to an unfair advantage over a rival lord or party. Many of the edicts the three former council members claimed to have seen were written by previous counselors now dead." He said quietly, "It would be impossible at this point to know, but I can't see why not. We know that Lord Amergin's father used one to take several farms from freemen living near his lands."

Kalamar had heard of that particular case, as it had quickly spread throughout the land. Terrence, when he stripped Amergin of Firewold and his nobility, returned all the land to living descendants, along with a sizable payment from the ill-gotten gains in the Firewold treasury. Amergin's son, Ion, had pleaded with Terrence for the chance to restore his family's honor. Terrence had relented, but it was a much-reduced property and Lord Owen was named the executor to oversee its proper function. The remainder had been divided between the baron himself and several knights of impeccable character.

In addition to the injustice of the situation, Kalamar wondered at the dangerousness of it. Large communities with a strong reason to hate the established order lived in close proximity but were mainly forgotten. This banishment situation had disaster written all over it. Especially with foreign enemies, they needed every warrior.

Kalamar said, "Thank you for showing me this," and turned to leave.

"May I inquire what you are going to do, my lord?"

Kalamar turned back and said, "Do you really want to know?"

Monahan grew a large grin over his face and replied, "No, my lord, I do not."

Kalamar laughed and replied, "You are wise beyond your years," as he continued out the door.

*****

Kalamar used his time walking back to Hayden to examine from all angles what he'd decided to do in Monahan's office. He knew it would make those who hated him even more vengeful. It might also create new enemies. He wouldn't be breaking any rules and laws that he knew of, but it could be seen as undermining the baron's authority.

He was currently popular with most everyone as his university was generating great excitement with the opening coming after this harvest season. This, however, could cause a great many problems. He knew it was the right decision but was now experienced enough to see many of the bad places it could take him and his close associates.

After seeing the marked map, it only took moments to locate the lands in question by scrying. He was pleasantly surprised to observe that, between them, there were tens of thousands of people. He wondered again how much the baron actually knew or understood. As an enemy, they could overwhelm half the barony, especially with those five lords all together in the south. More determined than ever, he decided to start with the largest and oldest community, Ardara. He quickly found a promising spot and teleported.

Extending his senses, he found no one nearby. He also found no traces of magic either man made or godly in nature. He stepped out of the woods north of Ardara, onto the path leading southeast to the central city. From his cursory earlier look, it was larger than Stormlake and he suspected that wouldn't be well received by the baron.

The path quickly opened up into miles of cleared farming land surrounding the exiled capital. Villages, hamlets and farmsteads broke up the fields of wheat, corn and potatoes. With the afternoon sun shining down, everything about the place appeared pleasant and peaceful. Those working in the fields would simply smile and wave as he passed, if they took notice at all. Clearly, this place was unused to threats of violence. He took that as a good sign.

It was an excellent day for walking and he'd enjoyed the several miles stroll before reaching the north gate. It was the first hour of evening and he joined the crowd heading into the city as they finished up their day. His rich clothing set him apart as noble and earned him pleasant curtsies heading in. Upon reaching the gate proper, he headed directly for the guards to introduce himself. He had no intention of playing the spy or being accused of unseemly behavior.

"Good evening," he began pleasantly. "I am Lordmage Kalamar Sylvicheld of Hayden Hamlet. I'd like to introduce myself to the Lord of Ardara."

The guards didn't lose their pleasant demeanor but did look a bit confused as they tried to place his name and home. "I'm not familiar with Hayden, my lord. Forgive my not knowing, but where is that?" It was honestly asked without suspicion.

"It is east of Stormlake," Kalamar replied.

That brought an immediate response. Their expressions quickly turned hard. Spears casually gripped before now trembled with tension. Passersby that had been casually observing stepped back as the guard responded, "Stormlake, you say?"

"East of Stormlake, actually, I said. I mean no harm but wish to meet with the Lord of Ardara. I believe he'll want to hear my words." Kalamar kept his voice even and calm. He made no sudden gestures. Stormlake may have forgotten these men but they had not reciprocated in kind. The crowd of onlookers was growing larger as both word and rumor were spreading like wildfire.

The gate captain, hearing the commotion, had come down from the barbican. He quickly saw the center of the disturbance and strode over. He looked Kalamar up and down and then asked his guard, "What is going on here?"

"Captain, this here noble claims to be from Stormlake and wants to see Lord KurZell."

The captain's eyes widened, but otherwise, he remained controlled as he asked, "Is that true?"

"Not quite, good Captain. I am from Hayden Hamlet, east of Stormlake, but yes, I do seek to meet with the Lord of Ardara."

"And may I ask, my lord, how do you get here from Hayden?"

"I teleported to north of the city."

"You what?" was the captain's uncertain response.

"I used magic to transport myself from Hayden to here," Kalamar calmly replied.

Now he'd stepped into it as swords were drawn and spears were leveled at him from the surrounding guards.

"You're a wizard!" the captain accused.

Kalamar decided not to split hairs and responded, "Yes. Is there a problem?" His master had warned him of places that feared and hated mages and that the best advice, short of fleeing for his life, was to keep them talking using a calm tone. If he could get them past their initial fears and let their rational mind regain control, he could salvage the situation. If not, he would have to teleport away before some idiot tried to skewer him.

"Wizards are servants of evil!" hissed the captain. "Everyone knows this."

"I can assure you, Captain, that I have dedicated my life to good!" He continued, "If you have any priests in the city, they can confirm the truth of my words." He added for good measure, "Don't you think you should inform your superiors of my presence? I will be happy to calmly stay here until they arrive to make a decision." He knew that most people under stress and presented with a confusing issue would leap at the opportunity to pass it off to someone higher up the chain of command. The more time he bought he hoped, the greater the chance they would calm down and see reason. He also hoped his sincere suggestion for a local priest would lend itself to a peaceful resolution.

"Yes, you need to stay right where you are. If you move, you will be killed." He did not turn his head but ordered one of his men to find Lord Ea and another to find Ghan Jean.

While outwardly Kalamar maintained his calm indifference, inwardly he breathed a sigh of relief. A ghan would quickly sort this out. He was still prepared to leave at a moment's notice, but his hope grew that he could still salvage the situation to everyone's benefit.

The crowd had only grown during all the commotion, but since it was boring to watch someone stand still, tensions began to subside. They picked up again with interest, not fear, as shouts of "Make way" were heard. The relief in the gate captain was palpable as he heard a voice shout, "What's all this ruckus about?"

Kalamar was relieved as well as the newcomer came into view. His aura was clear Saa'Vey and he was surely a high priest of at least fourth circle.

The captain did not turn his head, keeping his eyes on Kalamar, but said, "This man claims to be a wizard from east of Stormlake. He says he wants to see Lord KurZell." He had emphasized east in what Kalamar hoped was a sense of humor breaking through.

While the priest wasn't as old as Ghan Teague, he seemed to have the same irritation to foolishness that many experienced teachers had. "Well, of course, he's a wizard!" The priest huffed. "He's making no effort to hide it whatsoever! You'd have to be blind not to notice. Is that why you're scaring everyone?" he demanded.

"I'm not scaring anyone," the captain replied in a lower tone of voice, like a belligerent child caught doing wrong.

"Ghan," Kalamar began, sensing an opening. He bowed his head in respect but didn't otherwise move. "The good captain here was simply concerned and wished for confirmation of my honest intentions." The captains faced showed relief and gratitude for the gesture and several in the crowd nervously chuckled.

"Well, well, well," the priest said as he continued walking up to Kalamar. "He speaks! It seems someone managed to teach you some manners. Polite, respectful! That's what I always say. Isn't that so, Captain?"

"Yes, Ghan. Be polite and respectful," the captain replied by route.

Most of the tension had indeed been removed by the gruff, curmudgeonly manner of the high priest as Lord Ea KurZell made his appearance at the gate. Everyone bowed their heads in respect as he stepped from the shadows into the fading western light.

He was probably in his late forties or early fifties. Hair had gone mostly gray but still full. A weathered face, stern and uncompromising. His clothing was better made in mostly greens with yellow stitching. His quick gaze seemed to include everything. He was clearly comfortable with his authority.

"Who are you, and why are you here?" he demanded.

Kalamar responded in the same measured tones as before, "I am Lordmage Kalamar Sylvicheld of Hayden Hamlet, east of Stormlake. I am here to open trade between my lands and yours, my lord."

This was clearly not the expected answer or a direction he'd anticipated. "You wish to open trade between our lands!" Ea's tone was incredulous.

"I believe that's what the boy just said!" Ghan Jean added sarcastically. "You losing your hearing?"

Ea rounded on the ghan but with a smile on his face and in his voice, "No, I'm not losing my hearing." It was clear their relationship was comfortable and extended back years. It reminded Kalamar of his best friends, Garret and Mac.

"Surely, your advanced years haven't blinded you to the preposterousness of his words!" Ea continued.

Kalamar quickly but politely intervened, "My lord, Surr[34] Ghan, I understand my appearance and words are cause for careful consideration. Is there someplace that I may tell my tale in full? I believe that will help you understand the current situation."

"See, see!" Jean crooned. "Courtesy and respect! You louts seem to forget that! Surr Ghan," he admonished with a broad smile.

Ea stifled his own smile and said, "Very well. It seems you have won over this old fool, so we might as well hear your story. Come this way and let's make ourselves more comfortable."

The sun had not yet gone down as they made their way through the city to the main estate in the center. It appeared that Ea kept a less formal hall than Eddington as everyone who could crowded into the main hall to hear him speak. The hearth fires were ablaze and the lanterns lit to banish shadows from the hall. The comfortableness of the place reminded Kalamar of Nellis, so long ago it seemed.

The crowd grew hushed and Lord KurZell motioned for him to proceed. He did not have his master's talent for storytelling and he did not use magic to enhance his voice, but he felt he did a credible job nonetheless. He told his story from being invited east to serve his master to forming his mercantile concern, the Blue Rose Shipping, the repeating harassment from Hoff sorcerers and the constant attempts at surveillance. He spoke of the upcoming first year of Hayden University.

He left out all the infighting and nastiness as they had no place or part in his purpose here. He continued on to the orc attack on the southeastern border and his discovering additional lords in Eddington. He ended with his request to set up a shipping route for goods both going and coming to all the lords here on the south side of Stonewash River.

---

[34] Surr is an old tongue word for esteemed or valued. It is sometimes used before Ghan in a formal setting.

Even the abbreviated version of the last two years was a lot to take in and he finished to a hushed and thoughtful crowd.

"That's quite a tale, lad," Ghan Jean said. Ardara was definitely less formal, which Kalamar appreciated.

"How are you planning on getting them here, young man? I'm sure you noticed there's quite a bit of unaccommodating terrain between here and the rest of the lands," Ea added.

Kalamar held up his left hand, wiggling his fingers while replying, "Do you mind if I use a bit of magic to show you?" He wore a mischievous grin as he said it.

Jean started laughing. "Of course, lad. It'd do some people good!"

Ea's expression was a bit more reserved but he reluctantly nodded his assent.

Kalamar nodded. He didn't want anyone in the room to overreact. He murmured the words to a simple illusion. When he was done, a map of Eddington was created across the ceiling. He smiled as Lord Ea and everyone else continued to look on expectantly. He pointed up and grinned as everyone gasped.

"That's incredible!" Ea said.

"A simple illusion," Kalamar responded. "While you are correct, coming around Stormlake would be difficult until a proper road is built, I have something different in mind." As he'd spoken, he'd drawn red arrows to show the path he just described. He continued, "You may have noticed that the land is far more populated than in the past. My plan is to build a bridge across Stonewash River, here"—he drew another arrow—"at Moss Brook. If you can find or make a path north, I will get Moss Brook's permission for the bridge."

"Who are those villages to our northeast?" Jean asked.

"Sadly, they are others who have been banished. Ardara, Westfield, Mackenzie, Lubinn, Narrandell, BrodenForr and Fellate." As he called each name, he created a red arrow to point out the location. Murmurs and cries were uttered at some of the names as they had been known before their own banishment.

"My lord," one of Ea's own counselors began, "we should send riders to those towns north of us. We must make contact with Lubinn and Narrandell."

"I take it you already have contact with Westfield and Mackenzie?" Kalamar asked.

"We do. We will build the road to Moss Brook as well as to the other four noble houses south of Stonewash."

"Then I will get the bridge built and we can reunite the land and be stronger for it," Kalamar replied.

He was met with a few cautious affirmations. He hoped the baron and, just as importantly, the counselors, felt the same way.

*****

Kalamar stood on the northern shore of the Stonewash, looking at the bridge he'd built with a deep sense of pride. The lady of Moss Brook and its chancellor had been ecstatic about the bridge and had financed its construction. Just as he'd used magic to summon earth elementals to build his tower, he had called on the same ones to build the columns and support structure of the bridge. Cut planks had then been put down to make the crossing floor. The bridge had a stone arch at each end.

As a special touch, he'd created the crest of Moss Brook on both columns from the north and that of Ardara matching on the south. At the center of each arch, he'd added the three towers of Eddington. All were lit by magic and glowed during the night.

It had taken two weeks, two weeks to contact all the banished lords, call the elementals and build the bridge structure. Ardara had kept its word and found paths between the five southern lords and Moss Brook. Those lords and their families were even now waiting on the other side of the bridge. Other than workmen, no one had crossed it.

Kalamar turned to his right and saw, not just the lords and ladies of Moss Brook, but the lords of BrodenForr and Fellate as well. While there was yet no road for carts, pack animals could navigate the path and their lords had joined them for this special occasion.

Kalamar extended his arm to Lady Nia of Moss Brook and together they walked across the bridge leading the processional. The southern lords did not cross, so as to not break the conditions of their banishment, but waited patiently.

Kalamar made introductions and the party was soon in full swing, celebrating the momentous occasion. As he danced, admiring the joy and happiness present, he knew that some would hate what he'd done. With the sun shining bright and the air full of gay music, he just didn't care and would face whatever tomorrow threw his way tomorrow...

Chapter 15

prophecy

Kalamar returned home to be greeted by Viz. He glanced up as the cherub[35] flew into the room he used for teleportation. From his expression, he had some disturbing news.

"What's the problem, my friend?"

Viz's childlike voice was unusually somber as he replied, "That's the problem. I don't know. A Mallynne priest arrived moments before you did and is asking to see you. He hasn't said anything but I had a foreboding the moment he arrived."

Kalamar was instantly alert. As an angelic being, Viz would be sensitive to such vibrations. He left the room and crossed to the Floating Disk[36] built into the southeastern corner of the tower. It quickly whisked him and Viz to the main floor, where he hurriedly crossed to the waiting room.

Stepping through the door, he saw that it was Ghan Regan. "Hello Ghan," he said with a nod, "How can I be of service?"

---

[35] Cherubs are angelic entities that will serve a good person or cause. They are from the higher planes of existence. About two feet tall, the look slightly babylike in their mundane form, except for the wings. They are opposites to imps, infernal creatures from the lower planes who will serve for the pleasure of corrupting and stealing souls. Imps are wizened, emaciated creatures also with wings, but including a daggerlike tail. Where cherubs are pale white or blue with a golden glow, imps are black or green and appear to absorb light, creating shadows.

[36] A vertical tube would be built into a structure. A mage would then enchant a disk as a mode of transportation to float between the floors on command. They were often seen as vanity projects or an ostentatious display of power, usually by those who lacked the prerequisite power, skill and spells.

Regan had risen and nodded as Kalamar entered the room. He smiled in delight as he saw the cherub, but his expression quickly turned dour. "I need you to take me to Baron Terrence immediately!" he stated.

"Of course, Ghan. Are you ready now?" Kalamar didn't see any gear or belongings with the priest.

"Yes, but you are not. You need to get your gear of war." His declaration along with Viz's earlier warning combined to create a feeling of impending doom.

Kalamar had long ago prepared a specific spell that would call his sword and backpack to him on the utterance of a single rune which he now spoke. As both items materialized in his hands, he slung the sword belt over his head and left arm, buckling the belt around his waist to lock the sword's hilt over his right shoulder.

He then pulled his backpack over that and replied, "I am now."

"Then let us proceed," Ghan Regan replied.

*****

As Garret headed to the command tent with Ghan Mac in answer to a summons, he had to admit he was happier than he'd been in quite some time. He loved the life of a soldier and being here, training with four thousand men to repel any orcish threat to the barony, gave him a sense of purpose he couldn't deny. It was taking time and effort, but all the nobles, knights and soldiers were being forged into a real army.

There were accidents of course and even a death. A knight during a charge had turned left when the horn had sounded right. He'd snapped his neck as he and his horse crashed into another. In spite of this, or maybe because of this, a real sense of purpose and bonding had grown to encompass all those here in defense of their land.

They reached the main tent to find it packed with nobles and commanders with more squeezing in. Those already inside made room for him with nods of respect. It seemed that being the only warrior present who had actual experience commanding men in battle against orcs had raised his status in their eyes. In honesty, he found it a refreshing change, especially in the nobles. He took his place not far from General Shay and waited as the remainder entered.

The tent was standing room only, except for a small patch in the center. Baron Terrence said, "Send them in."

Murmurs of surprise began in the back as someone pushed through the crowd to enter the ring. Garret was equally surprised as he saw it was a priest of Mallynne, followed by his friend, Kalamar. His surprise turned to concern as he saw the expressions both wore.

"Ghan Regan," the baron began, "you have demanded this meeting in the name of your patron. How can we help the goddess of healing?"

That set the crowd murmuring and muttering, but before the priest could begin, someone else raised his voice and said, "Lord Kalamar! What are you doing here? You were ordered to stay in Stormlake."

Before Kalamar could reply or address the rudeness, Ghan Regan proclaimed, "He is here because the goddess commands him to be. Do you dare gainsay her in this matter?"

That caused a low and angry buzz among those present, whether in support or against was impossible to say.

Lord Malcolm quickly stepped up and said, "Ghan Regan, we ask that you please speak the goddess' will." All present quieted down to listen.

"Each night since the orc attack, our high priestess has had a terrible dream. The same nightmare. A dark storm rages in the heart of the orc lands. Terrible winds and destruction it brings to all it touches. It pours out in an unstoppable force that drowns all our lands in darkness and death." He paused here and let his words sink in. A real fear began to grow in the pavilion as all waited for him to continue.

"Each night Ghan Malise hears a voice in the storm, trying to call out, but each night it is futile. Each night, except this last night. Last night, the warning in all its horror was perfectly clear." He paused, drawing himself up as if to steel his spirit against the words.

Beware to all,
your doom is neigh.
Maidens will weep
and grown men cry.

A darkness soon
to cover the land.
Less longtime friends
can make a stand.

Through orcs' hearts
the path is found.
They must fly quick
or be run to ground.

Intrepid band,
to hunt death's gate.
As desperate shadows
must not be late.

Sacred artifact
must be found.
Or all in darkness,
forever bound.

Heroes must follow
the Warlock's lead.
Else hope's promise
will be a wasted deed.

The race against,
much more than sand.
All will be lost
by the faltering hand.

> The doom awaits
> the last sun's fall.
> It's paid by one,
> or it's paid by all.

The room itself seemed to have grown dark as each man's most-fevered imaginations were made real. It was deathly quiet as everyone watched the priest who'd gone pale at his own words, as if he'd been drained of life just to speak them.

Garret looked from the priest to his friend and noticed that Kalamar had just learned of this with them.

The room stirred to life, with most whispering either prayers for protection or asking a variant of "What does it mean?" This continued for several minutes, with the priest finally gathering himself and raising his hand for silence.

It came immediately. He cleared his throat and said, "My goddess was able to give us two clues to help. The first is the path will be found in the heart of the orc lands. The second is, unless the path is found and its end reached before tomorrow's sunrise, the quest will fail and all will perish."

An icy grip was felt by each man present given such an impossible timeline. Who could solve the riddle so quickly, much less reach the heart of orc lands, wherever that was? Real panic was growing when Ghan Teague called out.

"Who is this warlock to lead our heroes?"

Ghan Regan did not answer but simply pointed back to his right—straight at Kalamar. Garret could tell his friend was just as startled as everyone else by this. His friend's gaze went to the archmage and Garret followed it. He was startled to see an odd expression on the court wizard's face. It was a knowing look, as if something long suspected was finally confirmed. The look was gone in a flash and Garret had no more time to consider it as someone called out, "What is a warlock?"

It was Lord Crow who answered, "Warlock is a title that hasn't been heard since the founding of Calledon over 1,400 years ago. It belonged to an elite group of mages that were masters of battle. They were said to have no equal."

Garret caught the look on General Shay's face at this revelation. It seemed no surprise to him as he, like the archmage before, found confirmation, not confusion. General Shay called out over the growing chorus, "Warlock, do you have thoughts on this matter?"

Kalamar was startled at being addressed as such, but quickly schooled his expression and said, "No, actually I don't. But clearly, I don't have a lot of time to solve the mystery. Is there anywhere I can go to think on this?"

It was Lord Treavor of Northspring who quickly spoke up, "Of course, my lord, follow me." He matched deeds to words and quickly led Kalamar through the crowd and out the tent.

Garret caught General Shay's gaze, got permission and followed with Ghan Mac right beside. They swiftly caught Lords Treavor and Kalamar.

Treavor said, "Well, this is an exciting start to the day, I must say!"

It was such an outrageous understatement all of them smiled, with Mac replying, "The gods wouldn't want us to get bored and lazy!" To which they almost laughed. Almost.

It was Kalamar who next spoke as they entered Treavor's tent, "I don't suppose any of you know what the prophecy means?" His tone didn't suggest he thought they would answer.

Garret replied, "Actually, that's fairly simple. You have to find a path to death's gate and get us there before the sun rises tomorrow, or we all die."

Kalamar stopped and turned, stunned. "And how am I supposed to do that?" he demanded.

"Haven't a clue!" he responded with an insolent grin to which they all laughed. "But," he continued, "I will certainly follow wherever you lead."

"Hear, hear!" exclaimed Mac.

Kalamar was truly touched by the faith he saw in his friends' faces and replied, "Thank you. I couldn't ask for better companions!" No one said anything else as Lord Treavor sent his servants out of the tent.

"My lord," Treavor began, "please make yourself at home. If you need anything, just let me know. You can have some privacy behind that curtain, and we will be out here when you need us."

"Thank you, my lord," Kalamar replied and passed through to the interior of the tent.

*****

Everyone in the tent rose as Kalamar came out into the main portion. He'd spent most of the day in the same position, searching for clues with his magic. Anxious visitors and nosey busybodies had visited repeatedly during the day in hopes of learning something but Lord Treavor sent them on their way disappointed. Garret watched as his friend stretched, no doubt trying to work some circulation back into his muscles.

"Is there any food about?" Kalamar asked. "I'm starving."

They were prepared for this and Mac pointed to the table in the corner with bread, meat, cheese and a bit of wine already laid out. With a nod of thanks, Kalamar sat down and tore into the food. The five of them said nothing and gave him some peace to replenish his body.

While Kalamar had been searching for answers, Garret, Mac, Lord Treavor, Leopold and Zelig had put together arms, armor and supplies for their journey into the unknown. They'd tried to anticipate what they might need based on clues in the prophecy. The race and sands of time suggested the need for speed, so they packed light. Death's gate and shadows suggested underground or darkness, so they brought supplies for light. Other than that, they just didn't know. Lord Treavor had introduced Leopold and Zelig shortly after Kalamar left the room and a more unlikely pair he couldn't imagine. Leopold was small, wiry, and seemed to naturally disappear if you didn't pay much attention. With a nondescript face and dirty-blond hair, he could blend into any group and be quickly forgotten. Zelig, on the other hand, was a giant who towered over everyone at almost seven feet. His face had clearly been smashed repeatedly in fights of one kind or the other. His wild, coal-black hair and huge mustache combined to make him look formidable. He was clearly the strong, silent type who probably scared most people into giving up before the fight began. They had been best friends and inseparable since childhood.

Lord Treavor introduced the pair to Kalamar as he ate. Garret could see that his first instinct was to reject the two joining them but as Treavor gave a bit of their history and Leopold's knowledge of locks and traps, he clearly thought better of it.

Kalamar finished his quick meal with a large gulp of the wine and said, "I have discovered where we must go. It is indeed a race as the orcs are trying to break into the temple but have so far been repulsed. They've been at it for years and each attempt they get closer and closer. I have no doubt they will succeed by tomorrow sundown."

Lord Treavor asked, "If they have spent years trying to get in, how will you succeed in a single night?"

"They are using brute force to break down the defenses at the front door. We, on the other hand, are going to use stealth and guile while going in a back door, as it were," Kalamar responded calmly.

Leopold chimed in and said, "I like the plan already!"

Zelig responded, "You would," and grimaced.

"Well," Garret added, "if everything's settled, when do we leave? We have everything ready to go."

Kalamar replied, "Not until after midnight. First, the orcs are guarding the temple's perimeter and I want them at their most lax when we make our move. And second, I've exhausted most of my magic in the search and need some rest to recover it."

They all nodded and turned to Mac as he said, "This temple. Do you know whose it is?"

"I do not," Kalamar replied. "It is shielded in a way I've never seen or even heard of before. The power structures are quite alien to me. I could only get small glimpses from the magical tunnel the orcs are using and didn't want to alert them to my presence. They have a thousand priests working to tear down the protections it has. I've discussed what I found with Archmage Crow and perhaps he will discover something before we leave."

Kalamar stood up and said, "Lord Treavor, would you do me a favor and convey the general points to Baron Eddington. I really need to begin my meditations if I'm to recover any of my powers before we leave, but I'd like him to have some comfort that progress has been made and we have a plan of attack."

"Of course, my friend," Treavor said. "It will be my pleasure. Don't give it another thought."

Garret watched as Kalamar nodded and then headed farther into the tent to meditate, and Lord Treavor left the tent to make the report. He looked at the others and said, "I guess the soldiers' motto applies to heroes as well. 'Hurry up and wait!'"

No one responded, as there really wasn't anything to say.

*****

A strong internal clock was vital to high-level magical work and Kalamar used his to wake just before the first hour of night began. He then cast a simple scrying spell to quickly confirm the position of the orc's sentries and the location he wanted to teleport still appeared safe. The moon was low in the west, but he could confirm what he needed.

It was time, he said to himself and stood. Straightening out the kinks, he walked out to the main partition of the tent. A single lantern gave enough light to see that his team was ready and waiting. In addition, Baron Terrence, Archmage Crow, Lord Malcolm, Ghan Teague, General Shay and, of course, Lord Treavor were there to see them off. The silence was eerie and he had no wish to break it. Since the archmage didn't volunteer he'd discovered something important, Kalamar just nodded to the assembled group and then walked over to his friends. They gathered around, each putting a hand on his shoulders to make the connection.

Clearing his mind, Kalamar reached into himself and drew upon his powers. As always, he thrilled at the pleasure it created in him. Even in the void, this feeling was unlike anything else he'd ever known. The necessary runes burned in his mind and he slowly spoke them, each one with purpose, gathering, guiding, controlling and releasing the powers he needed to teleport him and his friends almost forty miles, deep into the Blackburn Forest and the orc's domain. One moment they were in the tent in Eddington and the next they were in a small forest glade, with only a brief flash of color and darkness in between.

The heavy scent of trees filled the air as the crescent moon shone down from the west, nearing the end of its journey. The sounds of the forest momentarily paused with their arrival but slowly resumed when they offered no threat. Kalamar then cast two spells, one to link them together so they could feel where the others were. Garret and Mac were used to this as they had practiced together in their training. Leo and Zel had been told what to expect and would learn as they went. The other spell gave them the ability to see in the dark, not like a dwarf or goblin but like an elf or cat. Again, they would have to adapt quickly. He gave them a few minutes to adjust and then, like ghosts, they passed out of the glade and north to the temple. They'd already discussed their order of march while he'd been resting, so no words were needed as they took their places.

Kalamar had chosen a teleport site about a mile away from where they needed to enter the shielding around the temple. The idea was to make sure no magical ripples disturbed the surrounding orcish spells and alerted them to their presence. Fortunately, the trees in this part were evergreen and only pine needles blanketed the ground. He discovered that he and Mac seemed to make the most noise, although precious little. Leo and even Zel were like a breeze barely felt, racing through the night.

He halted just at the edge of the orc's concealing magic and whispered, "We are about to cross a magic shield and on the other side is a guard post with three sentries. They must be taken out quick and quiet. I need to get past them to open the path into the temple itself."

"Leave that to us!" Leo replied.

"All right, step through where I step through," Kalamar responded. Turning to the orc shield, he delicately extended his senses into the shield itself. It was created with the power of a thousand priests and witch doctors, which made it strong. However, they didn't blend very well and that left tiny areas that wouldn't form smoothly or evenly. This made it possible for a mage with skill to send his power through. Once done, he could slowly expand that opening enough for a person to step through. While it felt like forever, it really only took a few minutes. He then cast a small illusion to color the opening just enough for the others to see it and pass through.

Once through, they could see the guard post and its sentries. Kalamar closed the opening he just made and released the illusion to fade. He left the guards to his friends and headed to the hairline fracture discovered in his earlier searches to repeat what he'd just done. The difference however, was significant. Instead of a horde of competing egos forced to work together, this was a single fused working, possibly by the god or power dwelling inside. The crack was caused because of the pressures on the western side by the invading orcs and was so small most would never find it. Even now Kalamar was unsure if it had been luck, skill, a guiding presence or a bit of them all that had allowed him to discover it.

He glanced over in time to see his friends setting up the dead orcs on their own spears to make it appear to a casual observer they were still guarding the area. He turned back to the temple shield and began. He had to be infinitely more careful here and it took much longer than he wished. Sweat was running down his face and neck when he was finally finished.

The pressure and focus were excruciating and he took a moment to mop his face and stretch out the tension in his body. Done, he turned to his friends who nodded readily.

Kalamar quietly spoke, "When we traverse this gate, you will be in a landscape wholly unfamiliar. I will be casting a glamour over each of us to change our appearance to fit in. We must look and act like a party seeking to pray at the temple. You must not draw your weapons or act hostile unless I give the word. If that happens, the mission will probably fail. We must pass through the entrance to the temple before sunrise. Understood?" He looked to each for confirmation.

"Mac," he whispered, "what I must ask of you will be hardest of all. You must hide your faith in your god. Any hint of energy from another power will alert whatever is inside." Kalamar knew it was cruel to ask this since it was like asking someone to cut off his right arm, but he knew it could be done, as Mac had described a test all priests went through with this as part of the training. He watched his friend grimace with remembered pain and then nod. Agony washed across his friend's continence and it was hard to watch as he made the soulful adjustments.

Mac took a few calming breaths and signaled his readiness to proceed. Kalamar then turned and stepped through, wrapping himself in the illusion as he crossed over. He turned and did the same for the others as they came through. During his search earlier in the day, he'd gathered enough information to understand what was required. He was dressed as a mage in this distant land, wearing only white kilt-like pants with a white hat that draped over the back of his head to his shoulders. He also had sandals on his feet. The others he outfitted as warriors, which included a breastplate of bronze over a white shirt and no headgear.

Kalamar gave them a few moments to orient themselves and he turned to the land itself. He knew of it only from his master's books. It was a desert land called Ghet, far to the south on the other side of the continent of Rularan. It had a single massive river that provided all water and life to its people. Occasionally there would be a beautiful green oasis found around a pool of water from an underground spring. This was what they saw. It was a living illusion. How it got here was a mystery they would probably have to solve to succeed in their quest.

"Walk where I walk" was all Kalamar said as he led them north and west to the temple's entrance. They came across one strange sight after another as they raced against the sunrise. It was fortunate the creatures they encountered didn't seem hostile, just mildly annoyed and they kept their distance to keep it that way. Eventually, they found a road and their progress was much faster. The only people they saw were illusions, as if dreams from the god inside. It was from these Kalamar had learned the proper manner of dress.

All these things paled in comparison to the temple itself. It was as large as a small mountain, shaped as a perfect pyramid. The temple entrance on the western side seemed a separate columned building built into the main structure. At the top was a cap made of some type of crystal that glowed with moonlight as it drew in the power of that celestial body. The covering of the construction was pure alabaster and glowed pearlescence in the night. Only the bottom twenty feet was painted. The background was red, and it had many figures and strange hieroglyphic symbols telling stories and great deeds they could only guess at.

Time was racing from the hourglass and Kal knew it. As they rounded the southwestern corner, they could see the magical tunnel the orcs were making to reach the entrance. It pulsed with terrible power and thrust like a spear from the western shield wall, straight to the entrance. All manner of creatures attacked in defense of the temple, but to little avail. While occasionally they would have success getting to the orcs inside, more would replace them in a steady stream.

The orc's strategy was simple. Hold during the night when the temple was strongest and during the daylight, extend the tunnel to the entrance. This was clearly the work of years and they were "oh so" close to the goal. The questers could see they would reach the entrance by the end of today and they put on a burst of extra speed to both avoid the orcish gaze and the sun's first rays.

Winded from the race, they paused before the main entrance to catch their breath. Knowing there was no time to waste, Kalamar scanned the pictures and scenes before him for clues. As soon as he was able, he began casting identifying spells to detect any traps or triggers that would prevent their entrance. Leo began his own examinations for the same reasons.

Having found none, they pushed open one of the massive bronze doors enough for them to squeeze inside. The sky had been lighting quickly, dispelling the night as the sun's rays raced down the pyramid's side as they closed the door behind them. It had opened without a sound, but it closed with a boom, echoing both within the cavernous chamber in which they stood and across the sandy plain outside.

Chapter 16

Death's Gate

nending darkness was all their panic-laced senses felt. The boom from the door reverberated through their bodies, not just their ears. There was no chance the orcs wouldn't hear and begin their own rush to breach the temple's remaining defenses.

Harsh breathing from their race against the sun was the only other sound as the remaining echoes faded from the closed door.

The inky blackness was impenetrable and absolute. Kalamar was about to cast a light spell when Zel whispered, "Look!"

Each of them turned in place until they found what he was talking about. Far in the distance, a pair of lights flickered like tiny specks against the gloom. As they stood, trying to calm their racing hearts, a second set appeared closer than the first. Then a third and so on as the lights slowly marched closer and closer to the questers' position.

Kalamar recognized what was happening, but Mac spoke first. "It's torches in sconces along the walls. They're igniting in pairs from the far end of the hall to this one."

"That's a terrifying effect," Leo offered quietly.

"I suspect it's meant to be," Mac replied.

As they waited to see what was heading their way, Kalamar extended his senses. Like the shields outside, a single presence filled all the temple. As expected, the most-concentrated portion was from the direction the lights were coming, into the very heart of the pyramid.

As the paired lights got closer, it became possible to see around them. It was a great hall, larger than the entire main castle at

Stormlake. It could probably hold ten thousand people from end to end. This was just the pavilion leading into the temple. Kalamar knew the pyramid itself only began after you passed through the hall.

The torches closest to them were finally lit. It was all done by some power. They saw no one walking the great hall, lighting them as they came. As far as they knew, there were still the only ones here. What the lit torches showed was both incredible and eerie. Hieroglyphs like those outside covered the walls. They were clearly telling stories of the power that resided here as he was the central character in almost every section. The images it showed of him were a giant being with a long-nosed dog or wolf's head. It was solid black with bright-red eyes and tall, sharp, pointed ears. None of the scenes showed anything remotely happy or lighthearted. They were filled with groveling worshipers and angry-looking priests directing fanatical followers.

"That's encouraging," Garret said with a low chuckle.

No one else replied. They just started down the hall.

*****

The temple was truly an alien nightmare, thought Kalamar. They stood before what they both believed and hoped was the final door. The grand entrance hall had been blocked by a massive obsidian statue of the temple's ruler, complete with snarling silver fangs and ruby eyes that glowed with a fire all their own. Its presence was palpable when standing before it and they suspected most petitioners never got beyond that point. Behind it, a smaller but grander entrance had led directly into the pyramid's great worship hall.

This room was perfectly square and peaked inside like an echo of the pyramid outside. The highest point appeared to be crystal like the outside apex, only inverted. It reflected light that it must gather from its outside inverse image. With the sun now ruling the sky, it bathed the hall in an angry-looking red and orange. Near the northern wall was an even larger, more terrible version of this temple's denizen and before it was what could only be a sacrificial altar. The altar was pure gold, constructed in some fashion that allowed it to maintain its shape and fulfill its terrible purpose. The intricately carved altar was large enough to allow for the murder of a dozen people, end to end, at the same time. It was caked in old dried blood in quantities that left no illusions.

After that were the killing traps. The entire place was filled with them. Poison darts, trap floors and collapsing walls were mixed in with distorting runes. These were designed to warp any uninvited guest's senses, making them easy victims for the traps. It had taken all his and Leo's skills to keep everyone alive through the nightmare of death.

Kalamar was exhausted both mentally and magically. He took from his pack a small vial and drank it. It was a last resort designed to temporarily restore his magical reserves. Without a doubt, he knew he'd need everything he had for the remaining tasks. As best they could determine, this room was far below the great worship hall and centered under the highest peak of the temple.

Both he and Leo had checked it twice finding nothing but this only increased their concern. It was an absolutely beautiful gold door inlaid with all manner of perfect gemstones. Its value was impossible to imagine. With a deep breath and final look around at his worn-out but determined companions, he reached out with his mind and gave the door a gentle shove. It opened without a sound.

They stepped inside to a smaller, pyramid room like the great worship hall. It was a complete copy except one small, frightening detail. Where above the temple's ruler glared down in insatiable rage, here the throne was empty. The bloodstained altar was still there although, thankfully, small enough only for one person. There were also the same four statues, one to each corner. They were ferocious man-shaped, dog-headed combinations with terrible fangs and claws.

As they made it to the center of the room, the door they'd entered through closed with a boom much like the entrance door. Before they had a moment to react, a single word reverberated through the room.

"SACRIFICE!" a deep male voice seemed to shout into their very souls.

They instinctively formed a circle in the center, backs to each other.

"SACRIFICE!" again blasted through the room.

The corner statues now stepped off their pedestals. "THEY'RE GOLEMS," Kalamar shouted.

"SACRIFICE!"

The golems stomped forward, raising their arms. It was certain they meant to bring them down and crush the insignificant intruders.

"SACRIFICE!"

Golems are a bit slower than the average person, so everyone avoided the first blows. But in such a small space, it was inevitable they would be squashed sooner or later if a solution wasn't found. An all-out melee broke out, with everyone hacking and slashing the enemy while avoiding those massive stone fists and claws. All the while, "SACRIFICE!" kept being shouted out as a counterpoint to the mad scrambling in the room.

Kalamar was quickly exhausting himself along with everyone else. They all carried edged weapons, which were next to useless against stone. They needed bludgeoning weapons like hammers and maces to have a real impact. In addition, the space was so confined that any of Kalamar's more effective spells would kill everyone including himself. He wanted to shout in rage at the impossible situation they were in. All the while, "SACRIFICE!" being screamed in the air was not only distracting but starting to damage his hearing. He seemed to be going deaf to the desperate exertions of his companions as they fought for their lives.

"To ME!" he shouted as he had one desperate card left to play.

"SACRIFICE!" came the relentless shout back.

He dodged another blow as he watched everyone scramble to his side. They were covered in scrapes from the shards of stone flying about the room. The air was filled with choking stone dust but finally he thought everyone was crowded in behind him.

He raised his sword high above his head in both hands. He was holding it by the blade and was going to bring it down on the hilt to shatter it, thereby releasing a last-ditch spell that would hopefully destroy the golems, but probably also collapse the room on them. He extended his shield in the hopes it would be enough to keep them alive.

Kalamar started to bring down the blade when he realized the golems had stopped moving. He blinked in confusion before he also realized the infernal shouting had stopped as well. He slowly turned to see equally confused looks on his three companions.

Three companions didn't seem right. Something was wrong and finally his wits rushed back to him. There were supposed to be four.

He spun around peering through the room as the dust slowly settled and saw the terrible truth. Zelig was laid out on the altar, his own hand still grasping the dagger he'd used to end his life. Everyone and everything in the room seemed to freeze in a terrible, disjointed moment.

"No!" shouted Leopold as he raced to his best friend's side. "No, no, no…" he kept saying softer and softer as he held onto his now lifeless friend.

Kalamar's mind was racing as the initial shock faded, but so were his senses. The presence that had been with them from the moment they entered the temple was now overwhelming.

He wrenched his gaze from the altar, the fresh blood growing in ever-larger pools and focused on the throne. As the dust further settled, it was terribly clear what had happened. The throne was no longer empty.

Seated in all his terrible glory was the master of this temple. The statues and images they'd seen throughout the journey here had not done him justice. They mostly got the features correct, but they could not possibly match the effect of the power rolling off him in waves. It crashed down on them like a waterfall, commanding them to grovel at his feet.

The warlock stepped forward and placed himself between this terrible being and his friends. They in turn left their spots around the altar and stood shoulder to shoulder behind him in support.

Kalamar would not grovel or even kneel to this terrible being, but he was also no fool. Respect must be shown, so he bowed deeply and his companions did likewise. As he finished this gesture, he looked up into the face of this being, expecting to see the snarling rage shown almost universally throughout the temple. He was surprised instead to see a thoughtfulness that could not be reconciled with the images. It seemed almost confused as it stared at something only it could see.

They waited as it slowly returned from its distant thoughts. Its massive head shifted slightly to now encompass them in its gaze. No one said anything.

"A million souls have been sacrificed to me over the millennia and not one has volunteered until this day." While it was not a shout like before, the power of it demanded your full attention. The giant, towering figure actually leaned forward as if to peer closer at his insignificant guests.

"This one"—he pointed to the altar—"the one you call Zel is showing me many things that are difficult to believe."

"YOU LEAVE HIM ALONE!" Leo shouted from behind Kalamar.

The massive head cocked to one side in disbelief.

"Your people are so different from mine," he continued. "Your values, your spirit." He paused again. "Even in death, Zel is trying to save your lives. Astonishing!" He paused again.

Kalamar had not been idle during this time. With nothing to lose, he'd extended his senses throughout the temple. He now had access to much of it and understood far better who this being was and what powers it had at its command—or had, as it were. The orc attacks had drained most everything from the being in front of him. Kane. Kane knew if they made it inside, he would be destroyed by the ravenous orcs' gods.

Kane was the keeper of the dead for the people of Ghet, but *his* temple had been exiled almost a century ago in a fashion Kalamar did not yet understand. With their god banished, the remaining temples were eventually abandoned. This had weakened him significantly. He was not a god of this world in the proper sense, but he was a power and that was close enough for the people of Ghet, who worshiped him.

"Great Kane," the warlock said respectfully. "The orcs will breach your temple doors within the hour. Every moment we waste here hastens your demise."

Kane was truly startled to hear his name spoken aloud in such a conversational way.

"In the past," he growled, "you would be sliced into pieces for daring to utter my name."

"Kill me and you only destroy yourself," Kalamar replied simply.

Kane's right fist clenched as if he would do just that, but he once again turned away to stare at something only he could see.

The fist slowly unclenched, and he said, "True," with a dark chuckle. "You are a remarkable people and according to Zel, you personally are even more so."

"Yes," he added before any of them could respond. "Yes, so be it." This last part seemed part of a separate conversation he was having.

"I'm offering you a deal, Kalamar Sylvicheld. A deal that will give you what you want and give me what I want. What do you say to that?" he asked.

"I need to hear it first," Kalamar replied carefully.

"So insolent!" he responded. "Extraordinary. Your goddess sent you here because the orcs are about to destroy me and claim the regalia of the Pharaoh! This talisman of my people gives the user control over Death's Gate. The ability to release and control the dead. They will surely destroy your world just as they will destroy mine. These are the terms:

"First, I will give you the talisman. With it, you will destroy the orcs and save my temple. Second, you will return here and learn from me. There is much I have to teach you and there is much I would like to learn about your people. Third, you will take the talisman from this place and hide it. Its power is what drew the orcs in the first place and with it elsewhere, they will abandon their pursuit of my temple's destruction. And fourth, you will tell no one of this agreement. It will be a secret kept by only those in this room," he finished, expecting an immediate agreement.

Kalamar wasn't ready to give him one.

"The first I have no problem with," he began slowly. "The second I have concerns, as I'm not willing to simply put myself at your mercy without binding assurances on your behavior. The third means I'm now exposing my people to significant risks and the fourth is out of the question. Particularly when considered with the second. I must also add an additional condition. You must release Zelig's spirit to us so we may return him to his people," he finished carefully.

Kane looked ready to explode. His fingers gripped the arm rest of his throne so tightly Kalamar thought it might shatter. They stared for some time at each other before he offered amendments to his counteroffer.

"The entire point of the goddess sending us was to get the talisman and keep it from the orcs. I must have faith she considered that danger before sending us on this mission, so I accept that one. I can also see the point of keeping the talisman secret, which would certainly include parts of this agreement." He continued, "As a compromise, I will tell only my master, the archmage Angus Crow. He is an outsider who can observe my behavior and make sure I am not compromised in some way and become a danger to my people. To the world at large, I will give the simple truth that we came to an agreement to defeat the orcs and safeguard the temple and its treasures."

Kalamar wondered what type of outburst his offer would receive and was surprised it was met with only silence.

"Your perspective is so different from mine," Kane eventually replied in his low, gravelly voice. "I look forward to your visits and accept your offer." As he finished speaking, he waved his left hand to the right wall and a small hidden door was revealed.

"The talisman is within," he began. "You must be told. You don't have to wear it all the time but once you accept it, only your death can separate you from it. You become its guardian for life," he finished solemnly.

Kal nodded and walked over to the cabinet. He sensed no traps and slowly opened the door. Inside, sitting on a simple stand was a golden decorative chest plate. It was almost like a heavy-looking necklace with a large flared wing centerpiece. It looked simple enough but the power it radiated was incredible. He extended his senses around the artifact and pondered the powerful link between it and Death's Gate. The gate was now quite visible to him. The doorway to a realm of death was hovering just above the altar. With this key, he could open and close that door and command any he released from its dark embrace.

No one should have this power, he thought. *What madman would even create such a thing?* But those were considerations for another time. He had to survive the next hour first. Slowly he reached out and took the talisman from its stand. Lifting by its chains, he raised it over his head and settled it on his shoulders. He shuddered as the links binding him to it began forming. With each link, however, his control of the talisman grew until he was its absolute master. None, not even Kane, could countermand his authority over the dead of Ghet.

Chapter 17

Where Mortals Fear to Tread

arret watched his friend take up the talisman with a knot in his stomach. He wanted nothing to do with this place and its evil god and saw only disaster from the terrible bargain just made. He knew he didn't have a better idea and they were out of time. He also knew it would accomplish their mission, but his fears against it were a powerful force. This, he thought, was why he was a simple soldier. *I can leave the deal making and the terrible compromises to other wiser heads.* He grimaced as a small sarcastic voice in his mind responded, "Like young Lord Allen?"

He banished that thought as he watched in horror as terrible forces started pressing against Kalamar. It looked like he was caught in a windstorm as his clothes seemed to float and flap around him and the veins in his neck stood out as he fought for control. He let out a sigh of relief as the effects seemed to subside and his friend returned to a semblance of normal.

He was about to ask how he felt but stopped short as the warlock turned directly to them. His eyes were black, as black as this terrible temple had been when they first entered, but that wasn't the worst. His face was stretched in a grimace—not pain but part joy and part despair. It was the most terrible thing he'd ever seen and his concerns for his friend's soul leaped to his throat.

Retching his head around, he looked at the temple's monster to see what he thought of all this. The expression of glee on that terror's face made him want to vomit. He quickly turned to Mac and felt a small measure of peace.

His best friend, Mac, had been with him his entire life. Throughout it all, Garret had watched him most closely. He was relentless in his devotion to duty and steady as a mountain. That's what he saw in that so familiar face, but this time there was something more. He couldn't describe it but he knew instantly what it was. His god Saa'Vey was there. He was looking out through his most-devoted priest and Garret knew no evil would slip past him.

He found his center again and turned back to Kalamar. The darkness was gone from his eyes and his expression was confident and clear. He wanted to shout at the victory of his friend over the terrible forces trying to corrupt his body and soul.

"Time to get to work!" Kalamar said with a grin and began drifting up to the ceiling radiating that ugly red-orange flickering light. He entered it and passed straight through like a wraith. As he drifted away, the flickering light changed to some type of scrying tool. Those left behind could watch him as he went straight up through the entire temple to its highest peak. As the warlock slipped out through the top, standing at the highest point, the scrying altered its perspective. They could see the entire temple as if from a bird's perspective.

The sun was setting but not yet finished as it burned red against the western sky. Below the orcs were working furiously to reach the temple's door. They were already on the lowest steps and the temple's stone defenders from earlier that morning were almost completely destroyed. Thousands of chanting and shouting orcs were in that tunnel, hacking and clawing to get through. Only his friend stood against the horde now. He knew even if they raced back through the maze to the front door, they'd never reach it in time. He turned his gaze back to Kalamar, wondering how on earth he could defeat that foe.

Kalamar, however, wasn't there. Or he was and wasn't. He'd shifted himself into a terrible monster, not the one whose temple they'd fought though, not Kane, but one he didn't remember seeing in any of the wall pictures. He was a giant like Kane, but his head was that of a terrible pale dragon with cold blue eyes and razor teeth. Down his back ran matching raised spines that became a long, sinuous tail. His hands and feet ended in terrible claws.

With a terrible roar, the dragon beast raced down the pyramid's side, over the roof of the entrance hall and leaped directly into the orc horde. Screams, shouts and wailing erupted as the warlock slashed, ripped, tore and bit unleashing a fury difficult to watch. Bodies and parts were being strewn in every direction. It wasn't a fight; it was a slaughter and step by step, the orcs were being driven back and the tunnel they'd created was shrinking.

The orcs, however, and especially their gods, were not about to abandon the fight. The thousands of priests channeling their dark god's powers shifted their tactics the moment the temple's new guardian appeared. They ceased to expend their energies to contain the temple's power as it was no longer necessary. Their new target was the temple's last guardian. If the temple sent a monster onto the field, they would send their own champion. They summoned a devil from hell.

There was a terrible ripping sound from outside the temple grounds deep in the orc hordes' ranks. It was followed by a deafening roar every bit as terrible as Kal's had been earlier. With its own shout, it raced down the tunnel, gleefully killing any orc unable to scramble out its way. A revolting, fleshy thud sounded as the two combatants hurled into each other. The devil was a bit smaller in height but meatier in build. It didn't have a tail but did have a wider mouth, more razor-sharp teeth and at least a dozen eyes.

The warlock's advance was stopped. The orcs weren't content to leave it a stalemate however, as they redirected their army around Kal and the demon to slowly began advancing again. Faster and faster they regained lost ground and were now making steady progress back to the temple doors.

Garret spun as a rotting smell assaulted his senses and a cold, chill wind filled the room. Over the altar, he saw a dark void open and a flood of pale spirits rush out in a blur. It was an endless stream of souls with haunted expressions, crying out in shrieks and moans. They disappeared into the fading fire at the top of the room, only to reappear at the temple steps slamming into the orcs. They dissolved in wisps of smoke and fumes like waves against the shore.

Some of the orcs collapsed while others seemed to go berserk attacking anything near them. Some resisted the assault, but enough didn't to halt their latest advance. A stalemate once again.

The warlock, however, had a new card to play. The sun was finally setting. It wasn't down yet, but long shadows were forming everywhere across the field and where they did, he rebuilt the broken golems that littered the ground. First one, then two, then a few became dozens. They stomped, hopped, charged and rolled into the orcs who had nowhere to go. Stepping outside the tunnel meant stepping outside their god's protection and almost instant death. On the other hand, a death match was going on between two terrifying giants that crushed anything near them.

Among the rising defenders, at the last moment, a colossus golem changed direction and crashed into the devil, trapping its leg for a few moments. The vicious beast then made a fatal mistake and released Kal to throw off the animated statue. The warlock wasted no time in grabbing its head and, with a brutal twist, ripped it completely off. With a roar of triumph, the dragon-headed guardian hurled it down the tunnel, knocking over the orcs in its path.

Darkness fully fell and the battle's tide turned for the last time. Leading his army of ghosts and golems, he routed the orcs from the temple grounds and destroyed their sorcerous tunnel. With a final shout of victory, he sealed the breach as if it never was.

Garret once again looked over to their host to see how he would celebrate Kalamar's victory. He was surprised to see a rather-thoughtful expression. It was as if Kane wasn't quite sure how he felt about what he'd just witnessed. Was that doubt, even fear, in his eyes? He was hopeful it was.

The warlock returned to their dungeon room the way he'd left. Thankfully, he'd shifted back into his mortal form, but Garret once again had a sense of unease. Power rolled off him in waves, much like the temple's ruler just an hour earlier. Triumph was written on his face, but so was power. The temple it seemed was under Kal's control, not Kane's. Was that Kane's cause for alarm? Was Kal actually in a position to set himself up as the new ruler of this place?

197

"Your enemy is destroyed!" the warlock proclaimed as he turned to Kane.

"So it would seem," Kane responded. "And a most-decisive victory it was."

Did Kane seem smaller? Garret thought. He physically towered over all of them but didn't seem quite as substantial anymore, like he was fading away.

"Thank you," Kal responded graciously. "I've sealed the breach and built the temple's defenses stronger than they were before. And as you said, once I take the talisman away, they will have far less incentive to bother you in the future."

"That is true," Kane added soberly. "As an additional show of gratitude, I offer you as much of this treasure as you can carry." He waved his right hand, and a doorway opened on the left, revealing a storeroom full of treasures fit for a king.

"That is very kind of you," Kal said with a smile as he walked over to the doorway. He then knelt down and placed a small box on the floor before it. He whispered a word, and in a blur, all the treasure in the room seemed to jump into his box. He closed it with a snap and rose, turned to Kane, and gave a respectful bow.

Garret gaped at the trick and looked to see how Kane would respond. A flicker of something he didn't recognize crossed Kane's face but then their host grinned and nodded his head.

"A fascinating display," he said. "And one I won't forget." Garret was unsure if that comment was a threat or praise.

"Then with your permission, Great Kane, we will be leaving and return to our people. They will be greatly relieved to learn of the successful result of the goddess' quest."

Kane nodded, and Kalamar created a magical gurney to carry their companion, Zelig, home. He also would swear he saw Zel's spirit leave the altar and settle over his now cold, bloodless body.

Garret quickly glanced at Mac, who nodded, confirming the release of Zelig's spirit.

Everyone gathered around Kalamar as they had before.

"I look forward to our next meeting, young Kalamar," Kane said right before they disappeared.

They reappeared in the same glade they'd teleported to on their way here. Garret watched as Kal seemed to diminish before his eyes. The vast powers he'd held just moments ago were gone and now he seemed his old self, the young talented mage he'd befriended two years ago.

"Whew!" Kalamar said with a small smile. "Am I glad to be out of there." He meant it to lighten the moment, and it did, at least briefly.

"But we lost a true hero in the process," he continued sadly and turned to Leopold. "I can't begin to express my condolences. We would have failed, as well as never left that place, without his noble sacrifice." As he said this, he placed his hand on Leo's arm in a comforting gesture.

"Thank you, my lord," Leo replied and said no more.

"We're going to make two more jumps. One to my tower, where I can remove the talisman and begin the process to hide it. The other back to Lord Treavor's tent. The reason I didn't travel straight to my tower is to throw anyone trying to follow off the trail. They will have felt it going south to where we are, but then it will disappear as my tower's shields are enough to hide the next jump."

They reappeared into a room with no windows or doors. It was exactly as Kal had described it to Garret, but without any markings or reference; they really could be anywhere, which was exactly the point. The warlock was making sure none of them could, even by accident, reveal a clue to its whereabouts. After Kal vanished and reappeared, he did indeed return them to the same location in Lord Treavor's tent. The startled lord jumped up from his camp stool.

"Praise the gods you're back," he said with obvious delight. "Were you successful?" he asked.

"Yes, my lord," Kal replied. "But we paid a terrible price. Zelig is the hero here and the only reason we succeeded."

Lord Treavor looked over to the gurney as it set itself gently on the floor, but he walked over to Leo, who'd followed it. Gently he placed his hand on Leo's shoulder and whispered what must have been comforting words as Leo nodded to them. Garret turned away to give them some privacy as they had their whispered conversation.

At its conclusion, Leo left his lost friend's side and returned to theirs while Lord Treavor moved to stand before them.

"If you are ready, I am commanded by the Lord Baron to bring you before him the moment you return," Lord Treavor said.

"We are ready," Lord Kalamar replied. "Please lead the way."

As they made their way to the command tent, Garret looked up and noticed it was almost the same time of day they had left. That seemed too much the coincidence.

They arrived to a much smaller group than when the Mallynne priest delivered the prophecy. Either Kalamar had gotten a warning to the archmage or Saa'Vey had informed the high chaplain. It seemed the baron wanted to limit the discussion until he was certain of the news. The talk quieted down as they stepped into the tent and a path parted for their entrance.

Kalamar bowed to Baron Terrence and began. He told the story in a precise and factual manner. He only broke his rhythm to pause and expand on Zelig's brave sacrifice. As any honorable leader, he spoke fully and favorably on the brave deeds of his soldiers and minimized his own contributions. The only change he made was to use truthful, but incomplete, wording concerning the agreement. No one interrupted through the telling and the warlock now stood still and silent allowing them time to absorb his words and consider their questions. It was the high chaplain who spoke first.

"That is an extraordinary report, my lord. And you and your team are to be honored." He paused before continuing. "So the talisman is now safely removed from the orcs' reach?" he asked.

"Yes, Ghan Teague. I've hidden it even from my valiant companions and will continue to guard, relocate and/or improve its defenses as necessary," Kal replied.

"What of this temple god?" Baron Terrance asked. "Is he so willing to let go of this powerful relic? Will he not seek it out once the threat to him is removed?"

"That is entirely possible, Lord Baron and I will not pretend to guess his motives or strategies. I will venture that as the talisman is now known to the warrior god and the healing goddess, it is my hope they will now lend their wisdom and power to its protection and concealment," Kalamar responded and there were several murmurs at this response. Once again, he could not guess whether supportive or dismissive.

General Shay asked a more open question. "What of the orcs themselves? It seems they suffered a grievous defeat. Will they now come seeking revenge or will they disappear back in their holes?"

Baron Terrance surprisingly spoke before Kal could respond. "That is an impossible question. Who can possibly guess their motives? What we do know is the prophecy seemed clear on us getting the talisman before they did, to prevent darkness from destroying our lands and Lord Sylvicheld has indeed accomplished that." He paused for a moment to scan the faces of those present. "The gods asked us to accomplish a great deed and we have done so. We must now trust it is concluded to their satisfaction," he added with finality.

Garret was disquieted by the baron's speech. Their lord had rarely shown any real deference to the gods, so there must be some other reason to declare the matter settled. He just wished he knew what it was.

"My Lord Baron," Kalamar spoke in the silence, "I would wish to discharge my obligations to the gods this evening for their warning and protections. Would you allow me to do so?"

There was an immediate excited noise throughout those in the command tent and the baron gave his ascent. No one would want to miss the opportunity to witness what Kalamar had mentioned as a treasure room. *If he wanted to change the conversation*, Garret thought, *he'd found the perfect way to do so.*

Garret watched with amusement as Kal had to almost shove everyone back to make room. Once satisfied, he knelt down and again produced the intricately carved box. Opening it with a murmured word, the treasure that had appeared to jump into the box now jumped out, standing just as it had in the temple.

After the initial gasps from those gathered, he was alarmed by the open avarice that settled on many of their expressions. It was a kingdom's treasury of gold, statues and jewels; and he was seriously concerned a fight would break out, leading to bloodshed at any moment.

"Archmage," Kalamar called out quickly, "would you be so kind as to divide the treasure into eight equal portions."

The request startled the onlookers and for the moment their curiosity kept anyone from acting rashly. The archmage did as he was asked and everyone was fascinated as he magically moved various pieces of treasure around and eventually created eight distinct piles.

"Ghan Regan," Kalamar said, "as your goddess brought us the warning, would you claim an eighth as thanks?"

The crowd murmured in understanding and were rapt in wondering which pile he would choose. After he made his selection, Kalamar called out.

"Ghan Teague, as we were victorious on the battlefield thanks in no small part to the warrior god's aide, would you now choose an eighth as thanks?"

Those present were now quite engaged in the spectacle before them—the game of dividing the treasure and guessing which each would choose. As a quest, the code of Saa'Vey made clear the treasure belonged to Kal as the leader, and he had sole responsibility for dividing it as he saw fit. If he had wished to keep every coin, nary a word could legally be spoken against him. That he was so generously giving it away was a wonder.

"My Lord Baron," Kalamar called out, "as our rightful leader and the reason we are all gathered on this battlefield, would you now claim an eighth?"

Many present were stunned at the generosity. There was no reason, legal or otherwise, to offer such a king's gift to the baron. Maybe a few choice pieces, but this was unheard of. Whatever Garret might have thought, the baron's expression made clear he thought this was simply his due. He strode around the treasure, appearing for all the world a miser, weighing to a fraction the value of the remaining six piles.

In the end, he chose the one Garret guessed he would. It did not provide him with satisfaction that he'd discerned the correct choice. It was the one most ostentatious with large statues and other vain display pieces. The healing priest had taken a simple pile of mostly coins and the warrior priest took the one that included some unusual weapons.

Garret stopped and stared at Kal as his mind finally guessed the purpose and reasoning for the number of piles. Whether guessed or predetermined, it also seemed clear the archmage knew the reasons and had separated the piles not only by value but by personal qualities of the choosers. That he guessed them so accurately was a bit disconcerting.

"As each here now knows," Kalamar began, "this quest risked not only our lives, but our very souls were in the balance. One of us"—he paused—"paid the ultimate price. The price not only to save our lives but to save the quest and the lives of all in our lands. It is the hero Zelig who made this sacrifice and we cannot say or do enough to repay him. As such, I would ask his best friend, Leopold, to step forward and claim the share Zelig has so deservedly earned so it may be provided to his family in absentia."

Garret forgot for a moment his own growing concern at the direction this was going to appreciate the genius of his friend's careful timing. Sooner or later, it would occur to some that the baron's portion was no bigger than the commoners. That the baron had earned none of it and the commoners risked everything would never be considered. But by choosing Zelig first, by highlighting his heroic sacrifice, the case would be clearly made that every warrior and most every noble could plainly see.

While Garret did not know Zelig before this day, Leopold's choice seemed right to him.

"Leopold," Kal said, "you have lost your best and childhood friend. I would ask that you choose next." Leo bowed low and then quickly made his choice.

"Ghan Mac," Kal continued. "Please," he said simply while indicating the treasure.

His friend Mac, had obviously guessed the nature of Kalamar's thoughts and wasn't going to give in without a fight.

"My Lord Kalamar," he began. "I am honored beyond words at your generous offer but I cannot accept. The vows of my order prohibit me from acquiring or holding any type of wealth. I serve at my god's pleasure and wealth holds no value to me." He finished this humbly and Garret knew he meant it. He also knew that Mac seemed pleased he could force Kal to keep the larger share he surely deserved.

Kalamar however, was grinning as he replied, "Ghan Mac, then you are welcome to dispose of your portion as proscribed by your holy order. Please." He was again pointing at the treasure piles.

Garret worked hard to keep his own smile hidden. He knew full well Mac's quiet pride and humility and was delighted Kal found a way around it. Mac deserved this as much as anyone.

"Captain Garret Walker," Kal said still wearing his smile. "Please."

He knew he had no graceful way out. So rather than give him any satisfaction, he quietly walked over and chose "his" pile. There were only two left. The one the archmage clearly knew he would want included a beautiful pearl-inlaid bow and several long spears among the other vast riches. It's the one he would have chosen had he gone first and Kal and the archmage knew it. That left the remaining pile to Kal, the pile that included several gold and silver books.

It seemed others had finally figured out the cleverness of the archmage as they broke into applause. For his own part, Garret grimaced, as having this kind of wealth would only lead to trouble.

Chapter 18

the dirty work

Ormand loaded his carry strap with wood from the storage pile and started making his delivery rounds. The sun had set long ago and his chores were almost complete. It was grunt work but when infiltrating a castle, you took the opportunities you found. He'd been working as "Schmit" for almost five weeks as the previous laborer had conveniently "disappeared." It happened all the time and no one gave it a second thought.

Since he'd done this type of work before, it was easy enough to blend in and quickly become an invisible part of castle life. While he hated tolerating the beatings and violence, it did provide him an excellent vantage point to gather the intelligence he needed for his current job.

No one at the top of society ever paid attention to those at the bottom unless the work didn't get done. They considered them beneath their notice and therefore spoke far too casually when they were around. Most servants knew more about what was going on than their masters and were happy to share it with anyone who'd listen. The difference however was, most were too scared to use it to their advantage. Ormand had no such inhibition.

Plodding his way across the main wall entrance, he stumbled and fell hard, spilling his woodpile.

"You sneak the wine cellars?" Carl laughed. Carl was one of the guards on duty tonight.

"Lazy sod-loving maggot!" Hanz cursed as he came over. "Pick that up and get your arse back to work." He added a few kicks to drive home the point.

"Yes, Captain, quick, quick I go." Ormand whizzed as he scrambled to dodge the blows and pick up the spilled firewood. Hanz wasn't a real captain, but it seemed all the mean ones loved to be called captain when their actual captain wasn't around.

"Just get back to work!" Hanz said as he kicked dirt in his face. Feeling satisfied, he strutted back to Carl to continue his bored watch.

Ormand briefly leaned against the door as he struggled to lift the wood back over his shoulder. As he did so, he placed a very special stick on the door latch brace. Muttering, he quickly shuffled away to the fading laughs of the soldiers on duty. *You won't be laughing much longer*, he thought with pleasure.

"Schmit" carefully finished his assigned chores. He'd learned long ago that acting like a spy would get you killed. But if you put your "real" work first, you would quickly be forgotten and then all kinds of opportunities would present themselves.

Acting far more hurt than he was from his earlier beating, Schmit stumbled again. He fell beside a well not far from the main gate where he'd left his stick. It obviously wasn't just a stick but instead was a powerful fireball just waiting for him to release it and destroy the gate. The gate had to be destroyed because his employer had assault soldiers in the fruit trees just outside, waiting to invade.

Ormand glanced up in the sky to confirm against the moon what he already knew. It was time. Still playing his role, he leaned over and wretched as if spitting something up. In between the hacks and spitting, he spoke the activation rune.

Boom! The world exploded in fire as not only the door but much of the overhanging wall vanished in a choking cloud of dust. He let the concussive force send him smashing to the ground so no one could possibly suspect him. He scrambled away as he heard screams from within, but also the shouts from the Lord of Ormsburg's forces outside.

The grand master watched as the confused and disorganized Volker defenders were quickly overrun by Ormsburg soldiers. He was waiting for something and finally saw it. Court Wizard Waldemar ran out of a side door with a couple of soldiers for protection. The court wizard scanned the scene and strode over to a place of his liking for a counterattack.

It was a good place, Ormand thought. Relatively isolated, but with a wide, open view to launch fireballs or lightning and crush the still crowded invaders. *There was just one small problem*, Ormand thought with a grin.

Scrambling again to a hidden vantage point behind the court wizard, Ormand picked up a small shattered board and hurled it at the wizard. Not with his arm—he'd not only miss but be seen making such a bold gesture—but with a simple second-circle spell that hurled it faster than an arrow and with as much force as a ballista.

It had taken a bit of practice to master this spell, but Ormand had spent years at it. The missile struck with his customary accuracy, almost ripping the head off the doomed wizard. The guards fled as they realized, without the wizard, they had no chance of survival.

Without the wizard's aide, the defending forces were quickly routed into the palace itself. *It wouldn't be long now*, he thought. Ormand stood and dusted himself off before casually walking over to Waldemar's corpse. He flipped it over and quickly saw the necklace he needed. He was almost gentle as he lifted it over the nearly headless body and stuffed it in his pocket.

Standing again, he turned to watch as Lord Liesel Ormsburg, his three sons and their personal guards strode into the main yard to claim their prize. Lord Liesel nodded graciously when he caught the grand master in his gaze. Ormand bowed in return. He hurried over as Lord Liesel beckoned him.

"A great victory, my lord!" he said while in his mind he went over all his options in case of treachery. He could teleport away or turn everyone and everything around him to cinders, depending on how things went. Sometimes people considered him a loose end that needed to be cleaned up.

Lord Liesel was beaming as he looked around and said, "Yes, yes, it is, my friend. I planned it, but you were crucial in carrying it out and I will not forget that. Your payment is outside as we agreed, but join us in the main hall when you have a moment. I have a treat for you," he finished expansively.

Ormand bowed low in thanks and humbly backed away. He didn't instantly suspect a trap; he always expected a trap. Only after Lord Liesel and his party were out of sight did he turn and head outside to the agreed-upon location. Using well-practiced stealth and his vast knowledge of spells, he determined there were no hidden assailants and there were no hidden traps on the chest of gold. Opening it, he found the agreed-upon thousand pounds sterling in gold. Without wasting another moment, he teleported himself and his gold home.

*****

Grand Master Ormand stepped through the main palace doors to a celebration in full swing. After returning home, he'd cleaned himself, scanned the palace of former Lord Truman Volker for tricks or traps and then teleported back for the other treasure he'd requested when he accepted this job.

He doubted he'd have any interest in the treat promised him and had considered just getting his reward and leaving. But he told himself, it was unwise to directly anger a lord and much of his business was working for such people. So expecting the worst, he headed to the main hall.

The dead were strewn everywhere. Not just soldiers, defending or otherwise, but servants caught in the melee as well. The screams and wailing coming from the main hall told him what was happening long before he crossed the threshold. Every woman and girl they could find was being raped and despoiled.

As he continued to Lord Liesel at the far end, he could see a few unlucky ones were set aside and guarded against the festivities. Closer he confirmed his suspicions. They were the pretty ones and would be sold into slavery. Virgins commanded a high price and noble virgins could make even a lord extremely wealthy.

Bowing low, he politely said, "My lord. I have come as requested. How can I be of service?"

"Ahh, there you are, my old friend." Lord Liesel was clearly in a festive mood with his extraordinary victory. Lord Gustav of Lacklly over a decade ago had been the last to so successfully raid and destroy a rival. He was still getting invitations from that triumph.

"Yes, my friend, yes, what a most triumphant day we've had. Yes, yes…" he trailed off.

"Reward, I've got another reward for you, my wizardly friend. See?" Liesel sloshed most of the wine from his cup as he pointed past his entourage to something in the corner.

"Out of the way, you fools," he said with a laugh. "Let the wizard view his prize!"

The indicated fools, which include his youngest son, quickly stumbled away from the direction of their lord's unsteady hand. Without the offending persons blocking his view, he could now see his prize. It was Lady Winola Volker. No doubt now, widow Volker. Standing under guard with an expression of pure hatred on her face, she was forced to watch the destruction of her life.

"My lord," Ormand began but was cut off.

"If I remember correctly, she had you beaten several years ago. Isn't that so?" he asked with a nasty leer.

"Yes, my lord," Ormand replied cautiously. "She accused me of looking queerly at her daughter. The fact I wasn't even in the building during the incident didn't seem to matter."

"Yes!" Lord Liesel shouted. "That's it. I knew there was some terrible injustice I was setting right." Ormand chuckled inwardly at the idea that anything Liesel did was about serving justice.

"Take her, my friend! Take her. Treat her as she so rightly deserves!" he said with a giggle.

Ormand didn't need to look around to know exactly what was expected. He also knew that all nobles stuck together and him being a commoner created a very delicate situation.

"My lord, I am honored beyond measure at such a priceless gift. But"—and here he had to be very careful; disagreeing with a noble was almost always a death sentence—"shouldn't someone more *worthy* enforce your good justice?" he asked as humble as he could manage.

"Nonsense! My friend." Lord Liesel giggled and Ormand knew it was useless to resist further. This wasn't about rewarding Ormand; this was about punishing Winola. She must have personally insulted Ormsburg so grievously he was replying in one of the worst ways possible.

It was a waste of his time, but he had no more objections to use without insulting Lord Liesel. As he walked over to Lady Winola, her expression made clear she'd heard every word and knew exactly what was about to occur.

"How dare you, insolent dog! Don't you lay a hand on me!" her threats became a running litany even before he reached her. He could hear Liesel and his cronies laughing hysterically behind him. Winola screamed as he grabbed her by the hair and dragged her to the nearest table. She was flailing her arms wildly but ineffectually, so he smashed her face into the table to end her resistance. The shouts of encouragement from his onlookers only grew louder in approval.

Not wanting to waste any more of his precious time on this foolery, he quickly ripped open the back of her dress and shifted his clothing aside. As he was finishing up, he glanced to the officer on his left doing the same thing to one of the better-looking servant girls. The pathetic leer on his face only made Ormand shake his head at the stupidity of it all. There were so many more important things to focus one's time on, but here Lord Liesel had his entire army wasting away on this debauchery.

He looked at the lady as he stepped back. She was weeping and pounding her fist in impotent rage. Another soldier rushed in to take his place. He turned to see Lord Liesel and his henchmen cheering the new man on. *At least*, he thought, *it makes all these fools predictable*. He quickly walked away.

Lord Liesel didn't even notice as he bowed and left the room to continue onto his real reason for returning. Master Waldemar may have been a fool but he was no idiot. In his library was a tome for harnessing the undead, not just making bone golems but actually linking and controlling self-animated undead. In the right hands, it was invaluable and the right hands were his own.

Waldemar's shields on the palace walls might have been weak, but those around his personal quarters were quite impressive. He reached into his pocket and removed the necklace charm he'd taken from the corpse. He smiled as the wards opened and he walked right in. Ignoring the sitting rooms, he hurried to the left where the library and study were.

Something slammed into his back and he spun in rage as pain seared his nerves. He stared in indignation at the pale-faced young apprentice staring back at him. Fear and determination equally vied for control of her features and she stepped back as he stepped forward. Two quick steps and the back of his hand sent her crashing into first the wall and then the floor.

How dare an apprentice interfere with a grand master? She turned over to face him and fear was now in complete control. *She needed a lesson*, he thought as he stood over her. Her eyes widened in panic as she now realized what was coming next. As he stood, reveling in that panic, a small voice asked if he was really any different from those in the main hall after all.

Chapter 19

maybe good isn't so bad

Vayden shifted the focus of his scrying spell and smiled. Not because of what he saw but because he could cast it at all. He'd spent most of his life magically crippled, but now, now his power burned bright inside his soul. He briefly concentrated and the spells he knew flared like fire in his mind. They were primed for his will to release. He shifted the scrying focus again just for the pure joy of it. No more would he have to…

His vision briefly caught someone who shouldn't be there. He redirected the focus in the direction he thought the target was walking. Sure enough, it was QuickKnife Quennell, a vicious member of the Red Rover gang in Tanners, a district in southeast Harrisburg. Quennell was far from his stomping grounds to be on Marble Street near Westgate. Not really thinking it through but flush with his new sense of power, he released the scrying spell and rushed out of his home to follow QuickKnife.

It was only a few blocks and didn't take long to spot him. This was a poorer area and Quennell wasn't making any effort to blend in. While Vayden wasn't a master thief like his best friend Coyne, he'd been surveilling people his whole life and set himself to the task.

One of the first rules was to never match your mark's speed and direction. You will quickly fall into their rhythm, giving yourself away, especially if they make sudden changes. You need to keep your own pace that just happens to take you in the same direction they're going. It's difficult, but Vayden had years of experience.

Another rule was to never focus on your target. Whether from natural gifts or experience, many people develop a sixth sense about being observed. You have to keep shifting your focus to things around your mark. His new master Kalamar, said the same thing. People will often sense they're being scried if you focus on them. Both the magic itself and the attention will sooner or later set off their natural alarms.

QuickKnife was heading into a less populated area and it would soon become impossible to follow someone of his skill. Making his best guess of the area he might be going, Vayden pictured in his mind an occasional client on the other side of this low-traffic area. He might lose him of course, but it would be far worse to be caught following.

His new course did cause him to lose sight several times but as he was traversing the most desolate part of Rat's Quarry, he caught sight of him going down Blair Ave and into a corner row house. Vayden was thankfully already going the same way, so he could simply continue on past.

As he got closer, his personal alarms flared as he noticed a seated man leaning against the wall of the house QuickKnife just entered. With a large workman's hat covering his head, he appeared to doze on the ground but Vayden had no doubt he was being studied as he walked up the street.

Vayden's mind raced as the list of options shrunk with every step he took. The smart choice would be to keep walking. He was forty feet away and only had a few steps left to decide. The problem was, someone in there needed his help and was pleading for it. He didn't know how, he just knew.

All casters learned spell work while standing up or kneeling comfortably. This made sense because casting required a great deal of focus and an even internal energy flow. Most never got themselves in dangerous situations, so as a general rule, this worked well. His first master had disagreed and so did his new one. Some things would always require stillness, but sometimes, particularly with lower-level spells, the rules could be bent. He began murmuring the runes to a sleep spell.

At twenty feet, he turned his head away from the lookout so as not to arouse suspicion. At ten paces, he turned back and released the final rune. He watched as the figure slumped further against the wall, but thankfully didn't fall over. Nodding to him and hoping to appear just giving a greeting, he stepped past him, opened the door and walked inside.

Relief flooded his system as there was no one in the main room. Fear quickly returned as he realized what an impossible situation he was in. He could still flee but the call for help seemed louder, like an incessant whisper. Quickly deciding, he cast one of the three spells he'd learned from his first master.

Message spells were generally to and from sorcerers. The effect was similar to someone whispering in your ear. But if you knew someone well and with a bit of practice, you could teach a non-caster to recognize the message and listen. He sent a quick message to his best friend. "QuickKnife in home on Blair Ave and Lake St. Help!"

Hoping his luck continued, he cast a spell he'd just learned from his new master. He let out a sigh of relief as the invisibility glamour wrapped around him. It wouldn't fool everyone but if he was generally quiet and still while staying in shadows, he had a chance.

He spent a few moments poking his head around doorways and discovered the main floor was momentarily empty. He heard creaking from upstairs and thought to go up but his mind said, *Down*, so down he went. The stairs went farther underground than would be normal. Vayden got chills down his spine as he heard voices murmuring when he reached the bottom.

It was a great storeroom that clearly went under several of the houses on the block. A smuggler's lair was his first thought and business was good. It was filled bottom to top. Crates stacked high and shelves brimming with, no doubt, stolen goods of every kind. Lanterns were evenly placed on the walls to provide just enough light to see by, but thankfully far enough apart they created long shadows.

He'd seen enough and needed to get out and get help. He placed his foot on the first step and his luck finally failed. It creaked and the voices stopped. He was about to race up the stairs when a voice cried in his head.

"Help me!" a small childlike voice echoed in his mind.

He was so startled he froze. Bewildered, an image appeared in his mind. He saw three men separate from each other and start walking through a maze of goods and shelves. His mind stuttered as he quickly realized he was seeing this room but from up high in a corner.

He recognized QuickKnife, but not the other two. He fled, but not up. QuickKnife was coming directly toward the stairs, so as best he could, he headed for another corner to buy some time. The images continued as if he was up in the corner watching the scene play out. He stumbled a bit as he tried to get used to seeing two different things at once.

QuickKnife paused at the noise, but one of the others changed direction to cut him off. He started casting a firebolt spell as fast as he could. It was disconcerting to see multiple images and he hoped he was timing it correctly.

Vayden turned the corner the same moment his closest tracker did. They were almost nose to nose as he finished the spell and the bolts slammed into the man before him. The shock on his hunter's face as he died; seeing it so close was a gut-wrenching experience. Time seemed to slow as the body collapsed to the ground.

"Run," the voice shouted, and he did, racing to another corner. He was desperately trying to stifle his panting as the fear and exertion fought to gain footholds.

Taking deep breaths, he regained some measure of control. He focused on the other image and realized QuickKnife was out of sight. The third fellow was now moving cautiously along the outside wall in his direction. Vayden squatted down low and cast another firebolt. It was difficult but he slowed the cadence as the other man was taking his time in the hunt. The second man jumped around the corner, hoping to surprise Vayden, but instead received five bolts in the neck and face. A gargled shout sounded before he hit the floor dead.

Vayden moved one more time. QuickKnife appeared in the images again. It seemed he was taking no chances and had climbed on top of the shelves and crates to ambush his prey. It was clear he knew where Vayden was as he slowly but surely headed his direction.

Vayden began another spell, not a firebolt but a second-circle acid globe attack. It was more powerful and took longer, but he hoped it would be strong enough to finish the job. He had no illusions about his chances if Quennell got close enough with his knives.

His nerves were fraying. He could see with his eyes the shelf top he expected his attacker to leap over. The image in his mind separately showed that same attacker methodically making his way over to the still and scared form standing in the corner, bracing for the attack. He watched as QuickKnife bunched himself for the leap. He could obviously hear the chanting no matter how low Vayden mumbled it.

Everything happened at once. QuickKnife Quennell leaped over the last shelf and came hurdling down, with both knives ready to sink death into his body. Vayden rushed the last two runes and hurled the acid globes at his attacker. As they hit, he realized he would die from his own attack if touched by any of the acid spray. He tried to jump out of the way, but only managed to fall on his face as QuickKnife crashed to the ground with a scream. Scrambling to his feet, he rushed another firebolt. As he reached the finial rune, he realized Quennell wasn't moving. His bolts slammed into a corpse.

Harsh breathing dominated the room. Relief flooded his system as he realized it was his own. He'd managed to survive what, now looking back, should have been his death. He started to shake as the energy rush from his earlier terror fled. He leaned back against the wall to keep himself upright.

"A little help!" the small voice said in his mind.

Startled, he glanced around. His mind finally connected the pieces, and he looked around and up to where the images had been coming from. A small pair of red eyes reflected the lamplight and as he squinted, he could just make out a cage of some kind hanging from the ceiling. He shifted his gaze and found what he sought—a tied-off rope leading up.

Slowly he walked over to the rope end. He was exhausted and his body didn't want to listen to any more commands. It took a few moments, but he finally untied the knot and lowered the cage to the ground.

He gasped as inside was a tiny dragon. Idiot! He berated himself. Not a dragon but a dragonette. Which, he mused, was just as startling. Dragonettes were almost as rare as dragons and would be used by some sorcerers as familiars.[37] They were worth a fortune to the right buyer. Dragonettes were intelligent and spoke telepathically among themselves and with those they deemed worthy. They didn't have a breath weapon but did have a spiked tail to inject a sleeping poison into their prey.

"You're the one calling to me as I walked by," he said, making the final connections.

"Yes, now will you let me out? I saved your life," he retorted.

"But only after endangering it in the first place," Vayden shot back.

The dragonette didn't seem the least regretful as he said, "Would you leave a person caged and trapped in here?"

"No," he replied thoughtfully. "I would not. Stand away from the door." It was locked, and he wasn't going to go searching for the key. He once again cast his acid globe spell while being careful to have it splatter away from the cage, not inside it. The lock dissolved along with parts of the door. The dragonette quickly shot out and up, circling in the shadows above.

"Thank you!" it shouted down in happiness. "My name is Burnt Toe by the way." It said by way of introduction.

"Vayden," he replied

"Someone's coming!" Burnt Toe said and disappeared into a corner. He could guess where because images reappeared in his mind, this time of the staircase bottom. He watched in dread. He

---

[37] A familiar is a creature linked to its witch or wizard. The most popular in common imagination is the witch with her cat; however, they can be almost any domesticated animal. Cats and dogs, birds and bats, snakes and lizards. Rare ones with far more intelligence can be found. Dragonettes are one of these. Imps are not true familiars but will play the role for the opportunity to capture the mage's soul. The benefits are significant. The mage can see and hear through the senses of the familiar. They also gain stronger mental powers, helping with the number of spells they can cast. The downside is, if they are killed (not die naturally), their master can be violently sick and/or mentally unstable for weeks.

was exhausted. Casting in battle was quite different than casting in the comfort of your home and he was not used to such exertions. The flames of the spells in his mind seemed low and flickering.

Relief made him cry out as he saw who stepped off the staircase.

"Coyne," he called, "am I happy to see you!"

Coyne was of medium build and medium height, which supposedly was ideal for his line of work. His problem was his face. He was handsome to the point of beautiful and no one could forget it or his flowing golden locks once they saw him. He was the one who taught Vayden how to disguise himself, as he needed such skills to ply his trade.

At the moment, he was expressionless as he studied everything, a slow side-to-side movement of his head as he memorized everything he saw.

"What kind of mess do I have to save you from this time?" he finally said with a smile. Two other members of his South Side Thieves guild stepped off the stairs as he spoke. They quickly spread out into the room, searching everything.

"Save me!" he bantered back. "What on earth gives you that idea?"

"Your desperate plea for help!" he shot back. "You're not so addled you don't remember sending it, are you?"

"I might have sent you an invitation," he replied carefully.

"Hmm," his friend said gravely. "I'm sure I remember a squeal for HELP!" he continued with a laugh.

Vayden laughed as well. "Very well," he began, "I may have been a bit nervous." He graciously allowed. He then proceeded to tell the story. By the time he finished, Coyne's two partners had finished their search of the basement. Apparently, there was a small tunnel at the far end. It led to the basement of a fence on Brick Lane. They also confirmed QuickKnife, Breaker Brad and Slow Coach were dead. Vayden hadn't heard of the other two; obviously, his friend had.

"I'm amazed you're still alive," he said with a tinge of respect. "You've stepped into it this time though. I don't envy you talking your way out of it, with your new speech problem," he finished with a grin.

Vayden's grin turn a bit sour. His speech problem was his new master's code of conduct he'd agreed to live his life by. Most weren't really a problem for him, as he didn't run around, beating and murdering people and he didn't steal stuff even with his best friend's occupation. There were two however, that directly interfered with life as he knew it. The first was bribing. He'd never taken a bribe, but that was only because he wasn't important enough to be bribed, *but* he'd certainly paid his share of them to stay in business.

The other and most difficult, was lying. Everybody lied, and he'd gone round and round with his master over this one. Kalamar had simply smiled politely and said he'd be amazed at his new life once he "kicked" the habit. People would trust him more and he'd gain new business where before they wouldn't consider dealing with him.

This would be his first major test. As a good person, he would have to report this. As a best friend, he couldn't tell them the whole truth. How could he possibly explain calling a master thief to save him? *Ridiculous*, he thought, but he'd sworn an oath. And the very powers that had saved his life today came from the man he swore that oath to.

He sighed as his friend grinned at the predicament.

"Don't hurt yourself laughing," he said sourly to his friend. "How much time do you need?"

"For what?" Coyne replied innocently.

"To take whatever you want from this place before I call the authorities?" he snapped back. "Did you hit your head walking down the stairs?" he asked sarcastically.

"What!" Coyne mocked with a grin. "Give us a half hour," he continued seriously. "But you have a bigger problem. Go upstairs before you call them."

"What now?" he said, shaking his head and started walking to the stairs. He'd forgotten about his "new" friend who decided he better leave also. Instead of just flying up the stairs, though, he decided to startle Vayden along with everyone else by landing on his shoulder.

"No!" Vayden shouted as Coyne's blade was already out and coming down to kill the monster attacking his friend.

"It's all right!" he shouted with hands outstretched. "He's with me," he said into the shocked expressions all around.

"What is that thing?" Coyne asked finally as he put away his short sword.

"A dragonette," Vayden replied. "It was a prisoner here and I'm setting it free."

"It's not the only one," his friend said cryptically as Vayden walked up the stairs.

Back on the main level, he couldn't help but notice all the blood on the floor. Fearing the worst, he followed the drag marks to the kitchen. There were five corpses thrown in a pile, including the lookout he'd put to sleep. Obviously, Coyne and crew were taking no chances. Shaking his head, he headed upstairs.

It was quickly apparent that, just like the basement, the top floor had been expanded through several of the other row houses, leaving only the main floor separate. After a moment's consideration, this made sense to Vayden as it would provide a veneer of normalcy to anyone observing from the street.

The first rooms were sleeping quarters and a dining, card-playing area. An interrupted game was strewn about. There was not a coin to be found, he noted wryly. Vayden took his time looking around so he could run out the sandglass on Coyne's one-half hour.

It was only after opening the last door that Vayden realized what his friend was talking about. It was a prison. Four cages to a side and a larger one against the far wall. There were six people in those cages, but only five were standing to stare at him. The last was laying on the floor, staring at nothing. He looked at each and they at him. He tried to guess what expressions rippled across their faces. Was he a new tormentor or perhaps a buyer? Was the monster on his shoulder some new terror? It was an impossible task.

In the back cage was a giant of a man, clearly a soldier by trade. Vayden made his way to him.

"All of you," he began addressing everyone, "have nothing to fear from me. The men who held you captive are dead." The collective signs and sobs were difficult to bear. He could only imagine what tortures were inflicted and why.

"Can you tell me who your tormentors were and why they captured you?" he asked.

The soldier looked from the creature on his shoulder and back to his face. "The only name that matters is QuickKnife Quennell. He's the sadistic leader of these happy killers. The reason we're all here is because he decided to move into this area and set up shop. The girls are here to keep his men company. The rest are here as punishment for standing up to him." His voice was low and hard. Like many soldiers, he spoke quickly and to the point.

"Do you know where the keys are?" he asked.

"The wall behind you" was the reply and Vayden retrieved them. As he began opening cells, he said, "It's quite a mess downstairs, so I'd ask that we stick together in going outside. I'll send for a healing priest to tend any wounds you have."

The soldier picked up the dead girl and they all waited. Clearly, they weren't going to leave her behind. Vayden led the way downstairs. It had the feel of a funeral procession, which seemed appropriate.

As he stepped outside and onto the street, he wondered at how bright and cheerful the sun and sky looked. It seemed wrong that it wasn't rain and storms after the horror experienced inside. Pedestrian traffic had picked up a bit as it was now midday.

Many kept their heads down and walked on by. This was a rough neighborhood and no good came from getting involved in the affairs of others. A few did stop and he asked that the constable be called, as there was murder in the house.

A boy went running off and thankfully, it wasn't a long wait before the local constable with a few assistants arrived at the scene. He told a simple story. Simple, his master said, was always best.

He'd been heading to see a business associate on Wafer Lane. As he walked past this home, he heard a cry for help. He headed inside and downstairs, quickly realizing he'd made a terrible mistake.

He was attacked by three men. He recognized one of them as QuickKnife Quennell. The call for help had been from Burnt Toe, the creature sitting on his shoulder. With its magical help, he'd been able to survive the assault and defeat the attackers.

After pulling his scattered wits together, he'd gone upstairs and found the prisoners currently standing behind him. With all the blood on the main floor he realized something else must be going on, he brought them out and called for help.

His story was all true but it obviously left out several details. The constable clearly thought so as well. Ordering them to stay put and leaving his men to make sure, he went inside to see for himself.

While the constable was inside, three important things occurred. A healing priestess arrived and began tending the wounded. A crowd gathered and the families of those kidnapped rejoiced with much weeping and happy tears. And finally, Granville Ouibrook, Lord and Protector of Westside District, arrived with a full entourage of knights. The unofficially named Rat's Quarry resided within his district, and he'd come to learn what the fuss was about.

The constable stepped outside just as Lord Granville rode up, demanding answers. He bowed to his lord and began with what he knew. Eight bodies of violent criminals, including the notorious QuickKnife Quennell, were inside. One local girl was dead outside. At this point, all the locals started shouting about hostages and kidnappings. The former prisoners added their tales to the confusing mix. It was quickly becoming a riot in the making.

"You!" Lord Granville shouted, pointing at Vayden and temporarily silencing the crowd. "Who are you and how are you involved in all this?" he demanded. Vayden had stayed quiet, but he clearly stood out as not belonging. His clothing was different, although not particularly better. And the dragonette on his shoulder surely had something to do with his inability to blind in.

He bowed, introduced himself and told the same story as before. A couple of locals had seen him walking earlier and chimed in with their supporting versions. The former prisoners did the same.

"Is that what your investigation found inside?" Lord Granville demanded of the constable.

"My lord. The notorious murderer, QuickKnife Quennell, is indeed dead inside, along with his two henchmen. All slain by magic in the basement. There are five men piled up in the kitchen killed with blades. Two of those are also wanted men. The others I am unfamiliar with.

"The basement is filled with what appears to be stolen goods but has been ransacked this very day. It was clearly a group of men. I cannot say one way or the other who they were or when they arrived. Only that they are gone."

Someone shouted from the crowd, "They arrived after the sorcerer. I saw the pack of them rush the house and then flee." And that set off the crowd again.

Lord Granville had clearly had enough. "SILENCE!" he shouted. "Enough! Wanted murderers, kidnappers and thieves are now brought to justice. As for the others, it was probably a rival gang watching for an opportunity for revenge. They'll get their due soon enough. For now, let us be thankful for the safe return of family and friends and sleep soundly knowing justice has prevailed!"

His knights knew their duty and took up a cheer, which was picked up by the crowd. Whatever additional questions the constable had, he would never raise them. His lord had spoken and it was done. Evil men were put down and no one was questioning how this evil was allowed in his area of responsibility. It was a victory for everyone and he nodded graciously to Master Vayden.

*****

Vayden was weary like he'd never felt before as he plodded up to his door. It was a deep-in-the-bones, worn-out feeling from the day's activities. He opened the door and Burnt Toe shot inside, evaluating his new domain. Apparently, he'd decided to stay for a while.

He turned to his other new house guests. Siusan had no home to return to and the family where she previously worked had hired another during her absence. Bringing up the rear was the soldier named Mckile and he'd asked to stay as a bodyguard in payment of his debt. If Vayden was going to go around doing foolhardy feats like today, *Mckile could come in handy*, he thought.

Shaking his head, he closed the door. Home at last.

Chapter 20

lessons

Garret and his men on that fateful orc attack were dismissed the very evening of the successful quest. It had been devastating to him. Being a soldier was his only ambition in life. As such, he would be eternally grateful his friend, Kal, had needed and hired him to be captain of his guard. He would be lost as anything other than a soldier.

The official reason for their release was to reward them for their heroic actions in protecting the barony. Each of his soldiers had been given one hundred pounds sterling, which with care, could certainly provide a living for the remainder of their lives. Since they were also capable of finding other work, they would probably live quite well. He didn't think it right, but at least his men were properly seen to.

But as Garret looked across the table at his friends, he could not believe what he was now hearing. The baron was reducing his army by over half. Over two thousand men were to be dismissed from service right before winter. No service bonus, nothing. It was simply inexcusable.

Many had no other skills, as they'd been soldiers their entire lives. Winter was when most paying work stopped anyway, so they would be unable to find anything that could keep them fed through the snows. It was a death sentence for all who didn't have families capable of providing for them until next spring.

The reason for doing so was equally impossible to believe. Over the last four years, Baron Eddington had been training soldiers and increasing his army to counter the threat warned about in the dreams and omens of the priests from various orders; dreams of darkness and disaster coming.

The baron and his council had now concluded the threat was over with the successful completion of the quest. Everything would return to before and the large expenditures directed to martial needs would be redirected elsewhere. As the priest themselves had made no such declaration, the real reason must be something else.

"It is my belief," Kal began quietly, "the real reason is to get rid of my master, the high wizard and then, by extension, get rid of me." The words fell heavy in the room. All three of them thought it, but none had wanted to say it aloud.

"The court wizard's position," he continued, "was created to deal with the growing threats to the baron and his court. If those are now over..." he let the question hang in the room.

"That is true. But part of that threat was the spying being done by mages from other lands," Mac said. "Even if they believe the official stated reason, that threat still remains," he finished firmly.

"True," Kal began. "But that threat can now be dealt with by Adept Bedelia. She and the other two mages can maintain the shields that my master created. They are not experienced enough to handle an escalation, but they can certainly continue the status quo."

Garret spoke for the first time, "And let's not forget the witch Amanda moved to Stormlake last year. Many of the nobles opposed to Kal and the archmage are very supportive of her. As a mistress of magic, they could see her as a backstop if things did escalate."

"Unfortunately true, my friend. I had not considered that," Mac said glumly.

"I think we are leading ourselves astray with this line of inquiry," Kal injected. "My master is quite capable of handling himself against any moves the counselors might make. The immediate concern is two thousand well-trained soldiers starving and angry at their mistreatment. I can't just hire them or even feed them, as that would constitute raising an army. Perhaps, even, that's their plan. Get me to do something they can describe as treason. I've certainly been known in the past to make rash decisions." He finished with a grim smile.

Both Mac and Garret chuckled. The adoption of Lily came immediately to mind.

"I had been about to suggest sending them out to Wildwood and I would personally pay for their supply from my newfound wealth, but that would be seen exactly as treason. Raising an army to attack the baron would be the battle cry," Garret said with disgust.

After some moments of silence, Kal said, "I could hire as many as one hundred for additional guards and such without raising too much suspicion. I suspect other friendly lords will see the same problem we do and, combined, could add a few hundred more." He paused before continuing.

"Those lords who dislike me will instantly suspect something nefarious. Possibly, they will hire as many as they can to counter what they suspect we are up to. Since many of them couldn't meet their noble requirements at the muster just called, that could be as many as five hundred more hired for the winter. Unfortunately, that still leaves one thousand men and their families hungry this winter."

"You would see those men hired by such hateful and petty lords?" Garret asked in surprised disgust.

Kal remained calm as he replied, "I would see the pettiness of those lords turned against them to feed good and deserving families."

Garret shook his head in apology. "I'm sorry Kal. You're right and I shouldn't have spoken so quickly."

Kal said, "I'm not offended, my friend. If you reacted that way, knowing me as well as you do, what chance do those lords have of seeing through this and reacting differently than we expect?" He finished with a clever smile.

"None at all, I hope, but this certainly makes my head hurt. Give me an honest enemy any day," Mac said, and they laughed.

"So what do we do for the remaining thousand?" Garret asked.

They were all quietly lost in their own thoughts until Kal chuckled.

"We build something big!" he said with a grin.

"They've harassed you with everything you've tried. What could you possibly build requiring that many men that they wouldn't stop?" Garret replied.

"Your university!" Mac interjected. "The baron is your biggest supporter and you have a waiting list a mile long. Every noble and merchant has been begging you to expand the student acceptance list." He practically bounced with excitement.

"Exactly. The expansion won't be ready this year but by next fall, with that many men working, I could probably triple the size of the acceptance class," Kal replied expansively. "And as you will recall, many nobles were quite distraught when I used my magic to construct buildings. So this time, I will be respecting their sensibilities and using the local labor force," he finished with a wolfish grin.

They all laughed. The nobles' previous complaints would be turned against them.

"Didn't you say you liked the stone recently discovered in the quarries south of the Stonewash?" Mac asked Kal thoughtfully.

"I did indeed," Kal replied. "That's an excellent suggestion," he finished, nodding to his friend.

Garret didn't follow that and said so.

Kal replied, "Because they will be in far-friendlier lands than the quarries of the north. It will be a far-better place for them to build new lives with their families and the work will strengthen our natural allies."

Garret nodded in understanding and said, "I am certainly glad you two understand politics as it makes my head spin."

"Nonsense," Kal retorted. "You're completely capable of understanding. You've just chosen not to."

"Politics use the same laws as war, my young friend," Mac explained. "The armaments and battlefield are different, but the strategies are exactly the same."

Garret was very thoughtful as he considered those words.

*****

Grand Master Ormand finished his last spell and looked around. He stood in the trees at the edge of Trent. The hamlet was a broken collection of hovels, where everyone knew better than to pay attention to anything. It was ideal for having a meeting with someone you didn't trust. In his case, that was everyone. He chuckled to himself.

The inn—it didn't have a name—had four entrances, which was also a benefit. Choosing one, he stepped inside and looked around. A serving bar and rickety tables widely spaced apart, were all the furnishings. The owner, a chubby man with a much-broken face, was behind the bar, using a dirty rag to wipe a mug. His wife and two children were at the fireplace, throwing what one hoped were meats and vegetables into a cooking pot for what might pass as stew.

Three tables were occupied. The closest were locals, big, dirty farmhands, no doubt drowning their useless lives with what passed as ale. Far to the left was a man being serviced by the woman in his lap. Ormand couldn't help but notice the slight magical aura she had. As this hamlet was not far from Pack 11 grounds, this wouldn't be unusual. The better-looking students would be whored out to gain coins and secrets from clientele. Since those so volunteered usually received better treatment and more food scraps, everyone benefited from the system.

The third table, far from the other two, held his colleague. Full Master Medwin was the Fifth of Pack 112 located far to the east. They'd developed a professional respect over twenty years of buying and trading information, to their mutual benefit. Medwin had called this particular meeting as he'd come across something of value to Ormand. *The questions would be what's it actually worth and how much he'd part with it for,* Ormand thought.

Medwin nodded and he sat down. It wasn't ideal, but it could have been worse. There were only two chairs. Medwin's was mostly to the wall. He slid his slightly to the side, but not enough to cause alarm.

Medwin smiled at the move, but said, "Welcome, old friend." Neither thought of the other as anything but rivals. Since they'd known each other longer than anyone else, it'd become a joke between them.

"Thank you, my friend. How's your ale?" Ormand asked politely.

"As delightful as always," he replied with a sour smile.

"That bad, huh." Ormand finished their verbal game and they sat for a few moments, watching everything and saying nothing. The client at the next table was starting to enjoy his service.

"I've heard something that will concern you, my old friend," Medwin offered.

"Lots of things concern me, as you well know," Ormand replied.

"That's true," Medwin continued. "But in this case, it seems you've made an enemy who wants your head." And with that, a wand seemed to slip like magic into his right hand, aimed squarely and steadily at Ormand.

At the same moment the wand appeared, the three smelly brutes stood, drew long knives and advanced to stand threateningly behind and to his left. The client at the second table threw off his entertainment, knocking the table over in the process.

The client's aura blazed with magical power. He was also a master wizard. Ormand had to hand it to his colleague. It was clever to use the girl's weak aura to hide the real threat's larger one. The inn owner's wife hunched over her brood in a vain attempt to protect them if violence actually broke out. He couldn't see the owner from his current position but didn't hear any movement from that direction.

Ormand didn't move. He looked into his "friend's" face and saw only a vicious smile.

"Can you share whom I've so offended this time?" he said slowly and clearly. He didn't want to risk the assumption he was casting a spell.

No one moved as Medwin considered this. Finally, he replied, "It seems Lady Winola Volker has an old-fashioned brother who feels he must defend her honor. As I'm sure you understand, he can't very well take it out on Lord Liesel Ormsburg so he's decided to settle for…"

The entire inn exploded in a massive fireball. It was centered on Ormand and radiated outward, smashing through most of the rickety walls holding up the roof. As he looked around, the grand master was rather surprised the roof still held. It was a Dead Man's Pyre spell he'd used. Most people couldn't even attempt it, as it was extremely tricky to cast and even more so to hold. It was a sixth-circle fireball centered on the caster that radiate out to destroy anyone and anything around you. It came in very handy against treachery.

"Are you surprised, my old friend?" he asked Medwin's burnt corpse.

He bent down and said, "Thanks for the gift!" as he yanked the magic wand out of the crispy hand. Any magical item was valuable and wands were extremely versatile as well. He spun as he heard a groan.

It seemed the knocked-over table had shielded the magical distraction from death.

"Get up!" he barked as he watched her eyes flutter as consciousness returned.

She turned pale but did as she was told. He watched carefully as she looked around, seeing the destruction he'd wrought. She didn't cringe or whine as she accepted the inevitability of whatever came next. He appreciated that.

"Can you be useful?" he asked gruffly.

She didn't hesitate. "Yes, Master," and she bowed low.

"It's Grand Master," he said. "You work for me now."

*****

Vayden used to be intimidated when he came to Guild Master Crevan's estate. It had always represented the pinnacle of what a commoner could aspire to. Its location on Rose Petal Way was just a street over from one of the three noble areas in the city. The guild, Gentlemen's Acquisition Guild, had been created by Mr. Edward Pierce at the city's founding. The purpose was to supply the uncommon items of value nobles needed, without having to deal with the commoners. While gentlemen had quickly stopped running it after the second generation, it had continued to be the guild that supplied finer items for the wealthy community.

Part of its exclusivity was the exorbitant annual membership fee. Currently, at two hundred pounds sterling, it kept all but the most determined out. It guaranteed only the highest-quality people and service. Vayden's former master had been a member and the only thing that saved him in the first year was, his former master had already set aside the money for the next year's fee.

Vayden had started judging each year's success by calculating how many days it took to earn that year's fee. There were many years he'd almost starved to death setting aside the money to keep his membership. Once lost, it was lost forever.

Compounding the problem, many of his late master's clients had abandoned him and, ever so conveniently, their debts. A thirteen-year-old boy didn't get very far demanding payment for services rendered by a dead man.

He'd struggled and fought and starved for it but kept the membership. Because of that however, he'd always felt he didn't really deserve to associate with them. He'd come to this grand estate four times each year for meetings and been reminded how far below the other members he was. This year however, was different. He'd not only earned this year's fee but collected the next two years as well.

Master Kalamar wasn't just his master in magical studies, he was his biggest client. He was buying every book, piece of furniture, old map, picture and assorted odds and ends Vayden could get his hands on. That wealth brought notice and opened doors to new business and opportunities.

His growing variety of both spells and powers now allowed him to keep up with his competitors and their vast lists of informants. His newfound wealth now brought informants his way too. He and his master had discussed at length the difference between paying for information and bribing someone to compromise their oath of service.

Vayden was just beginning to understand his master's discussions about behavior. He behaved differently and was more confident and sure of himself. Everyone around him picked up on those changes and responded accordingly. He behaved as if he had worth and they treated him as such. When he'd been poor and felt unworthy, they treated him that way. It sometimes seemed he was replaying the scenes of years gone by and getting different results.

His master warned it didn't mean he should be arrogant and treat people badly, but generally, if you treated people with respect, they would reciprocate. And that respect started with respecting oneself. It was a very different perspective indeed.

The meeting played out similarly to the hundred meetings before. They discussed trends in the city and surrounding area. They discussed the latest behavior and wants of the nobles and how they might fulfill them. And they congratulated individual members for wining particular auctions or acquiring something notable for a client. Vayden rather enjoyed being among that last group. He had a second purpose for being here, however.

"Master Slone," he said as everyone was heading for the exit. "Might I have a moment of your time?" he asked politely.

"Of course, Master Vayden." Slone paused from throwing his cloak on and waited politely. He was older than Vayden by a decade or so and had generally been polite if not kind over the many years they'd known each other. Part of that, no doubt, was because they'd never really competed for business, as Slone had a specific, and generally loyal, set of clients. Vayden knew only too well that Slone worked very hard to make sure they stayed loyal. That was the problem he hoped to address.

One of Slone's clients was Lady Mirbella Dunlorr of Shadyside. He'd learned through his growing resources she was looking to hand over all her needs to Master Garth on Bakers Lane. Garth already handled all the common needs of her estates and seemed to have convinced her of the efficiency of one broker for everything.

Vayden waited until the nearest members had given them a bit of space and said, "Master Slone. I have a desk set with matching shelves I was hoping you could take a look at." He began vaguely to gauge his response. The response was very bland, so he continued. "I understand you're an expert on Guybrick furniture." Now he saw real interest. He knew it was Guybrick, or he wouldn't be mentioning it.

"I must confess," he continued, "there are some scratches and a few chips, but maybe with the right restorer it could be salvaged." He added, "If it really is Guybrick that is, the mark is worn and it's possible it could be a forgery. That's what I'm hoping you could tell me." He finished.

Slone was practically dancing on his feet. Since Guybrick died almost a century ago, it would be impossible it didn't have scratches and chips. They'd be seen as proof it wasn't a forgery. And if the mark was still there, even worn, it would vastly improve the value and authenticity.

"As you know," Slone began, "I have a client who loves Guybrick." He paused. It would be very rude to actively steal a client from a fellow member, so he was putting his claim in early.

"That's why I came to you," he said simply.

"There are not many pieces left unclaimed," Slone continued. "It would be unusual to find one after all these years." Vayden just nodded.

"Still," he continued brightly, "if it is a Guybrick, it would be quite the discovery. How did you come by it?" Knowing where it came from would be part of documenting its history.

"At the RussLarnt estate sale last month," he answered. "I was mainly interested in the library, but they wanted to be rid of everything."

"They didn't know about the desk?" he asked breathlessly. They both knew the RussLarnts were one of the oldest noble families in Torrence.

"It was stacked in an old storage room filled with other furnishings. That's what caused some of the marks it now has I'm afraid. All the pieces were an older style so maybe they redecorated at some point," Vayden concluded. It seemed only the wealthy had the option of growing weary of a style and deciding to change everything. He'd never really understood it, but he was certainly willing to profit from it.

"I tell you what," Slone said, trying to tamp down his excitement, "why don't I come by in the morning and take a quick look. How does the second hour of morning sound?"

"I can make that work," Vayden agreed with a smile.

"Excellent!" Slone replied. "Until tomorrow." He practically waltzed out of the room.

Vayden turned as a chair was dragged across the floor.

"Master Orville," he said politely. "I didn't realize anyone was still here."

Orville got up slowly from the chair. He had retired from business years before but still attended the meetings. He had an excellent memory and his advice could be quite sage.

"Did I fall asleep again?" he said with a laugh. Vayden didn't believe that for a moment.

"I doubt that, Master," he said good-naturedly. "You still run circles around me. Always have." He laughed.

"That's very kind of you, young man. Very *kind*," he said with special emphasis on "kind."

"Help an old man to the door, will you?" he asked.

"It'll be my pleasure," Vayden replied, putting words into action.

Chapter 21

opportunities

"You unsophisticated cow!" Hannelore spat. "You have no idea how to deal with a wizard's invitation!"[38]

"I will break you! You weak-willed trollop!" Otylia shot back.

"How dare you, you backstreet whore! You couldn't—" Hannelore began.

"Enough!" Ormand demanded as he stepped around the threshold into the entry parlor of his house. "My office immediately!" And with that, he disappeared, using the stored magic in his home's shields to reappear in his study.

Rivalries were one thing, but his new students' hatred of each other was getting out of hand. He settled himself at his desk as the required knock occurred.

"Come in," he said and unlocked, then opened the door using the same magical reserve he'd just tapped for his teleportation spell. It was always important for others to be reminded of how far above them you were. It maintained respect and discipline.

He watched as they entered. Otylia and Hannelore centered themselves on his desk. Hannelore was the former student of the now-dead Volker Court Wizard Waldemar. He'd brought her along with his other prizes from the successful Ormsburg raid. Waldemar had been a thorough teacher and her general magical knowledge had been

---

[38] A wizard's invitation was a magical construction used to send formal greetings or declarations from one mage to another. They could be as simple as an improved message spell or as complicated as a temporary conversation spell allowing instantaneous discussions between the parties involved.

broad and extensive. As she'd been with him the longest, normally, that would make her senior and to the left. But she'd just completed her apprenticeship under his instruction and was a First Circle Initiate.

Otylia was an Adept Second Circle, but barely. The packs only trained to kill and lost many students with their forcing programs. Their students were turned into efficient killers but little else. As she had beauty, they'd also given her some training on seduction and eavesdropping spells to assist in her additional entertainment role.

He studied them carefully as they stood quietly and without expression, as they'd been taught. They would speak only when spoken to. He was their master and they had much to learn, both of magic and life and they needed to learn quickly. After careful consideration, he decided on his course of action.

"This petty squabbling has to end," he began calmly.

"You," he continued, looking at Otylia as the senior, "have power and toughness, as you were thrown in with killers to survive or die."

"And you"—he looked at Hannelore—"were shown the finer things in life. Instructed in the ways of high society and social graces."

Turning his attention back to them both, he said firmly, "Yet both of you ending up in the exact same place."

He watched them carefully as they grasped his meaning. All their supposed advantages over the other and they ended in identical situations.

"The world as you know, will use you and kill you anytime it chooses." He paused. "But only a fool looks to add enemies to that list for petty reasons." He waited a moment to let that settle.

"I, as your master, am using you to extend my power. In return however, I'm teaching you and giving you tools to advance yourselves and better your position. Both as witches and in life. You don't have to like it or like me, but you're both intelligent enough not to spurn it.

"Each of you have talents and skills the other doesn't. That is an opportunity to develop your own power in areas you don't currently possess. You don't have to like each other, but to waste this chance to learn new skills is stupidity for its own sake!"

He paused to give them time to absorb his wisdom in this.

"Now, I don't care whether you take this opportunity or not. It is entirely up to you. However, if you don't end the pointless bickering, I will!" He watched as their faces paled with understanding.

"Hannelore, as you have experience with a wizard's invitation, you will answer the one at the door. As you are doing so, you will show Otylia what and how you are doing it. Is that clear?"

"Yes, Master," they both replied.

"Begone," he said, dismissing them with a wave.

*****

The wizard's invitation had come from Lordmage Kalamar Sylvicheld. It was a request to meet in a glade west of Hoff and just north of the Badlands.[39] The request was to discuss an exchange. Ormand had studied carefully the site, looking for any traps. He'd also observed the lordmage's appearance with one other person as the invitation stipulated.

Grand Master Ormand looked around after teleporting to the meeting site. Spring was in full bloom as winter had finally been banished. The day was overcast but warm as the sun's rays soaked the earth with its power.

"Thank you for agreeing to meet with me," Kalamar said with a polite bow.

Ormand studied his opponent thoroughly. The intelligent, decisive young man he'd seen several years before had grown into a power to be reckoned with. His aura was so stable, so intense, Ormand suspected non-casters could sense it even if they couldn't see it. Remembering his instruction to his students earlier in the day, this man was not one to make an enemy of lightly.

"Of course, lordmage. I was only too happy to receive your invitation." He bowed politely in return. "To what do I owe the privilege of this encounter?"

---

[39] The Badlands are a collection of small towns and villages just west and south of Hoff. It's rumored the headquarters of the Raven-spike Assassins guild operates from there to avoid any interference from Hoff's nobles.

"We have a guest," Kalamar pointed back to the other man present, "who wishes to"—he paused here as if considering his next words—"immigrate to Hoff," he finished with a smile.

Ormand shifted some of his attention to the other man standing about ten paces behind and to the left of Kalamar. He was a wizard, a master by his aura's strength. Long brown hair and a neatly trimmed beard highlighted his average features. Something about him was familiar, however.

"Ahh!" he said out loud, instantly regretting it. Uncontrolled outbursts gave your opponent advantages. As he'd started though, he needed to finish as if he'd meant it. "You are the former First of Pack 70," he finished with a smile.

The man bowed as Kalamar said, "Correct. Hoag has been our guest since the incident last year. It seems, however, he finds our"—he again paused for the right word—"society is a bit stifling for his taste. So rather than creating an incident with possibly dangerous consequences, he'd like to be reintegrated into Hoff's society. I was hoping you might be willing to help with that." The lordmage finished.

"And what is that worth to you?" he asked quickly to buy time to consider the extraordinary advantages this could bring him.

"Me?" Kalamar asked with a shrug. "Nothing," he answered his own question. "But to Hoag, that's a different matter. He understands the difficulties presented and is willing to work for you. As *your* man," Kalamar emphasized.

The grand master once again turned his attention to Hoag. To have a master wizard in his sworn service[40] even for a fixed time would give him a great deal of power.

"Why would you give up such an advantage?" he asked. It seemed inconceivable to so lightly discard such a tool.

---

[40] While sworn service is mostly known as an oath of allegiance to a noble, it is not exclusively such. Nobles resent and try to suppress it, but such oaths are frequently administered in guilds or other power structures. A student's bond to his or her master or mistress is another such bond. They can be sealed by wizards or priest which, in many ways, makes them stronger than the noble version.

"Hoag is our guest. Not a prisoner," the lordmage answered simply.

"And if your former guest were ordered to do something against your interest?" Ormand asked shrewdly.

"Then I would deal with the situation appropriately," Kalamar replied with steel in his voice.

Ormand nodded but tried another tack. "Aren't you concerned someone you released might"—and here he paused, searching for the right words—"cause harm to others?' he finished delicately.

"I am concerned that leaving here you could 'cause harm to others.' Should I stop you from doing so?" he asked not as a challenge but as a simple question.

Kalamar continued before Ormand could respond. "If I started forcing everyone to act as I saw fit, I'd quickly become the very thing I oppose. Hoag came to us as a guest. He caused no harm while with us and has decided to leave. I have no moral or legal authority to stop or harm him just because he might do something I would oppose. If he, one day, decides to cause harm to those I'm dedicated to protecting, then I will take whatever action is necessary at that time."

The grand master nodded in understanding. He thought that kind of righteous sentimentality was foolish, as the world didn't work that way. However, as he was profiting from it, he had no intention of arguing the point. Life would make his point for him soon enough.

"Hoag," he called to the other man, "you are willing to enter my service in return for me giving you a new identity in Hoff?"

Hoag walked forward and said, "Yes, Grand Master. I am willing to faithfully serve for five years in exchange for giving me a new identity as a master wizard in Hoff."

Ormand considered this carefully. He wanted more, but five-year service was a considerable time, all things considered. He would gain much while risking very little.

"Very well," he finally replied. "Come forward and swear."

Chapter 22

a startling discovery

Vayden hummed to himself as he walked home on Carters Way. It was a beautiful summer morning and he'd just had a successful interview with Laurence, the estate manager for Lady Rona Yaltwain. His recent successes were getting him noticed and this in turn was gaining him access to new clients.

He'd had a dozen of these this year alone and while most didn't pan out, some did. His business was doing better than ever. In addition, his master had increased his orders this year for furnishing, books and all things related to learning. He was having to expand his reach beyond the city to meet the growing needs of his increased clientele.

Vayden stopped mid-stride as he recognized where he was. Just ahead was his longtime nemesis. While his fortunes had vastly improved, hers had declined and he couldn't muster the energy for sympathy. She had a whip-sharp mind and tongue and was a gifted merchant. While they generally dealt with different clientele, whenever their paths did cross, she seemed to go out of her way to hinder him. Even when that meant some other person made the deal. It had been beyond frustrating over the last decade.

Fortune had turned her face away, it seemed. *She was having to close up shop*, Vayden thought pleasantly as he stepped into her storefront.

"What do you want!" Mirielle snapped at him as he walked in. Tall for a woman, her auburn hair was pulled back in a tail from her face, showing sharp, angry lines. Her hands were now on her hips, as if daring him to step farther into her shop.

"I thought I might buy something," he said pleasantly while staring her down. She needed every penny no doubt and couldn't afford to turn away *any* customer.

She snorted, showing what she thought of that. What she said was, "Fine. Just don't break anything." She started to pretend to dust something while keeping her eyes on him.

He smiled and nodded, walking over to the closest wall shelves. There wasn't much left as she'd clearly been selling out of her faster-moving items. There were two books on a high shelf. He stretched to pull them down and started looking through them.

"How much do you owe?" he said casually over his shoulder. When he didn't get an answer, he gently set the books down on a lower shelf and turned around. Her face was flushed and she looked like she'd rather die than give him the answer.

"A hundred and eighteen pounds, thirteen shilling and four pennies," she finally replied as if the answer was pulled from her throat.

He casually looked around the shop and said, "You don't have it."

Vayden didn't intend for his comment to be insulting but he would swear she'd have punched him if they hadn't been separated by the counter.

She managed to contain herself somewhat and snarled, "Are you going to buy something?"

"Yes," he said as he turned away from her. This conversation wasn't going the way he'd pictured and the currents in the room were making him unbalanced.

"What do you want?" she asked as if choking on glass.

What he meant to say was "Everything in the store." What he actually said, though, as he turned around and stared deep into her large, bright-green eyes was, "Everything!"

She gasped as they both realized what he'd just meant. His mind raced as he saw her clearly for the first time. His body ached to hold her and a fire burned in his veins at the thought of her. How he couldn't have known this before was beyond his comprehension.

She stood stock-still. Mirielle was like a bird caught in the gaze of a serpent, afraid to move lest it strike but knowing it would strike if it didn't move. She began to tremble as her mind raced down unknowable paths. He watched unblinking as her will began to crumble. Her defenses were falling before his eyes as she rejected all the excuses conjured to reject his proposal.

In his mind's eye, he clearly saw his old master's image gloating. *Yes*, it said. *She'll be yours soon. No more torments and insults. You'll be the master forever.*

Another image appeared, however, of his new master. It said nothing but just looked at him with a tinge of sadness, a slight disapproval of something only it could see.

He looked back at Mirielle and watched as her shoulders slumped. She was actually leaning forward, as if drawn to him in some unfathomable way, those beautiful green eyes getting closer and closer.

His old master shouted in glee, *Almost yours. Keep at it and victory is assured!*

His new master just continued with that same sad smile. Its image didn't say anything and he knew it didn't have to. He wrenched himself away with what sounded like a sob. Like a drunk, he staggered over to the far wall to pant heavily as he gathered his wits. His old master was shouting every imaginable insult at his stupid failure. Such an easy victory. *She was almost yours!* the enraged image screeched.

He hurled a few insults at himself. She was now going to tell him off, throw him out and give him a tongue lashing as he'd never heard before. He heard her steps as she walked from behind the counter. She was going to physically throw him out the store. He'd be embarrassed before the whole world for his failure.

She stopped behind him and he waited for the blow to fall. He flinched as her fingers touched his shoulder. Drawing a deep breath, he turned to face her full fury and scorn like a man.

Vayden was confused as it wasn't fury or scorn on her face. It was something completely different that he couldn't seem to find words for. It was shy and bold. It was excited and reserved. It was happy and nervous.

She reached out for his hand and quietly said, "I should show you the rest before we conclude our negotiation," and with that, she led him from the shop's main parlor into the rest of the house.

Vayden's spirit soared to the heavens. This kind of victory was unfathomably better than anything his old master's empty and hateful philosophies could ever accomplish. Never again would he doubt the new path he was on, or the price it required. He looked on his old master for the last time and banished him forever.

Chapter 23

a deal concluded

Kalamar put down the last scroll. Rolling his shoulders, he looked around at the temple's library. He'd truly enjoyed his time here. The people of Ghet had an expansive knowledge of the world in which they lived and he'd learned a great deal studying the works of their greatest minds. He far better understood their people and society.

They were a people with a thousand gods. These beings were not true gods but powerful entities. They could not channel the faith of their believers nor could they supply power for their priests. Basically, all casters in the land of Ghet were mages assigned to their god's guild. The guild controlled what was taught to whom and jealously defended their spells and knowledge against all rival guilds who might try to steal them.

Almost all of these gods were local spirits whose power or name didn't extend beyond the local village or town. While they appeared immortal to their followers, most were not. They generally would live far beyond mortals, but they would not live forever.

There were 126 of these gods whose spheres of influence were far greater and correspondingly their power. These gods had their central temples in the City of the Gods. This city had a single road from a single entrance. The city formed a square and was impossible to enter without one of the gods' permission. The farther one walked along this road, the more powerful the god. Each temple was larger and grander than the next until the traveler would reach the king of all the gods. The ruler of them all.

For millennia, that god was Sha the Sun God. Unlike his brothers and sisters, he was a true god, as his power flowed from and to his people. His priests were true priests, drawing directly by faith on his power.

Eventually, he and his consort, Vreek the Earth Goddess, had a child. This child, Rhatu the Falcon Lord, was groomed by his father to take his place. Sha passed to his son the knowledge of true godhood on the condition that he would never share it with another. In this, Rhatu failed. Whether because of love or deceit, he shared the forbidden knowledge with his wife, Kohsaut, the goddess of beauty.

In punishment for this betrayal, Sha left the realm and removed his temple from the city. He took his palace and his authority to the sun itself. He thrust the mantel of leadership on his son and withdrew all support from the gods. This decision unleashed chaos across the land.

Sha had provided order for the gods and the people. Rhatu could not. Soon the gods began warring among themselves. They quickly formed alliances both for defense and to attack their rivals. Violence ruled both day and night and they all suffered.

The people learned with their very eyes gods could die and many were killed in the power struggles that ensued. The City of the Gods dwindled from 126 down to 111. Rhatu and Kohsaut realized Kane was their greatest rival and if he could be defeated, they could impose peace on the rest. A grand alliance was formed for this very purpose. While this alliance didn't have enough power to destroy Kane, they could, and did, banish him over a century before Kalamar's quest.

Kalamar now understood why magic never blossomed in Ghet. There was no freedom to explore or innovate. The godly guilds rigidly controlled all knowledge and refused any questioning. He also understood why all the temples practiced human sacrifice. It was in this way the gods, through their priesthood, could temporarily boost their strength to enact a greater effect, either in defense or as a demonstration of their power.

Knowing how Kane arrived here and suspecting what he wanted, Kalamar had always suspected a trap or trick to help restore the death god to his rightful place. It puzzled him exceedingly that it never came.

Kane had answered every question fully and honestly, as far as he could tell. No subject had been off limits in their discussions. Kalamar himself had gained extraordinary abilities and skills in strengthening his power and spells, particularly necromancy, as this was Kane's primary area of control and the focus of his worship.

While he was certain Kane had learned a great deal from him during his time spent here, he'd deliberately not shared his greater magical abilities and Kane had not once asked him to. He knew Kane needed something from him; he just couldn't determine what it was.

During their study together, an understanding had formed. Kalamar's visits would end once he'd read every tome and scroll in the library. He had to admit, it saddened him that he'd now finished the last one.

Getting up, he left the library, heading for Kane's private temple at the base of the complex. It was here they'd first met and here Kane stayed when not strolling the grounds. Kalamar waved a controlling charm to deactivate the temple's many defenses and cursed his foolishness for not realizing it sooner. How much effort could they have saved on the quest if he'd just recognized the need for such a charm and created one on that long-ago journey?

Putting aside his regrets, he entered the private temple for the last time. He bowed politely and waited to be acknowledged.

"Kal, my friend," Kane said. Kalamar wasn't sure how to take the idea Kane used his abbreviated name like his closest friends and family did. It disturbed him on some level he couldn't quite articulate.

"Great Kane," Kalamar replied. It seemed a satisfactory honorific, so he'd used it during their time together.

"You have finished in the library and so our time is at an end, my friend. I trust you are satisfied I have fulfilled all my terms?"

"Yes, Great Kane. I am satisfied. Are you satisfied I have fulfilled all my terms?" he asked in return.

"Yes, my friend. You have more than satisfied the terms and so I release you from our agreement."

With his greater understanding of power, Kalamar could actually feel the release on his soul. It was beautiful and awe-inspiring to see what most mortals never even guessed at. He also noted the effect it had on Kane. Just as Kalamar did, Kane grew stronger, and to his new senses, freer as the oaths were completed and their obligations to each other ended.

Kalamar watched closely to see if now, at the very end, Kane would enact his plan to return home but nothing happened. He just sat there, pleasantly smiling at him.

"You will always be welcome here, my friend," Kane spoke solemnly.

"Thank you," Kalamar replied, meaning it. With that, he turned and headed for the exit.

*****

Kane watched his new friend as he left the temple. *That young man's power was extraordinary,* he thought with a grin. It had pleased him greatly to watch as Kal time and time again tried to determine how Kane would use him to further his own ends, only to fail.

Kane began to laugh and it rumbled and shook his entire temple. He didn't have a trick at all. He had seen, when they first met, the path Kal would take. It wasn't Kane who manipulated him; it was Kal's petty rivals who would do all the work. They would set his feet inescapably upon a path that would give Kane everything he wanted. And there was nothing Kal would do to stop it.

*****

Far to the south and west in the land of Ghet rested the crumbling former temples of Kane. They were derelict and in disrepair, but not wholly abandoned. Even though their god was banished, the needs of the dead continued and a small but loyal few did what they could to meet those responsibilities.

Each of those priests and priestesses now looked around in wonder. For the first time in a century, they heard their master's voice. His laughter echoed through the empty halls and they rejoiced. He would soon be with them and they would be restored to their rightful position once more. Their humiliating exile would soon be at an end.

Epilogue

Never in all his years had Lord Malcolm attended a council like this. The passionate voices reverberated around the room in counterpoint to the howling winter winds outside. A messenger had miraculously made it through the deep snow and storms to tell of an attack. A farmstead within Lord Alan Ferguson's domain had been attacked and destroyed by outsiders from the north. The only clues found were, it was a large party of brigands and magic had been used. The newlywed couple had been murdered most foully and everything had been taken or burned to the ground. A party of six had set out to give the warning, but only one made it.

The debate that raged was whether to send a party out immediately, which would certainly result in that party's death, or to wait until spring to give it a chance to see justice done. The champions of the opposing perspectives were equally surprising.

For the immediate departure was Lord Willem Vestrum, whose nature was always to wait and see where the support was before stating his own opinions. The other side was led in most uncharacteristically passionate fashion by Lord and Archmage Angus Crow. He always made his cases carefully and thoughtfully. This debate had brought out something entirely different.

The central arguments were devolving down to honor.

"How can the people of this land trust in the just leadership of our lord and master, Baron Terrence Eddington, if his own men will not risk themselves in defense of their lives?" Willem snapped.

"The people of this land will trust the baron's leadership by his thoughtful and intelligent use of authority. Sending a troop of young men to their death won't inspire anyone," Angus shot back.

"By hiding behind castle walls until the danger is past?" Willem demanded

"By not wasting lives," Angus retorted. "Success in bringing justice to those so foully slain will ensure the people's appreciation and loyalty. Not reckless behavior and foolhardy ploys."

"That is the coward's choice!" Willem snapped.

"*ENOUGH!*" shouted Baron Eddington. "That is completely uncalled for and unwarranted. The archmage has argued passionately and effectively on a wise course of action."

Malcolm breathed a sigh of relief. While he understood Willem's arguments and they had merit, they were the easiest but not the wisest choice. He looked over to his friend the archmage, expecting to see relief but saw only stifled rage.

"With that being said," the baron continued, "there are times we must send our knights and soldiers, even to their deaths to fulfill honor's requirements. This is one of those times."

Malcolm could not believe what he was hearing. It was suicide to send out a troop into the worst winter they'd had in decades.

"Lord Willem, you are the keeper of knights. Who is the young warrior who will lead our brave soldiers to see justice done?" Eddington asked.

Willem's voice was now calm and measured as he replied, "My Lord Baron. As you know, I keep the roster of all unmarried knights in our realm for just this situation. I would be doing all our brave soldiers a disservice if I didn't put forward the name of the most qualified knight to succeed. As such, I cannot submit the next knight in the roster but must instead submit Knight Kalamar Sylvicheld. Only he has the skills and talents to see your good justice done."

Everyone gasped. Everyone except Angus Crow. He had clearly seen what the others had missed. This was Willem's opportunity to get rid of Kalamar once and for all. Malcolm had always wondered who the leader was of those that opposed and sabotaged the lordmage. While he'd never been able to prove it, he now didn't have to. The cloak of disguise was off for all to see. His quiet, behind-the-scenes efforts were no longer necessary.

That roster was meant to give untested knights an opportunity to prove their valor. It was never meant to send a proven lord with lands and responsibilities on a quest for glory. However, Willem had found a loophole. Every knight was married by the time he claimed lordship in the baron's name. Every knight but Kalamar.

Malcolm turned to his lord and master, hoping he saw through the plot just revealed. His hope turned to ash in his mouth.

"Lord Willem speaks true," Baron Terrance stated. "Lord Kalamar is the best chance this troop has. And while it is unorthodox to choose him, he matches the requirements of the law and mine is the rule of law." He paused to glare around the table. Everyone turned their eyes away but the archmage. It was the baron who turned away from him as he continued.

"Archmage, I trust you will inform the lordmage of the council's will and instruction," Baron Eddington said. "This council is ended." So saying, he stood and left the room.

Lord Malcolm Cherrheld was disturbed more than he could say, even his final statement, "the council's will." He'd never used those words in his life. It was always "his will." For the first time, he was sharing the blame with everyone instead of shouldering the responsibility himself.

Malcolm waited until last to leave the room. As he shuffled out, feeling every one of his sixty-two years, he would swear he heard laughter.

About the Author

The author currently resides in a small, quiet corner of South Carolina. He's been a lifelong devotee of fantasy stories since his best friend lent him a copy of *The Hobbit* in middle school. The passion in those pages has inspired him to create and write ever since.

The stories may be fantasy or science fiction, but he does a great deal of research to make them as believable and realistic as possible within the overall architecture of the written universe. It is the smallest details that can make the largest turning points. He's also spent decades studying magical systems and is himself an energy practitioner.

It is his greatest literary wish to provide others a few adventurous hours vacation from the sometimes-mundane world we occasionally find ourselves in.

Cover Art by Cheryl Reynolds

CPSIA information can be obtained
at www.ICGtesting.com
Printed in the USA
BVHW030811200123
655609BV00019B/371/J